PATTERNS IN THE DARK

BOOK FOUR

LINDSAY BUROKER

Patterns in the Dark

by Lindsay Buroker

Copyright © 2014 Lindsay Buroker

Cover and Formatting: Deranged Doctor Design

No part of this book may be reproduced, scanned, or distributed in any printed or electronic form without permission. Please do not participate in or encourage piracy of copyrighted materials in violation of the author's rights. Thank you for respecting the hard work of this author.

This is a work of fiction. Names, characters, places, and incidents either are the product of the author's imagination or are used fictitiously, and any resemblance to locales, events, business establishments, or actual persons—living or dead—is entirely coincidental.

FOREWORD

Thank you for coming back for another adventure in the Dragon Blood series. Patterns in the Dark picks up right after the events in Blood Charged (I don't think our poor heroes have even gotten a chance to shower yet). I hope you will enjoy helping Tolemek find his sister (and maybe a dragon, as well!).

Before you jump in, please let me thank my beta readers Cindy Wilkinson and Sarah Engelke for helping me make this a better story, and also my editor Shelley Holloway for putting up with my disdain for commas. Lastly, let me give a nod to the cover art designers at Deranged Doctor Design. Thanks to them, the novels are now available as paperbacks, as well as ebooks.

CHAPTER 1

THE TWO-MAN FLIER SETTLED ONTO a recently harvested taro field, the wheels sinking so deeply into the mud that Tolemek wondered if they would be able to escape later. Granted, the jungle-filled Mavar Island didn't offer anything as sophisticated as airstrips—or roads—but this seemed a dubious alternative. This thought was reinforced when brown-skinned men in grass skirts ran out of the village bordering the far side of the field. More than one carried a spear. Tolemek leaned forward to touch the shoulder of Lieutenant Cas "Raptor" Ahn, the pilot and the new love in his life, though there had been precious little time for loving of late. "Should we be readying weapons, or is that the welcoming committee?"

Not surprisingly, Cas's Mark 500 sniper rifle already rested between her legs. He had gotten used to the idea that she slept with it sometimes; after all, he had been known to sleep with a few vials of incendiary goo under his own pillow, at least in enemy territory.

"The colonel's dad is supposed to have been here for a couple of months," Cas said. She looked over at the flier that had touched down ahead and to the right of theirs.

Her commander, Colonel Ridgewalker Zirkander, appeared to be too busy rummaging for something in the cockpit to notice the villagers' approach. His passenger, the raven-haired sorceress Sardelle Terushan, was paying more attention to their surroundings and had her eyes on the approaching villagers. The young man piloting the third flier, Lieutenant Duck, was watching them, as well, and tapping his fingers on the firing mechanism for the craft's machine guns.

"That doesn't answer my question," Tolemek said. "There are plenty of men who'd like to shoot Zirkander. His father may be every bit as loathsome to these people."

"Loathsome." Cas snorted.

Zirkander sat up, waving a postcard in the air. "Found it." When he smiled, the chin strap of his leather cap dangling down to his white scarf and pilot's jacket, he admittedly didn't look much like a despicable villain. He was more the dashing sort whom women wanted to bed and whom men wanted to drink with, but Tolemek still had a tendency to find him irritating. Zirkander had been shooting down Cofah dirigibles for longer than Tolemek had been in the Cofah military, and during Tolemek's years as a pirate, Zirkander had shot down plenty of those airships too.

Sardelle leaned forward, touched Zirkander's shoulder, and whispered something.

"Ah, yes," Zirkander said, nodding toward the villagers. No less than a dozen of them were navigating the muddy field, grass skirts flapping about their legs as they ran. They would be close enough to throw those spears soon. "It's possible this isn't a sanctioned landing strip."

"It's possible they've never seen a flier before and think we're demons, here to pillage their homeland," Sardelle said.

"Demons? I was hoping for children of the gods." Zirkander threw a leg over the lip of the cockpit and jumped to the ground, mud spattering in all directions. It hardly mattered; the whole team was grimy after surviving that volcanic eruption on Cofahre. "Watch my back, will you?" he called up to Sardelle, then strode toward the approaching villagers, carrying nothing more than the postcard.

Cas shifted in the cockpit, emitting a grunt of irritation.

"Problem?" Tolemek wondered if he should get out or remain in the flier. His own reputation as the "Deathmaker" was even more loathsome than Zirkander's, at least among some peoples. But the pirate fleet he had been a part of had never visited this remote island, and he doubted the natives would know of him.

"He usually asks *me* to watch his back," Cas grumbled. She rested the barrel of her rifle on the windshield, clearly intending to do so whether Zirkander had asked or not.

"He probably doesn't want the natives perforated with bullets," Tolemek said, trying not to let it bother him that Cas felt some possessiveness toward another man. Zirkander had been her commander far longer than Tolemek had been in her life. It was natural that she cared about keeping him alive. This logic only partially reassured him.

"I wouldn't perforate a random native," Cas said. "Give him a shave maybe, but not perforate him."

At Zirkander's approach, the villagers had slowed down, with three breaking away to go up and talk to him. The others kept their spears to their shoulders, poised to launch. Not all of those wood-and-stone weapons were pointed at Zirkander—Cas and Duck were being targeted, as well. Or maybe it was the fliers in general that had the natives spooked. The Iskandians styled their aircraft after the dragons of old, with bronze hulls, outstretched wings, and propellers at the noses of reptilian snouts painted with flaring nostrils and rows of fangs.

Tolemek was positive Zirkander didn't know the language, but that didn't keep him from talking copiously as he gestured to the volcano at the center of the island, the jungle stretching inland, and the sea beyond the fields and the village. He finished with holding the postcard out to the villagers.

"Is his dad's picture on there?" Tolemek guessed. He had seen a few mass-produced mailing cards, but that one looked hand-painted.

"Yes," Cas said.

"You're certain because you've seen it before or because your eyes are better than mine?"

For an answer, she merely smiled over her shoulder at him. Her impish, freckled face was dirty with ash and engine grease that had a tendency to fly back and spatter the pilots as they flew, but attractive, nonetheless. Her smiles were rare, and they always warmed his heart—and other things too.

Zirkander turned his back on the natives—either bravely or

foolishly so, given the spears still pointed at him—and strolled back to the fliers. "I didn't understand a word that fellow said," he announced, "but we've either been invited to dinner or to *be* dinner."

"Did they recognize your father?" Tolemek asked.

He didn't care about dinner or the natives. The only reason they were making this stop was because Zirkander's father might be able to identify the flowers that Tolemek's sister, Tylie, had painted on the door of her asylum wall before being dragged off to… wherever the Cofah had taken her. That mural, and the message painted in red, were burned into Tolemek's mind: *Help me. They are taking me here.* Unfortunately, the tropical setting and the foliage in the painting were the only clues he had as to where *here* was. If Zirkander's father couldn't tell them, this trip would have been a waste of time, and Tolemek didn't know how much time he had.

"Yes," Zirkander said brightly as he reached his flier. He lifted a hand to help Sardelle down. She touched it briefly on her way over the side, but hopped into the mud without assistance.

"Did they seem happy about it?" Cas asked, her rifle still resting at the ready. Several of the villagers were heading back across the field, but a few were waiting. Guides or guards? It was hard to tell.

"They gave each other long looks that were hard to decipher."

"So long as they can decipher what our rifles can do," Cas said.

Tolemek climbed down, looking toward the jungle beyond the cleared fields and pulling a roll of paper out of his inside vest pocket. Even though he had memorized his sister's mural, he had also taken the time to painstakingly draw a reproduction during the flight, something he could show to people they encountered. Tolemek doubted he would be so lucky as to find the spot on the first stop, but he scanned the surrounding foliage, nonetheless, hoping to spot the flowers from the painting. The vine-draped trees, plants with huge leaves, and dense green canopy were appropriate, but he didn't see any of the purple, blue, or red flowers from the image.

"Do you want me to wait with the fliers, sir?" Duck asked. "Those shifty fellers there look like they might have naughty thoughts on their minds."

The remaining natives *did* appear interested in the fliers, and not in an oh-what-fascinating-new-technology-has-come-to-our-island way. One kept pointing at the wheels, and another was frowning at the snout of Zirkander's craft while shaking his spear in an agitated manner.

"You sure you're not just looking to avoid that possible confusion over dinner, Duck?" Zirkander asked.

"'Course not, sir. But I could keep watch and mosey around in the jungle a spell, see about replenishing our stores. There's a lot of fruit hanging on those trees back yonder. Might be *besyluch*, eh?" The lieutenant had apparently grown up in a very rural area of Iskandia. Though Tolemek's understanding of the language had improved tremendously since meeting Cas and spending time with these people, he still struggled to grasp some of Duck's slang.

"Let's wait until we talk to my dad," Zirkander said. "He can tell us what these people think of strangers foraging in their jungle. Besides, even though I gave those men my most affable and charismatic smile, I'm not convinced they fell in love with me."

"Because they weren't women," Sardelle said dryly, giving him a playful swat.

Tolemek hoped he and Cas reached a degree of familiarity where she felt comfortable swatting *him* in public. He didn't know if that would happen, though. Sardelle wasn't hugely flirtatious, but Cas was so reserved that she could make almost any woman seem wanton in comparison.

"Oh? I've been told men find me charismatic too. Isn't that right, Tolemek?" Zirkander wriggled his eyebrows.

"No."

"Damn. I've been lied to." Zirkander stepped toward Sardelle, took her hand, and waved at the fliers with the other as he asked her something softly.

She nodded. "I will. We don't want anyone stealing our

special cargo."

The vials of dragon blood. Most of it had gone back to Iskandia with Apex and Kaika, but Tolemek was glad they still had some with them. He didn't know if it would be of any use in finding his sister, but he hoped to keep some to study in his lab once this was all over.

"Good." Zirkander extended a hand toward the villagers. "Now, I believe our escort is waiting for us."

Duck looked longingly toward the jungle, like he ached to go exploring, but he jogged to fall in behind his commander. Sardelle squinted at the fliers for a moment—setting some magical booby trap?—then joined them. Tolemek and Cas took up the rear, she with her rifle cradled in her arms and he with a few handmade weapons and vials of useful concoctions tucked into the various inside pockets in his vest. He had left his tools and microscope case in the flier, but he still clanked softly as they navigated the mud. Cas quirked an eyebrow at him but didn't say anything. She was too busy glowering at the way the natives surrounded them, muttering to each other and pointing with their spears toward the village. Two men remained behind to watch—or guard?—the fliers. Maybe they thought the dragon-esque aircraft could move and cause trouble of their own accord.

"Thinking of you having a dad is stranger than a she-wolf with extra teats, sir," Duck told Zirkander as they plodded across the muddy field, dead leaves and a few dud plants rotting where they had been cast aside.

"Yeah, I hear that a lot." Zirkander gave his lieutenant a bemused smile.

"I just mean that you're the boss. At least, you have been since I joined Wolf Squadron. You're the big hero in the hangar, so it's hard to picture you... Did he bend you over his knee and paddle you when you were a bad boy?"

Cas snorted—at least Tolemek thought that was what the noise in her throat signified.

Zirkander coughed. "I... don't think that's an appropriate question to ask your commanding officer."

"Can I ask it?" Sardelle asked.

"Not in public, no."

"Later?"

"Maybe. To answer your question, Duck, Dad wasn't around much when I was growing up—or after that, either. Mom handled most of the discipline."

"Oh." Duck scraped his fingers through his short dark hair. "Did *she* paddle you?"

Zirkander gave him a baleful look—or what passed for one from him. Tolemek hadn't seen him truly irked very often. The night Zirkander had thought Tolemek had been a threat to Sardelle—and the Iskandian capital city—had been one such time.

Even though Zirkander didn't answer, Sardelle was grinning. This image must have tickled her.

Oh, we're all tickled, spoke a voice in Tolemek's head. Jaxi. He hadn't heard from the sentient soulblade since the battle at the volcano and had thought she might be done talking to him.

I was napping. I had to work hard to keep you alive back there.

Yes, I understand you were invaluable. Tolemek glanced toward Sardelle's waist, where the soulblade hung in an innocuous-looking scabbard that didn't hint of the special nature of its occupant. He had never considered himself quick to flatter, but it seemed wise to stay on the good side of a powerful magical artifact.

It is. And I'm just hopping into your head to warn you to keep an eye out. They have a shaman in the village, and these people do not *like the fliers. They've seen Iskandians and Cofah before, and even a dirigible or two, but they worship dragon gods here, and they think the fliers are positively blasphemous. Sardelle and I are watching out for magical problems, but you should ask sniper girl to watch for the mundane.*

You can't ask her yourself? To Tolemek's knowledge, Jaxi had never "spoken" to Cas, but he wasn't positive.

Sardelle says I shouldn't pop into people's heads without warning.

You didn't warn me first.

We considered you an enemy then. One doesn't have to be as polite with one's enemies. Besides, it's easier to talk to those with dragon blood.

Tolemek didn't respond to that. It had been a surprise—and a blow to his ego—to learn that some of his inventions worked not entirely because of science, but because he had unknowingly caressed them into working using his latent magical talent. In hindsight, it made sense, since he had known his sister had magical talent. In her case, he had never seen it as anything more than a curse—it had made her mentally unbalanced, and their father had put her in that asylum "for her own good."

We already told you, dragon blood doesn't make anyone crazy. Something else is going on there.

I know. We're almost there. Let me talk to Cas.

They had reached the end of the field and were walking up a path that meandered between the mud and thatch huts. A few double-hulled canoes were tied to a single dock that stretched into the lagoon beyond the village, but it was a foregone conclusion that these people didn't get off their island much. All of the inhabitants wore the simple grass skirts, with most of the women walking around as bare-chested as the men. They whispered from the doorways of the huts and pointed at the strangers.

Tolemek was relieved that most of the points went toward Zirkander and not him. He didn't know if it was because Zirkander was leading or because they saw a similarity between him and his father, but the fact that Tolemek's face wasn't known here was a good thing. There were numerous ports where the Deathmaker was wanted dead or alive. But mostly dead.

"Sardelle thinks we may have some trouble," Tolemek murmured to Cas as their guides slowed down, holding up hands to stop the group. "Apparently, there's a shaman."

"The sword talking to you again?" Cas murmured back.

"I think she likes me."

Don't flatter yourself. I talk to Sardelle's soul snozzle too.

Tolemek blinked. *Her what?*

The pretty boy the grass-skirted girls are ogling.

A trio of teenage girls hiding behind clothing hung to dry were *indeed* looking in Zirkander's direction and giggling. Tolemek decided it had more to do with that goofy leather cap than any superior handsomeness.

Whatever you need to think to feel virile, Deathmaker.

Does Zirkander find your interjections as charming as I do?

Doubly so, I assure you. I'm his favorite sentient sword.

Cas nudged Tolemek in the ribs and tilted her chin toward the doorway of one of the bigger huts. A gray-haired man with numerous necklaces and bone needles piercing his nipples walked out utterly naked, aside from his jewelry. He carried a carved bone cudgel that made the hair on Tolemek's arms stand up. Another older man walked out, this one bald and carrying a rifle nearly as nice as Cas's.

"Hope that wasn't something taken from the colonel's dad after they ate him," Cas muttered, her finger resting lightly on the trigger of her weapon. The idea of starting a fire fight from within this growing crowd of people made Tolemek uncomfortable. He had come for information, not to slay people—and he wasn't looking to be slain, either.

"Dad doesn't carry firearms," Zirkander said. "He's a peaceful explorer."

"What happens when the natives aren't peaceful?" Duck asked.

"A lot of the stories he told me as a kid involved running, swinging from vines, and swimming dangerous currents. I'm not quite sure how his strategies might have adjusted now that he's almost seventy."

The naked man—was this the shaman?—strode toward Zirkander with his cudgel held aloft and his well-endowed penis aloft, as well. Nobody looked at him as if this were odd.

"It's to intimidate you," Sardelle said. "I think they're a part of the *magnolushian* sect."

"Obviously." Zirkander cleared his throat and looked squarely at… the top of the man's head.

Tolemek had never heard of that sect, but he was suddenly glad Zirkander was the pretty one here.

The shaman stopped in front of Zirkander, pointed at his face, and jabbered in an irritated tone. He pointed toward a rocky promontory up the beach, jabbered more, pointed in the direction of the fliers, and jabbered even more.

Zirkander smiled and held out his postcard again.

The shaman slapped his hand away, almost knocking it to the ground.

"Sardelle," Zirkander said, "any idea what the appropriate thing for me to do here would be?"

"Yes, but I don't think you're going to do it."

"Does it involve taking off my pants?"

"And being larger than him, yes."

"Uhm, I'm just not as excited about this whole situation as he is."

Sardelle drew her sword and stepped forward. Jaxi's scabbard might not be that flamboyant, but the soulblade herself was another matter. She immediately flared to life, blindingly bright even in the tropical sun. People stepped back, raising their arms to shield their eyes. The shaman's hand tightened around his cudgel, but Sardelle twitched a finger, and the weapon flew from his grip. He growled and lunged for her.

Zirkander whipped out a pistol even as Cas stepped forward, her own rifle aiming at the shaman's chest, but Sardelle said, "Don't," and everyone halted, except for the shaman, who flew backward, his bare ass landing in the sand. She pointed her sword toward the bald man next to him and stared into his eyes, her own eyes cold, her face carved from granite.

Tolemek shifted uncomfortably. He had rarely seen Sardelle openly unleash her power, since it could get her killed for being a witch in Iskandia, and in Cofahre too. The reminders of what she could do were always disturbing. There was a reason the common man had been afraid of the magic wielders in prior centuries, eventually banding together to rid the world of most of them.

The bald man dropped to his knees and pressed his forehead to the sand. The rest of the villagers did the same, though the shaman was very slow to do so, and he glowered as his head descended.

Sardelle's eyes grew wide, her expression chagrined. "That's not what I... I was just trying to win the cock contest."

"Glad someone was equipped to do that," Zirkander said. "Is there any chance you can find out where my dad is?"

She nodded. "Over on that promontory. They're not happy that he's been here so long. The chief is hoping we'll leave soon and take him with us."

"What's the shaman thinking?"

"That he wants to stick a knife into my chest—and yours too."

"Mine?" Zirkander protested.

"His wife was looking admiringly at you."

"Wonderful. All right, group. Let's head up the beach before they get tired of kissing the sand."

Nobody rose to stop them when Zirkander and Duck walked toward the lagoon.

"Sardelle?" Tolemek asked. "Are you communicating with them mentally?"

"Jaxi is, yes. Neither of us has a clue about the language, so it's rough."

He unrolled his sketch. "Can you see if they recognize any of these flowers?"

"I'll check." Sardelle's eyes closed halfway as she gazed down at the shaman. A long moment passed, and Tolemek shifted from foot to foot. He doubted anything would come of the inquiry, but maybe these people traveled to various islands in their canoes. Maybe someone had come from another tribe. Maybe—

Sardelle shook her head. "Neither the shaman nor the chief is familiar with that foliage."

Tolemek sighed and headed after the others. He caught Cas glancing back toward the shaman, who was still glowering in their direction, his eyes promising they would hear from him again.

CHAPTER 2

THEY WERE BEING FOLLOWED.

Oh, Cas didn't see anyone when she looked back along the beach, but the jungle hugged the sandy shoreline, its dark interior offering thousands of hiding places. Monkeys shrieked from the treetops and rattled the branches. Brightly colored birds squawked, flying away as the group walked past. Nobody, human or animal, was happy to see the foreigners, and Cas hoped they could find what they needed and leave quickly.

She could feel the tense impatience oozing off Tolemek as he strode along—she had to hurry to keep up with his longer gait. Zirkander, Sardelle, and Duck were moving quickly, too, or at least they were until they reached the rocky outcropping. It marked the end of the beach, with rocks stretching out into the water as well as inland, and there was no choice but to go up.

"There are people up there," Sardelle said. "In a cave. A large cave."

"Do you want to lead the way?" Zirkander quirked an eyebrow at her. "Seeing as how you have the biggest sword here." Genuine humor warmed his face, and he didn't sound bitter or annoyed that Sardelle had been the one to deal with that odious shaman.

Sardelle grimaced, probably at the situation rather than him. "No, you can lead. You've seen my climbing skills." She gazed back down the empty beach.

Zirkander started toward the rock wall, but she stopped him with a hand to his forearm.

"One other thing. That shaman… He wasn't accustomed to combating other magic wielders—I sensed that quickly—but he *does* have power. Some other specialty that doubtlessly makes sense for his people and this environment."

"So he's a threat, even if your sword is bigger," Zirkander said.

"I definitely sensed that he was already plotting unpleasantries for us when we were leaving."

"I did too." Cas thought about mentioning her hunch that someone was watching them, but *everyone* probably felt that way already. "We might want to hurry."

Sardelle picked her way up the steep slope.

Despite his invitation that she lead, Zirkander went up at the same time she did, giving her a hand here and there. Sardelle was wearing practical leathers, rather than one of her usual dresses, and appeared quite capable of climbing on her own, but she accepted his assistance now and then. Cas wondered if she should let Tolemek do things like that for her more. It was probably important for the man to feel manly and useful, and she had a tendency toward being brusque and rejecting help. Tolemek hadn't complained, though, and he shouldn't have any reason to feel useless next to her. It wasn't as if Cas could fling villagers around with her mind. She could shoot holes into them if necessary, but that wasn't always the ideal approach.

Cas kept her back to the rocks, watching the beach and the jungle until Zirkander, Sardelle, and Duck made it to the top. Tolemek paused halfway up, waiting for her.

Cas clambered up, having to stretch to find handholds. Annoying how the seven gods had made so few trees, walls, and rocky promontories with the climbing needs of five-foot-tall women in mind. She glanced at Tolemek, wondering if he might offer her a hand at some point, but he merely nodded encouragingly at her. She decided she appreciated that—she didn't *need* help, and he knew it. But at the same time, he waited to make sure.

As soon as she reached the top, she faced the beach again, watching in case someone headed in their direction. She didn't have that dragon blood that Sardelle and even Tolemek had, but her neck hairs were dancing.

A flash of orange caught her eye. It did not come from the village, but from out in the fields. Thanks to the jungle, she could barely see the spot where they had landed now, but she leaned out and frowned.

"Someone threw a torch onto one of the fliers," she announced.

Zirkander had been walking across the flat section of rock that lay ahead, but he stopped, his head jerking around. "What?"

"A brand is burning in front of one of the windshields."

"Whose?" Duck asked.

"Uhm, that's the colonel's," Cas said.

"Wonderful." Zirkander looked at Sardelle. "This isn't because I wouldn't take off my trousers, is it?"

Sardelle wore that distant expression she got when she was accessing her magic. "I don't think so. It's those two guards that stayed behind. They're stalking around the fliers and experimenting. I've protected them, so the fire won't do any damage. Jaxi will keep an eye on things too."

Zirkander turned around again, though his voice floated back to them. "*Some* men get to meet their fathers down at the pub for a beer when they want to spend time together. *I* have to fly halfway across the world and deal with spear-wielding natives who hate my flier." Cas almost missed his lower mutter of, "I *knew* I should have brought my dragon with me."

"His what?" Tolemek muttered, heading across the rocks at Cas's side.

"He has a figurine he hangs in his cockpit for luck."

"I… see."

"A lot of pilots do," she said, feeling defensive on Zirkander's behalf. Every now and then, someone teased him about being superstitious, usually someone who had no idea how dangerous the job was.

"Do you?"

"You're looking at it." Cas patted the side of her rifle.

Tolemek snorted softly. "Brings good luck, does it?"

"Good luck to me, bad luck to the targets."

As they walked, Cas glanced back often and kept an eye toward the jungle, as well. Maybe she didn't need to be so alert, with Sardelle and her sword seemingly aware of everything around them, but she didn't know what else to do. This was so different from her usual missions, and she felt superfluous. She had contributed little, aside from shooting at a few Cofah scientists back at the volcano base. When they weren't flying, she wasn't sure what to do with herself. She wasn't even sure if she and Duck should be here, or if Zirkander should be here, either, for that matter. That other colonel, the one he had dumped along the Iskandian coast somewhere before they left, had been in charge of this mission, and technically, the squadron wasn't even on that mission any more. Zirkander had assigned *himself* to this quest of finding the source of those dragon blood vials and making sure the Cofah couldn't continue to get their hands on them. Even if it seemed like something the king would approve of, Zirkander was making decisions without consulting his chain of command, and that was never a good thing in the military. Cas hoped everything worked out and that he wouldn't get in trouble—again.

"That's impressive," Tolemek said, pointing ahead of them.

Cas had been so wrapped up in looking behind them—and worrying about her concerns—that she hadn't noticed the carvings in a rock wall rising up ahead of them. Two massive dragon heads framed a rectangular opening. Time had worn the edges from the carvings, and the sea air had pitted the stone, but the monolithic statues remained identifiable—and imposing as they gazed out at the dark blue ocean and choppy waves beyond the lagoon. The cave opening wasn't large enough to drive a flier through, but a real dragon might be able to fold up its wings and slip inside, at least judging by the skeleton erected in the museum in the capital. Her experience with "real" dragons was nonexistent. Like the rest of the civilized world, she had believed them extinct until that blood had shown up.

"Maybe we'll find some dragons with blood to share right here," Duck drawled, walking up to pat one of the statues.

Sardelle shook her head. "It's possible this was a dragon rider outpost a millennium or more ago, but there aren't any dragons here. I would feel it."

"I'll take your word for it," Duck said, giving her a wary look. Even though he seemed to have made his peace with her vocation back at the Cofah volcano base, he still wasn't comfortable with the idea of a sorceress on the team. Not that Cas was entirely, either.

Zirkander stuck his head into the cave.

Cas almost offered to scout ahead, but she continued to sense that trouble, if it came, would be from behind them, not ahead of them.

"Er, hello, ladies," Zirkander said, a strange note in his voice. "I don't suppose any of you has seen this man?"

The rest of the group approached the cave entrance, but paused on the threshold. With Sardelle, Tolemek, and Duck spread out in front of her, Cas couldn't see much. She was debating whether it was dignified to crouch down and look between Tolemek's legs when a distant voice called out from somewhere in the cave depths.

"Hello?" the drawn-out note echoed from the walls. "Do I hear an Iskandian voice?"

"Dad?" Zirkander called.

A long pause followed his question, punctuated only by the splashes of the waves battering at the rocks fifty feet below.

"Ridgewalker?" came the distance-muffled voice.

Tolemek shifted sideways, looking down at Cas. "His parents actually use that name, huh?"

"I think his father is the one who picked it," Cas said and made a move-aside motion. "Wanted him to be a mountain climber."

Tolemek pressed his back to the side of the stone entrance, so she could slip into the cave. She paused on the threshold, too, in part because she was in awe of the vast cavern that opened up inside, the walls covered with pictographs, hieroglyphics, and petroglyphs, and in part because six pretty young women in grass skirts were standing on the ledge inside. Like the rest of the villagers, they saw no need for shirts. They were looking curiously at Sardelle, Tolemek, and Duck, and whispering among each other. Two of them held stone knives. Cas didn't see any other weapons, and she was confident she could deal with the women if they decided to attack. They weren't close to the threshold, anyway. Rather, they stood near the far side of the ledge, about fifteen feet from the cave entrance. A rope bridge extended across a chasm to a tunnel on the far side, and narrow stone staircases carved into the walls ascended and descended from the ledge, disappearing into darkness above and below, darkness the sun's influence couldn't reach. Despite the possible routes from the ledge, a single rope attached to the base of a dragon statue carved from a stalagmite snaked across the stone floor and disappeared over the edge.

"It's me, Dad." Zirkander walked to the edge by the rope and peered down. "We could use some help if you're not too busy doing… whatever it is you're doing down there. Are you upside down?"

"Examining carvings on the underside of this ledge, yes." A scrape and a couple of grunts drifted upward. He—it occurred to Cas that she didn't know Zirkander's father's first name—sounded like he was at least twenty feet below them.

"Does Mom know about this harem of women you have helping you?"

"It's less a harem and more of a death squad. The mean-looking ones with the knives have orders to cut my rope if I disturb the sacred temple." More scrapes sounded, along with the clank of metal against rock. A moment later, a wiry man with shaggy white hair and a shaggy beard pulled himself over the side. He was attached to the rope by way of a harness that went around his waist and through his legs, but he soon unclipped himself and stepped away from the edge. The sleeves of his loose, button-down shirt were rolled up, revealing lean, ropy arms, and despite his seventy years, he had proved fit and agile as he pulled himself into view. He wore cut-away trousers that fell to the knees and lightweight, close-fitting shoes for climbing. "Ridge, it *is* you. I don't believe it."

"It's good to see you still alive, Dad."

They started toward each other, lifting their arms for a hug, but Zirkander's father snapped his fingers before they met and pulled a leather-bound notebook out of a bulging pocket. "One moment. I don't want to forget…" He patted himself down, pulled spectacles and a pen out of a shirt pocket, and started sketching something on a page that didn't look like it had room to hold anything more.

Zirkander lowered his arms, his lips twisting wryly as he

met Sardelle's eyes. "For those who were wondering about my childhood, I assure you this is a representative glimpse."

"Actually, we were wondering about the paddling, sir," Duck said.

"You had a fabulous childhood," Zirkander's father said without looking up. "What boy has the kinds of freedoms that you had? To study whatever you wished? To play however you wished to play? To roam wherever you wanted? I would have *adored* such a childhood."

Cas wouldn't have minded more freedom during her childhood, but judging by the continuing wryness on Zirkander's face, it hadn't been that perfect.

"You would have adored having a father who was never around?" Zirkander didn't sound bitter, exactly, and had probably accepted his past at this point in his life, but his tone *was* dryer than usual.

"Better than one who's always standing over your shoulder, judging your every move, insisting you become someone you don't want to be."

"That's the truth," Tolemek muttered.

Cas met his eyes, a wry smile of her own on her lips. He responded with a similar gesture. They had figured out early on that they had some of the same grievances when it came to fathers.

"Certainly, I would have been pleased if you had decided to come with me on my explorations, but you became a fine young man, despite your insistence on traveling in those flying deathtraps." Zirkander's father held up the journal. "Does that look like an Anksarian number seven? I think it does. I'm finding more and more evidence that suggests they were colonizing these islands millennium before the Iskandians even knew they were here. Do you know what this means?"

"You're going to find the Lost Treasure of Anksari Prime before you die?" Zirkander asked.

"Seven gods, I hope so."

"I'm happy for you, Dad. Did you want to meet my team and hear why we're here?"

"Mom didn't send you?"

"I don't think Mom even knows I'm out of the country."

"Oh. Huh." Zirkander's father scratched his jaw with his pen, apparently not realizing he was using the nib, because he left a black streak on his cheek. He pushed his spectacles up into his hair—the snarled tangles had no trouble supporting the frames—and considered Cas and the others.

Zirkander spread his arm toward the cave entrance. "That's Lieutenant Duck there, the big-eared fellow ogling the women." Duck flushed and jerked his wandering gaze away. "That's Lieutenant Cas Ahn, best marksman on Wolf Squadron. Tolemek, a Cofah scientist who's come over to our side."

Tolemek tensed, watching Zirkander's father warily, but the man's expression didn't change as his son ran through the introductions. If he spent his life in places like this, he might not have even heard of Tolemek; of course, Zirkander hadn't introduced him by his infamous Deathmaker moniker, either.

Zirkander shifted his arm so that his hand extended toward Sardelle. "And this is... ah..."

Sardelle lifted her eyebrows.

"Your soul snozzle?" Tolemek suggested, his eyes glinting.

Cas hadn't heard the term, but she got the gist and had a feeling Tolemek's humor was piqued at the chance of embarrassing Zirkander.

"Sardelle," Zirkander finally said, leaving off any further explanation as to what she did or what she meant to him. "Team, this is my father, Moe Zirkander."

"You can call me Rock Cheetah." Moe smiled, almost hopefully. "Or Rock. Or Cheetah."

"But you don't have to," Zirkander said. "My father has always lamented having what he calls an ordinary name. Thus perhaps explaining his need to give me an unordinary one."

"The women have always called me Rock Cheetah," Moe said. "Because of my blazing mountain climbing speed. It's less blazing than it used to be, I'll admit, but I can still ascend a peak faster than the boy can take off in his flying contraption."

"Mom doesn't call you that," Zirkander said.

"She did when we were younger."

"She's told me the story of how mortified her parents were when you first met and introduced yourself as Rock Cheetah."

"Fine," Moe said. "*Other* ladies, then." He nodded toward the women in the grass skirts.

"I'll wager twenty nucros that they call you Old White Man in their language."

Moe put his journal away and started coiling his rope. "It's *Strange* White Man, thank you."

"Sir," Tolemek said, stepping forward. "The reason we're here is that Zirkander believed you'd be able to help us with... a quest." He withdrew his roll of paper.

"A quest? I assumed this was some military mission."

"We're a mixed party of military and civilians," Zirkander said. "With two missions that happen to coincide with each other. Tee has some flowers he needs identified. More specifically, we need to know where they can be found."

While Tolemek unrolled his drawing for Moe, Zirkander joined Sardelle at the cave mouth. Her arms were folded over her chest. It was always hard to read her face, but Cas guessed she might have been peeved at not being introduced as Zirkander's lady friend, love of his life, future wife... whatever it was they had decided they were to each other. It was none of Cas's business, so she stepped back out into the sun to make sure nobody had approached while the team was inside.

"Sorry about that," Zirkander murmured to Sardelle, his voice just loud enough that Cas could make out the words. "My father is more open-minded than most, not to mention oblivious to racial tensions much of the time, but I wasn't sure I could reveal your occupation in the first two minutes he knew you."

"It wasn't my *occupation* I thought you might share with him," Sardelle said dryly.

Zirkander paused. "Oh. Right. I mean, I thought *that* would be obvious from the way I gazed adoringly at you from across the cave."

"Nice save, sir," Duck said.

Sardelle's snort wasn't quite in agreement.

Two seagulls squawked and leaped from perches high in the rocks above the cave. Cas frowned in that direction. Anything might have startled them, but now that she was out in the open, she once again had that feeling of being watched.

"Everything all right, Ahn?" Zirkander asked.

"I have a bad feeling about this island and these people," she said.

"Will it make you feel better to learn that you're not the only one?"

"It'll make me feel better to leave."

"Let's check on that, then."

Zirkander didn't have to go far. Tolemek and Moe had come closer to the entrance, to look at the drawing in the sunlight slanting inside. Cas twitched when she realized the women had disappeared. The rope had been pulled up, so they must have gone across the bridge or up one of the staircases. It bothered her that she hadn't noticed—and that there was apparently more than one way in and out of that cave. She should be watching in both directions.

"Not a very good drawing, is it?" Moe asked, his spectacles on his nose again as he studied Tolemek's handiwork.

Tolemek stepped up to his shoulder, frowning down at him. Moe was a couple of inches shorter than he and had a smaller frame than Zirkander too. "I was drawing it from the back seat of a flier while an Iskandian pilot with the nickname Raptor bobbed and weaved through the clouds like a drunken crow in a storm."

Cas squinted at him. "It's not my fault there's so much turbulence in the air off the eastern coast of Cofahre. Duck and the colonel were having just as much trouble keeping a steady course."

Moe looked up at Tolemek, who still cut a grim figure, even if he had lost the spiked bracers and other pirate regalia he had favored when Cas first met him. He might have a handsome face, but his bare, muscular arms, battle scars, and the ropes of black hair falling about his shoulders made him look more like a warrior—or a particularly menacing hoodlum—than a scientist.

"Ah, my apologies. I thought you might have purchased it in some bazaar."

"No," Tolemek said coolly. He pointed at the flowers. "That one is purple, that one is blue, and that one's red."

"Yes, I guessed that was the case. That's a *marsoothimum*."

Sardelle nodded—she had already identified that one for him.

"That one is a... oh, I don't know the proper scientific term for it, but the natives call them blood bellies, because they're carnivorous and eat flies and other insects. The blue one is a *keshialys*? I think that's the word. They're all over the mountain meadows above the tree line on Tsongirs Island."

"Tsongirs Island?" Tolemek asked softly, his gaze flicking toward Cas. His face was still, but his dark eyes brimmed with tamped down emotion. "Is that where all of these flowers can be found?"

"No, the *marsoothimums* are farther south. And the blood bellies, where did I see those?" Moe dug out his journal again and flipped through the pages.

Cas kept her focus toward the rocks and the approach to the cave, but she glanced toward his journal and saw surprisingly good drawings, everything from maps to seeds, cones, and flowers to reproductions of hieroglyphics and rock carvings. Small but tidy script accompanied most of the images.

"Ah, here's my sketch of the area." Moe tilted the book toward the sunlight, revealing a map of equatorial islands not far south of Cofahre. He produced a stubby charcoal stick. "Saw the blood bellies there, the *keshialys* there, and the *marsoothimums* are all through here," he said, touching different islands as he spoke. He drew lightly on the page, shading in areas. "Possible intersection points... Rat Island and the Bolos Keys, but none of those volcanoes has the altitude necessary for the alpine *keshialys*. I should know. I would have climbed them if they did."

"Volcanoes," Zirkander said. "I was hoping we'd seen enough of those for a while."

"Most of these archipelagos were formed by volcanic activity, but most of those volcanoes are also long extinct." Moe tapped a large island in the shaded area. "I think Mount Demise is the only likely spot, here on Owanu Owanus."

"Mount Demise?" Duck asked. "That sounds about as promising as being chased naked through the woods in winter by a starving mountain lion."

Several sets of eyes turned toward him.

"Has that happened to you?" Zirkander asked mildly.

"Not... recently."

"That's the Iskandian name for the place," Moe said, "but it's based on the legends from the local people. There's a relatively sophisticated native civilization that hugs the coast and has a city in the biggest harbor, but if you get even a half mile away from the beach, the jungle is extremely dense and wild and filled with deadly predators. Just getting to the mountain—which is an extinct volcano—is next to impossible by land. I believe it wasn't until dirigibles came along that the island was fully charted and the mountain named, though even those maps are vague. There are a few waterways visible from the air, and the dense jungle canopy makes it impossible to see the ground in most places. It's believed there are whole tribes of people back in there who have never had contact with modern civilization. Some are said to be cannibalistic. I haven't heard of any significant archaeological finds back there." He sniffed, as if to dismiss the entire island as unworthy of his attention.

Tolemek had a different reaction as he stared intently at the map, repeatedly mouthing, "Owanu Owanus," as if to burn it into his mind.

"Does that mean you're not going to volunteer to come with us, Dad?" Zirkander asked.

"Oh, I couldn't possibly. I still have work to do here."

"Hanging upside down and showing off your backside for the local ladies?"

Moe glanced at his butt, then waved a hand in dismissal. "Don't be ridiculous. I know the locals aren't excited about my presence, but I am *this* close to finding the coordinates to the Lost Treasure of Anksari Prime." He pinched his fingers together in front of his son's face. "Besides, it's another month before the *Evening Sun* freighter returns to the other side of the island to pick me up, and I'm not getting in one of those airborne deathtraps with you. That's a certainty."

"You've climbed twenty-thousand-foot mountains. How can you possibly be alarmed by the idea of flying?" Judging by Zirkander's long-suffering tone, he and his father had shared this argument before.

"Because I was attached to those mountains by ropes." Moe twirled the end of the coil slung over his shoulder. "There's *nothing* attaching your fliers to solid earth. I'm amazed you haven't dropped right out of the sky and crashed yet."

"That usually only happens when someone's shooting at me."

"You're going to die up there one day, and your mother's going to be all alone."

"I don't think it's *my* company she's always missing," Zirkander murmured.

Tolemek cleared his throat. His face remained neutral, but Cas knew him well enough to sense the impatience in the tense way he held his shoulders. "This city on Owanu Owanus... Is there a harbor? A dock? Do ships come and go?"

Zirkander nodded at Tolemek. "Good question. Ships that travel to Cofahre perhaps? Or that are part of a mail system that might eventually get cargo to Cofahre?"

"Yes, to both," Moe said. "It's technically under Cofah dominion, but Owanu Owanus doesn't have any natural resources that have been discovered, so the empire hasn't shown any great interest in it. Right now, the only population center of any significance is run by criminals and caters to pirates."

"Pirates?" Zirkander looked at Tolemek.

Tolemek shrugged. "I've never been there. The Roaming Curse operated mostly in the Northern Hemisphere and was an air-only fleet, so we didn't often dock in harbors that didn't offer accommodations for dirigibles. But this sounds like a place where your crates of dragon blood might have originated."

"That's what I'm thinking."

"Are the criminals accommodating to non-pirate visitors?" Cas tapped the barrel of her rifle.

"If you bring enough money, I should think so," Moe said.

"You know much more about this place than we do," Zirkander said. "Is there no chance that you'll pause your work here for a time and come with us? Duck has room in his flier, and we can return you to this very beach when we're done."

Before he finished speaking, Moe was shaking his head. He shook it particularly vehemently at the mention of a flier ride. "Here. The island isn't far away, nautically speaking." He held open his book for Zirkander's perusal. "I'll allow you to copy the map if you're quick about it. I need to get back to work. As I said, my time here is limited."

Zirkander's jaw tightened, but he didn't try again to convince his father to come with them. He scrutinized the map for a moment, then pushed it back without writing anything down. Cas had never known him to get lost and trusted that he had memorized it sufficiently to find it from the air.

Sardelle hadn't left the cave mouth or motioned to any of them, but Zirkander looked over his shoulder, meeting her eyes for a long moment. It was almost as if they were communicating. Maybe they were. The sword could talk to people in their heads, couldn't it? Cas shifted uneasily. She might have accepted that Sardelle was a sorceress, but she found the idea of her commander engaged in a telepathic conversation strange.

Zirkander cleared his throat. "We left our fliers unguarded, Dad. We may need to—"

A rock smashed to the ground a few feet away from him, breaking and sending stone shards flying.

"Take cover?" Tolemek asked.

Cas reacted to the attack instantly, raising her rifle and aiming for the top of the promontory. Nobody was standing up there, at least not in view. She searched for movement, the promise of a further attack. A coconut might have simply fallen from the tree branches up there, but rocks didn't usually drop out of the sky unannounced.

The tree branches. One shivered, leaves moving against the blue sky. A monkey stood on the limb. It lifted a furry brown arm and shrieked. There wasn't anything in its hands, but another rock lofted from atop the cliff. Cas thought about shooting it, to break it apart, but it was just as easy to avoid the head-sized projectile. Everyone skittered toward the wall for protection. The rock sounded like a cannonball when it landed.

"I can't believe a monkey threw that," Cas said. It must have weighed twenty pounds. That monkey didn't look big enough to be more than thirty or forty himself.

"What?" Zirkander asked.

"I see monkeys up there, but that's it. No people."

Another rock sailed over the edge, this one lofted in such a way that it landed closer to the group.

"Does this happen often, Dad?" Zirkander asked.

"No."

"Let's get off these rocks then."

Cas waved for the others to climb down first. *If* she found a target, she would shoot to cover their backs.

"Someone must be up there and out of sight," Tolemek said as he jogged for the edge. "Monkeys don't throw rocks at tourists."

Sardelle and Zirkander paused at the top of the climb down, giving each other long looks.

"Owls don't attack fliers, either," Zirkander said, "but we've seen that when shamans were around."

Sardelle said something, but the jungle erupted in noise, as if every animal in a five-mile radius had decided to shriek, roar, or caw at the top of its lungs.

"Go," Zirkander barked, waving to all of them. He jerked his hand for Cas to come too.

She wanted to guard their backs as they climbed down, but more rocks were sailing out of the jungle, some fist-sized and some head-sized. They were falling by the dozens now, and dodging them—or shooting them to break them apart—was less and less likely. Cas slung her rifle over her back on its harness and rushed after the others.

A small rock ricocheted off her shoulder, and she grunted at the sting. Getting hit by one of the big ones could bash her head in. Zirkander was right. Better to find cover before worrying about shooting attackers, *especially* if those were monkeys up there throwing rocks. It sounded ridiculous, but she couldn't believe that a troop of villagers could have climbed up there without her noticing it.

She picked her way down the rock wall much more quickly than she had gone up. Rocks small and large rained down all around them. Duck cried out, then cursed.

In her haste to reach the bottom, Cas slipped, her foot flying off a ledge and her knee slamming into the boulder. She dangled there for a moment, her hand's grip tenuous. An arm slid around her waist.

"You're almost down," Tolemek said in her ear.

He held her until she reestablished her grip, then climbed the rest of the way to the beach beside her.

"Thanks." Cas ripped her rifle off her back again, glowering at the jungle. They had reached the sandy beach, but the attack hadn't stopped. Rocks, coconuts, and sticks flew from the shadowy depths of the trees. She couldn't see much except the occasional movement of a branch, but she fired twice into the canopy, anyway, hoping the loud noise might startle their attackers. All it did was incense the jungle—the cacophony of shrieks and screeches increased to an ear-splitting level.

Zirkander grabbed her arm and jerked his head toward the village. Cas couldn't hear his shout of, "Let's go," but she read it on his lips just fine. Sardelle, Moe, and Duck were already pounding down the beach.

Cas didn't argue. It wasn't as if she could do anything by shooting into the jungle without a target. The crack of her rifle hadn't done a thing to startle the creatures in there.

She ran after the others with Tolemek and Zirkander on either side of her. She had to sprint to keep up with their long-legged strides, and she winced, knowing that they weren't running as quickly as they could. They were waiting for her, making sure she didn't fall behind. She hated feeling like a burden.

Ahead of them, Sardelle pointed at the jungle edging the beach. She, Duck, and Moe veered toward the trees. They probably wanted to avoid running through the village, or maybe they simply hoped the group would make a less easy target with trees all around. So long as there was a path they could follow, and they didn't have to cut their way back to the field—nobody had brought a machete.

A head-sized rock flew out of the trees toward Moe's head.

"Look out!" Zirkander shouted.

Cas feared Moe wouldn't hear him over the howls and shrieks. At the last second, he must have seen the projectile in his peripheral vision. He jerked an arm up to protect his head. The rock bounced off an invisible barrier a few feet before it reached him.

Moe stumbled, clearly surprised by the otherworldly protection. Duck grabbed his arm to offer support. Moe waved it away and ran faster, outpacing Sardelle and Duck to lead the way onto a narrow trail between the trees.

A coconut skipped off the beach a couple of feet in front of Cas, Tolemek, and Zirkander. Fearing they didn't have a sorcerous shield protecting *their* group, Cas ran faster. Sweat slithered down the side of her hot cheeks, and she was panting, but her pride wouldn't let her slow down. She made it to the trail first, racing down the packed sand after Sardelle and the others.

The attack from above didn't abate. If anything, the noise was louder in here, with the green canopy of leaves blocking out the sky and bouncing sound back down to them.

A shaggy brown beast leaped down from above and landed on the trail ahead of them.

Zirkander cursed and grabbed Cas by the shoulder. The ape towered ten times the size of a monkey—bigger than any of them, as well—and it clenched one of those head-sized rocks in its massive grip. Cas fired at the same time as it threw. Her shot took the ape in the chest, but the boulder arced straight at *her* chest. She tried to dodge to the side, but was pulled down by one of the men.

"Look out," she said, as if that wasn't the most useless warning in the world—but she didn't want to be pulled to safety only to have one of them be hit.

Zirkander leaped past her, with his pistol in his hand. Even though she had struck the ape in the chest, the creature hadn't fallen. It was shrieking, its arms flailing at the trees, as if to call down more attackers. Zirkander shot it twice in the head, then plowed in, his utility knife in hand.

Tolemek had been the one to tug Cas out of the rock's path, and he rolled off her, letting her up. She gave him a quick, one-armed hug, her rifle still in the other hand.

"On second thought, maybe I'll let the colonel go first," she said.

Zirkander had driven the ape away. It was staggering into the undergrowth and didn't look like it would make it far.

"What?" Tolemek yelled.

Cas shook her head and started up the trail again. They couldn't hear each other above all the noise. This was madness. She kept her eyes toward the branches above them, hoping to catch the next interloper before it landed on the trail, ready to hurl something at them. She never would have thought she would be shooting at animals in self-defense, Duck's stories of hungry mountain lions notwithstanding. She could only assume the shaman in the village had something to do with this.

The trail brightened ahead, the sun's rays slanting through the trees. They burst out of the jungle, splashing into the mud of the harvested field and nearly running into the backs of the others.

Cas stepped around them, trying to see why they had stopped. Her mouth fell open. What had Sardelle said before? That a burning brand had been thrown on one of the fliers? All three of the aircraft were in flames, huge individual bonfires with smoke pouring into the sky. Dozens of men with spears stood around the pyres, their backs to the heat as they faced Cas and the others. The shaman was there, his head lifted, and his eyes cold as he glowered in their direction.

"Sir?" Duck asked, his own pistol out, but his face full of alarm. Cas barely heard the word, but she knew what he was asking. What were they supposed to do *now*?

A rock slammed into Sardelle's barrier and bounced off. The attack was still coming from the jungle, but she seemed able to deflect it—for now. But what about the fliers? Would the fire damage them beyond repair? The hulls were metal, not wood, but there were certainly parts that could burn. The villagers must have smothered them with wood and pitch or the island's equivalent.

Cas stepped forward grimly. She had four more shots in her rifle and two boxes of ammo in her utility belt. She hated the idea of wantonly killing natives who just wanted to get rid of the threat to their people, but if they succeeded in destroying the fliers, the group would be stuck here. And Cas was *not* going to lose another flier. She had already crashed one in her young career.

"Jaxi, no," Sardelle barked. Cas wouldn't have heard the words at all, but had been stepping past her when she'd called out. Sardelle's gaze shifted back toward the village, concern in her eyes.

Though Cas was reluctant to look away from the natives—a few of them were stalking toward the group now, their spears raised to their shoulders—she risked a glance. And then a second glance, as her mouth tumbled open again.

Huge plumes of black smoke rose from the village. At least ten of the thatched roofs were on fire, great orange flames that leaped even higher than those on the fliers.

The villagers halted their shouts, and a stunned silence fell over the field. Even the yammering in the jungle stopped. Then a woman screamed in the village. The men who had been stalking toward Zirkander and the others turned and cut across the field toward the smoking huts instead. The shaman glared his hatred at Sardelle, but he ran in that direction, as well.

When it was clear they wouldn't threaten the group further, Cas lowered her rifle. Zirkander was already charging through the mud, toward the fliers. Cas chased after him, though she wondered how they would put out the fires and how much damage had been done. What if it was already too late?

But, by the time they had splashed across the field and to the closest fire, the flames on it had faded. All of the fires dwindled. Cas looked back toward Sardelle as she lowered her hand. She wiped her brow then walked across the field to join them. Moe was looking back at her, too, his mouth open, a perplexed expression on his face.

"About not revealing her occupation in the first two minutes he's known her," Tolemek said, "is it all right after the first *twenty* minutes?"

Zirkander rubbed his head. "I'm not sure."

"It doesn't look that bad, sir," Duck called from the top of his flier. He knocked a few charred brands off the hull. "In fact, I don't see any damage to the exterior at all."

"I think we have Sardelle to thank for that." Zirkander nodded to her.

She was striding toward them, mud spattering her leathers, her face grim as the smoke from the village rose behind her. Cas wouldn't have wanted to be the native who got in her way. She shouldered her rifle and jogged to her own flier. She didn't know how much time they had before the villagers put their fire out and returned their attention to them, but she assumed leaving sooner rather than later would be good. Tolemek was already up there, scooping charred wood out of the cockpit and cursing, shaking his hands after touching the still-smoking embers.

Moe stopped before reaching the fliers. "I'm not sure how I'm going to return to my work after all of this—" he pursed his lips and frowned at Sardelle and at the village, "—but I shall wish you luck and take my leave of you now, son."

"Dad, it's not going to be safe for you to stay."

"Of that, I'm certain. I'll make my way across the island and catch that boat in a couple of weeks."

"It would be better if you came with us now."

"In that benighted contraption?" Moe pointed at the dragon snout painted on the nose of Zirkander's flier. "I think not."

Zirkander looked to Tolemek and tilted his head toward his father. Asking if he had anything to knock out Moe? The way he had that obnoxious Colonel Therrik? Even if Tolemek did have another pill, Cas doubted they could trick Moe into munching on it at the foot of a flier. Tolemek shook his head. Cas pulled herself into the cockpit, but she didn't miss the long look Zirkander gave Sardelle. Once again, she had that creepy feeling that they were talking to each other in their minds.

Cas decided to worry about getting her own flier airworthy, rather than what was going on down there. But she wasn't surprised a moment later when Moe collapsed, and Zirkander caught him in his arms.

"Duck, give me a hand, will you?" he asked.

"Uh, sure, sir." Duck jumped down from the other flier. "Is he sick? What happened?"

"He's napping. Let's put him in your—no, better make it my flier. He's going to wake up hotter than a flagpole under the summer sun."

Duck scratched his head. "Napping, sir?"

"Yeah, he's old. Old people nap. Here, take his arm."

Sardelle wiped her brow again. They were all sweaty after the sprint through the jungle, but her shoulders had more of a slump to them. Cas had no idea how much magic a sorceress could do, but she looked like she was the one who needed a nap.

"Took care of most of the mess in here," Tolemek said from the back seat of their flier.

Cas nodded, watching Sardelle as she said a word to Zirkander, then headed to Duck's flier.

"I would be disturbed that she can make people fall asleep out of nowhere," Cas said, "but I guess you can do the same thing, so I would have to be disturbed by your potion-making skills too."

"You aren't?"

"Not… as much as I was."

Cas sat in the cockpit and, after checking to make sure no villagers were running back toward them, fastened her rifle into its special rack. Smoke and flames still danced on the thatch roofs, but she didn't hear any screams of pain. That was good. The people were running buckets of sea water up from the beach. Even though they had been troublesome, she hoped their village wouldn't be too badly damaged.

"You know it's mostly an illusion, right?" Tolemek asked.

"What?"

"The shaman's hut is really burning—I think Jaxi did that. But the rest is an illusion, to distract them."

"Oh. How can you tell?"

Tolemek grimaced. "Don't ask. I still can't believe that all my life I had no idea that I had... strange talents. Or sense. Something. But I wasn't surrounded by magic users, either. Just my untrained sister." He rubbed his face. "I wish I'd gotten her out of that place earlier."

"I thought you did and that you determined you couldn't help her."

"I did. But I still... I was running around, trying to find a solution for her from a distance, when I should have been keeping an eye on her. I had no idea the emperor... What could the government possibly want with her? Did she lead them to the dragon somehow? *Is* there even a dragon?" Tolemek slumped back against his seat.

"We'll find her," Cas said, switching on the flier, feeling the hum of the propeller.

"Ahn?" Zirkander asked.

She gave him the ready sign. It was time to find Tolemek's sister and the source of the dragon blood.

CHAPTER 3

THE SALTY SEA AIR WHIPPED at Tolemek's hair as he leaned out of his seat to peer at lights in the darkness ahead of and below them. The torches and lanterns of a city? He wasn't familiar with this part of the world, where hundreds, if not thousands of chains of islands dotted the ocean. Airship pirates rarely stopped in the area, both because of the dearth of dirigible ports he had mentioned and because there wasn't a financial incentive to visit. With few people, fewer towns, and even fewer shipping lanes, neither the islands nor the seas around them saw much wealth passing through. He had also heard that hurricanes often afflicted the area, though tonight, the sea and the sky were serene, without a cloud blotting out the burgeoning stars.

If this was their destination, they should descend soon, but Zirkander's voice hadn't sounded over the communication crystal yet. Tolemek checked on the other fliers, the faint glow of the control crystals lighting the back seats and cockpits. He couldn't see much of Duck, but Sardelle was slumped down in her seat, dozing after expending all the energy their escape had required. Moe had woken an hour or two ago. Judging about the amount of over-the-shoulder gesticulating that had been going on throughout the flight, father and son were having a long conversation. Moe pointed toward Sardelle more than once. Tolemek didn't know if it was because he had figured out she was responsible for knocking him unconscious or if it was simply because of her... occupation, as Zirkander had called it.

Moe might not be thrilled by the revelation that the group had a sorceress in their midst, but Tolemek admitted a selfish sense of relief at her presence. It took the onus off him. Moe Zirkander might be distracted from the mundane world by his own research, but Tolemek was certain *every* Iskandian had heard of the Tanglewood massacre. Were his involvement to come to light, Moe might object to helping the perpetrator of that incident hunt for a sibling. Tolemek hoped he had enough information to go on already and that he wouldn't need the help of either senior or junior Zirkander again.

"We'll most likely have to land on the beach near that town," came Zirkander's voice from the crystal in the cockpit, just audible over the wind, "but the moon is coming up, so let's fly around the island and see if there are any clearings closer to the mountain."

"We could use some fresh supplies, sir," Cas said.

"I know, but it sounds like a hellish trek through the interior to the mountain. Days on foot, hacking at foliage and vines to make a path. If there's a chance that we can set down right at its base, or even on some plateau, we would save ourselves a lot of trouble."

Tolemek leaned forward, touching Cas's shoulder to warn her he was about to shout. "Your father is positive those flowers only grow above a certain elevation?"

After a pause, Zirkander said, "Yes."

"I agree then. Setting down as close to the mountain as possible would be ideal, *if* this is the right island. It might be wise to ask around in that city and try to verify that it is. Find out if Cofah soldiers have been seen passing through with interesting crates." Maybe someone had even seen his sister.

Duck cleared his throat. "The colonel's lady friend would like a bath and requests a stop in the city for the night."

Zirkander sighed. "I knew it."

"That people want to bathe, sir?"

"That this would turn into a democracy as soon as the civilians outnumbered the soldiers."

"We're three and three, aren't we, sir?" Cas asked.

"I'm told my dad counts as two people because he's older than the rest of us combined."

Tolemek wasn't surprised when Zirkander got smacked in the back of the head, though it didn't seem that heartfelt.

"Maybe just than you four combined," Zirkander amended.

"Regardless, let's check out the island before heading to the city. I see a few fields down there. This is supposed to be a slightly more civilized town than the last one, pirate-infested or not. But let's pick a spot farther away this time."

As the conversation finished, the lights of the town passed below them, and a dark landscape replaced the dark ocean. The moon had risen, but Tolemek didn't see much on the ground, except for the dense black canopy blanketing everything. If rivers or other major terrain features parted the curtain of foliage anywhere, he couldn't pick them out. The extinct volcano rose up from the center of the island, but it was coated with the same thick foliage as the rest of the place.

"Dark down there," Duck said.

"I don't see any breaks in the canopy," Cas said. "No lights or structures, either, not visible from up here, anyway. There's— Sir, don't crash."

Her tone never changed, but the words startled Tolemek until he spotted Zirkander's flier dropping below the level of the others. It swooped toward the mountain, dipping so low that its running lights illuminated the lush green leaves of the treetops below. Monkeys—or some nocturnal relative of monkeys— shrieked in protest. Cas stayed aloft, though she followed along, frowning over the side as Zirkander dipped into valleys and canyons, as if he was looking for something much more important than a landing spot. They circled the entire mountain like that.

"Sorry, Sardelle," Zirkander said over the crystals. "I don't see anything. And there's not a clearing in sight. I don't think this place has ever seen a forest fire."

"Sorry, Sardelle?" Tolemek wondered. She hadn't said anything.

Not aloud, no, came Jaxi's mental intrusion, along with a surprising burst of emotion he had never received from the soulblade. Yes, her thoughts had been urgent that night in the capital, with that bomb threatening to destroy much of the city, but this was different. She almost seemed... giddy.

Good guess, genius. There's a dragon down there.

What? Tolemek shifted his attention from the mountain to Duck's flier. Sardelle was definitely awake now, her eyes wide as she leaned over the side of the craft, gazing into the darkness below. *You can tell?*

Obviously.

Can you talk to it? Tylie might be his priority, but Tolemek couldn't help but be intrigued by the idea that a living, breathing dragon might remain in the world. Besides, if it was here, then it was likely his sister was here too. Providing the Cofah hadn't moved her again.

I'm trying. I should be able to reach him. He's down there. It's possible he's ignoring me. If so, that's quite rude.

He? Tolemek had never imagined a dragon having a gender. In the books, they all tended to be referred to as it or she, perhaps because of their beauty.

This one might be pretty, but he's definitely a boy. Damn, we're leaving.

Zirkander's flier had come back up to a safer height above the canopy—something the white-faced Moe doubtlessly appreciated. The three aircraft sped back to the east, returning to the coast and the lights near the water. As they descended toward a field, Tolemek touched his vest pocket, feeling the crinkle of his drawing and wishing he had more to guide him to Tylie.

In the darkness, the landing was rough, but he kept his mouth shut about it. The look Cas had given him when he had defended his drawing by complaining about the turbulence could have shriveled the balls off a dragon.

I don't know about that. Dragons have big, sturdy balls.

You know this from the historical documents? Tolemek asked. *Or because you checked?*

I suppose it's more of an assumption, given that everything else about dragons is big and sturdy.

So you didn't check. The image of the soulblade magically lifting a dragon's leg to look flashed into his mind.

That sounds like a way to get one's hilt snapped off one's blade. Or to be melted. From what I've read, dragon fire is potent.

Tolemek frowned over at the other flier, wondering why Sardelle's sword was in his head so much. The other craft hadn't come to a stop yet; it was still wobbling, the wings tilting, as Duck struggled with the uneven ground. This field *hadn't* been harvested, and the air smelled of crushed pineapples. Sardelle wasn't looking in Tolemek's direction. Maybe she didn't know how mouthy her sword was being. Actually, it wasn't so much the mouthiness that made him twitchy, but the fact that Jaxi seemed to be monitoring his thoughts. Surely, he had proven that he wasn't a further threat to the Iskandians at this point. Were the others still suspicious of him?

Nah, I'm just listening for thoughts of dragons. It's too bad we sent back the historian. I've been wondering what could cause a dragon to ignore my telepathic questions. I thought you might have some knowledge in that head of yours, between the chemical formulas for substances that kill people and the gooey feelings for your woman.

Maybe it just doesn't want to talk to you, Tolemek suggested.

That's hard to imagine.

Is it? Huh.

"You ready?" Cas was looking back at him, frowning slightly. Maybe she had asked more than once. She had already turned off the propeller, tugged off her cap and goggles, and grabbed her gear.

"Yes." Tolemek unfastened his harness and decided not to mention mouthy swords.

He climbed down, joining the rest of the group on the ground. Something poked the side of his calf. Rows of lumpy protrusions stretched out ahead of them. His guess had been right. They were the tops of pineapples, the fruit almost ripe enough to harvest. He wouldn't have guessed that a town run by criminals would bother with agriculture, but maybe sea pirates liked pineapple in their rum.

Cas stood next to him, her arm touching his. Though Tolemek was eager to begin his search, he also looked forward to perhaps somewhere private tonight with Cas. They had scarcely had any time alone together since this crazy mission started.

"We'll see if we can get lodgings here tonight," Zirkander

said when everyone had gathered around. He patted Moe on the shoulder. "My father says we'll need a guide to make it through the jungle and to the mountain. He hasn't been here himself and isn't familiar with the area. He also says that, even if he had been here, he wouldn't guide me anywhere except into a communal pit toilet, because I kidnapped him. Apparently, he didn't appreciate my method of forcing him to spend time with me."

"It was fine until you started swooping all over that mountain," Moe grumbled, gripping his stomach with one hand. "We nearly crashed three times. My bladder isn't as steel-plated as it once was, you know."

"We weren't anywhere close to crashing, Dad."

"Tell that to the stain in your back seat."

"A piece of information that further ensures I'll never join your commander in his flier," Tolemek murmured to Cas, taking her hand.

She stiffened, and he worried he had been too presumptuous. She was in soldier-mode, keeping an eye on their surroundings, and not likely thinking of togetherness. But after a moment, she relaxed and said, "I prefer to keep you in *my* flier."

He appreciated the response, though he sometimes wondered if they would ever feel as comfortable around each other as Zirkander and Sardelle always appeared to be. Cas so rarely showed affection if anyone was around—and sometimes even when people *weren't* around—that Tolemek sometimes struggled to know when she wanted to be touched. He cared for her, more than he probably should, given the short time they had known each other, and it stung a little that he wasn't certain if she felt as strongly. But maybe the fault was his own. Had he been too distant, too obsessed with finding Tylie? Maybe he should make it clear to Cas how he felt.

"Sardelle," Zirkander said, "do you think you can protect the fliers again?"

"For tonight, yes. If we leave the area, you may need to hire a guard. Or find another way of protecting them." Sardelle sounded tired, despite her nap. Or maybe distracted. With the jungle rising on three sides of the field, the mountain was not visible, but she gazed in that direction, regardless. Maybe she could feel the dragon too. Or maybe Jaxi was yammering in her head about it.

Soulblades do not yammer. We provide useful and insightful commentary.

Tolemek declined to comment. Maybe if he ignored Jaxi, she would stop poking into his thoughts. He had the impression of a haughty sniff, but no more words drifted into his mind.

The group headed down one of the paths through the field. The beach and the ocean stretched away on the side that wasn't dominated by the jungle. Up ahead, the one- and two-story buildings of town spread inland. Along the waterfront, numerous docks stretched into the bay, several with ships tied along them. Lamps burned on a few of those ships, mostly sailing vessels rather than ironclads, but a few had smokestacks, as well as masts.

"Those are pirate ships," Sardelle said as they approached the outskirts of the town. "Most of them, anyway. There are a few fishing boats and a Berthnian freighter, as well. I don't see any Cofah ships."

"I told you this was a pirate outpost," Moe said.

"Your head might be in danger, Zirkander," Tolemek said. "Pirates don't like you."

"Not any of them? I thought you had decided I have endearing qualities."

"I've decided not to kill you."

"Because of my endearing qualities?"

"Because Cas likes you," Tolemek said. "*She* has endearing qualities."

Zirkander stopped at the end of the field and gazed out at the ships. In the darkness, one couldn't see the cannons, guns, and harpoon launchers bristling from the decks, but Tolemek knew they were there. Given the number of ships out there, the town would be crowded too.

"I wonder if there is a library or any type of repository of knowledge here," Moe said. "As long as I'm here, it would be shameful not to do some research. Do you want me to help your people find a guide before I go my own way? I suspect I'm more experienced in that area."

"You're leaving us already, Dad?" Zirkander took his arm and led him away from the group, though his low voice was still audible to Tolemek. "We've barely spent any time together."

"We just spent hours together."

"Hours in which you were railing at me for kidnapping you and telling me about how many men throughout history have met horrible ends because they dallied with witches. That hardly counts as spending time together. Besides, I'd like you to get to know Sardelle."

"Ridgewalker, you have a mission for the king, and I have a quest I would like to complete before I die, a quest I'm hoping won't be overly waylaid by being stuck in this lawless den of iniquity until I can find passage on a boat."

Lawless den of iniquity? Who said such things?

Moe clapped Zirkander on the arm. "It's been good seeing you, but we must not let our personal feelings keep us from achieving the greatness that lies within."

"Have a beer with us, at least. While you're helping us find a guide."

"A beer? So long as the lighting is sufficient so I can go over my notes while we drink. I believe there's a reference to Owanu Owanus in some of my early entries from last year."

Zirkander moved back to the group. "Sardelle, will you come with us to look for a guide and to help ensure that my head stays attached in this—what was it?—den of iniquity?"

"*Lawless* den of iniquity," Sardelle said.

"Yes, right," Zirkander said. "Cas, Duck, and Tolemek, we need provisions and lodgings for the night."

"And to ensure that the Cofah have actually been here," Tolemek said.

"You don't think they have? Ah, I forgot to mention it. Our sentient sword can sense that there is indeed a dragon here. It seems inevitable that the dragon blood originated from this port."

Tolemek sought a way to explain that the blood was only of

moderate interest to him. What he wanted to know was whether *Tylie* was here. Just because she might have been once didn't mean she still was. He didn't want to waste days—or weeks—marching through the jungle to some mountain of death if she had already been moved. "I intend to ask if anyone has seen my sister." He braced himself, expecting Zirkander to argue.

"That's fine, but you keep an eye out for your head too," Zirkander said. "I imagine there are a few pirates out there who would also be happy to kill you."

"*I'll* keep an eye out for his head." Cas patted her rifle.

"Good. Duck?" Zirkander dipped into a pouch and pulled out a few coins. "For the provisions and lodgings. Try to get a good deal. The general didn't send a huge pile of money along for us to use."

Doubtlessly, because the general hadn't expected his team to fly halfway around the world on some secondary quest. Tolemek kept the thought to himself, since this secondary quest worked in his favor.

"Where do you want to meet up, sir?" Duck asked.

"Just stay with Tolemek and make sure he knows the name of the place you find. We'll get the information from him." Zirkander smirked wryly at Tolemek.

Tolemek supposed that meant he wasn't done having Jaxi pop into his thoughts that night.

Duck scratched his head. "If you say so, sir."

When the group reached the first of the docks, they split apart, with Zirkander and the others heading into the city. Tolemek kept walking along the waterfront, waving for Cas and Duck to follow him. He doubted he would find any old allies on the docked pirate ships, but if there was a port master who took fees, he might know about any Cofah ships that had come through in the last few months.

"Might be trouble up ahead," Cas murmured, tilting her chin toward a pack of dark figures laughing and joking as they made their way up one of the longer docks and toward the city.

"Maybe not," Duck said. "They already look drunker than hogs that busted into the cider house."

The men turned off the docks and down the beach, pointing toward one of several well-lit taverns lining the waterfront. Their route would take them past Tolemek's group.

He stopped and leaned against a post near the water. "Let's let them pass."

He turned his shoulder, not wanting to be recognized. Too bad he didn't have a cloak with a hood on it, though the garment would have looked silly in this tropical climate, with a muggy breeze drifting in off the sea. Cas had teased him often about his hair, and he wondered now if he should have cut it back in Iskandia. Even if he wasn't wearing his pirate clothing any more, he *did* have a distinctive look. He thought about asking Cas if she would like to engage in a round of kissing, to *ensure* he wouldn't be recognized, but she was the image of the professional soldier as she watched the men amble past, her rifle cradled in her arms, her finger resting near the trigger.

One of the men in back noticed them, but he didn't slow down or look twice. As the group moved away, Tolemek started to relax until he spotted a boy standing in the shadows of a bench on the other side of the beach. As soon as Tolemek looked at him, the boy darted away, springing for the closest alley.

Cas started to lift her rifle, but paused, probably noticing the youth of their spy. The boy jumped the sleeping form of a drunk man and disappeared into the alley.

She sighed. "I think someone recognized you."

"Let's hope we'll be leaving before it matters." Tolemek pointed to a shack standing at the side of the longest and widest dock. "I want to see if the port master is there."

"It's late," Duck said. "He's probably gone to bed. Or to drink."

"That does seem more likely around here," Cas said.

Tolemek headed for the shack. "If he's not there, his records still may be."

When he lifted a hand to knock on the door, faint snores drifted out to him. He tapped three times. The snores didn't stop. He tried the knob, and the door opened.

Tolemek squinted into the single dim room, making out a desk by a shuttered window but not much else. "Anyone have a match?"

With a soft rasp, a flame flared to life beside him. Duck held the match aloft, revealing file cabinets in addition to the desk, as well as the source of the snores, a bearded man lying facedown on a cot, a pistol jutting from his holster. His arm hung to the wooden floor, an empty bottle next to his open fingers.

"Drinking *and* sleeping," Duck said. "I was right."

"I'll wait outside while you question him," Cas said. "Be quick. There are more people walking down the dock."

Duck found a lamp on its side under the desk and lit it.

Tolemek stepped inside and pulled the pistol out of the man's belt, crinkling his nose as he did so. He might not smell that fresh himself, after the fighting in the lab and the flight from the volcano, but this man had been wallowing in his own body odor for weeks without thinking to hop in the bay out there. The snores faltered when the pistol was removed, but then continued. Tolemek patted him down, making sure he didn't have any more weapons, then jostled his shoulder.

"No taxes today," the man slurred. "Holiday. Go way."

"I bet there are a lot of holidays around here," Duck said.

Tolemek pointed to the file cabinet. "See if there are any halfway decent records, anything about Cofah ships and suspicious crates." He jostled the drunk harder. "Wake up. The dock's on fire."

The man's bleary eyes opened. "Wha?"

"I need to ask you some questions."

The man's surprise turned to suspicion. "This isn't the library. We don't answer no questions. You pay your taxes?"

"The colonel's dad will be happy to know there *is* a library." Duck pulled a half-eaten sandwich out of the top file drawer. Judging by the greenish tint to the meat hanging out of it, it had been there a while. "Halfway decent records may be expecting too much though."

"I see that." Tolemek grabbed the drunk's shirt. "You *will* answer questions. If you want to return to your nap and be left in peace. Just a few. Do the Cofah ever come through here?"

"Get off me." The man grabbed Tolemek's wrist. "Who do

you think you are?"

Tolemek almost didn't respond with his name—Zirkander hadn't lied; there were pirates who would happily see him dead, just because he had been a prominent member of the Roaming Curse, an outfit a lot of rivals detested. But if his reputation had made its way down here, it might be of some use. The main reason he had cultivated it was so people would fear him and leave him alone. It sometimes meant less force was required to deal with enemies as well.

"Deathmaker." With his free hand, Tolemek pulled a small vial out of a vest pocket. He tipped it upside-down and right-side-up in front of the drunk's eyes, letting them focus on the viscous blue liquid inside.

Muffled voices came through the door. Those men talking to Cas? He almost turned his shirt grip into a chokehold, so he could hurry the questioning along, but he reminded himself that Cas could take care of herself. Her five-foot height and hundred pounds in size might make it tough for her to beat thugs into the ground, but she could keep them from getting into beating range with that rifle.

"What is it?" the drunk port master whispered, his eyes locked on the vial.

A lubricant for thwarting rusty locks and hinges, Tolemek thought. "A horrible poison that eats through your skin, through your muscles, and all the way down to your organs, where it turns them to mush and disintegrates your bones."

The drunk gulped.

Tolemek nudged the cap with his thumb. "If I dribble a single drop onto you..."

"Cofah been here," the man blurted. "Beginning of every month. Real regular like."

Tolemek didn't lower the vial, but he let his grip on the man's shirt loosen slightly. "Doing what?"

"Bringing in men and taking some crates. I seen 'em."

There was the proof Zirkander needed. As to what Tolemek needed... "They ever have a girl with them?" Without taking his eyes from the man, Tolemek withdrew a picture he had drawn of Tylie and held it up. "About seventeen—dark hair. Sweet, innocent face. Cofah."

The drunk shook his head. "Never seen a girl. Just men. Soldiers. Oh, and in the beginning, there were some men who weren't in uniform but were carrying lots of equipment. They had to hire a bunch of porters just to get it off the dock. Not many horses here. Livestock draws out the predators, you know."

"You're *certain* there was never a girl?" Tolemek found his hand tightening on the man's shirt again.

"Certain."

"Nobody else works this position who might have been on shift when she came?"

"No." The drunk lifted a hand toward Tolemek's wrist, but paused, eyeing the vial again. "Listen, nobody would bring a girl here. Can't hardly get any women to come stay for the pubs and brothels even. The jungle's dangerous. Wicked predators. Cannibals. Ain't none of those porters that went with the Cofah ever come back."

"Maybe they sneaked her in." Duck closed the cabinets. "Oh, ask him if he ever saw a dragon. Nobody could miss that."

"Dragon?" The drunk's eyebrows drew together, and he glanced at the empty bottle on the floor. "One of them 'kandian dragon fliers?"

"No." Tolemek released the man, frustrated with his answers, but believing the words.

A shot fired outside.

Tolemek lunged for the door, visions of Cas taking a bullet in the chest flooding his mind. Duck was sprinting for the exit, too, and they crashed into each other. Growling, Tolemek shoved him aside and jumped through the doorway first, his fist raised. He had put away the vial and clenched a small metal ball now, this more of a bomb than a lubricant.

Cas was standing where they had left her, as calm as a swan on a lake. The two men who had been walking down the dock earlier were on the beach now, hustling away, one hunched over and the other gripping his shoulder. Helping him walk?

"What happened, Raptor?" Duck asked.

"They realized I was a woman," Cas said. "Apparently, there aren't a lot of them here."

"Are you all right?" Tolemek could see she was, but bristled at the idea of some thugs propositioning her—or worse. He was tempted to throw his bomb after the retreating pair, but forced himself to lower his arm. Cas had taken care of it.

"Fine. First, they thought I was some boy spying on them. They weren't that bright. They..." She stepped out from under the eave of the shack and frowned at the sky out over the ocean. "That's not a pirate vessel."

Tolemek followed her gaze. A dirigible floated above the horizon, its oblong balloon large enough to blot out a large group of stars and part of the moon. "It's not Cofah, either," he said, noting the lack of a ship's wooden frame beneath it. Instead, a metal cabin hugged the underside of the envelope.

"Looks Iskandian." Duck glanced at Cas. "Someone coming to check up on us? On the colonel?"

"That's a civilian model, not a military one," she said, "but we better tell Zirkander. It's a long way from home."

Tolemek walked toward town with them, but his thoughts were on the drunk's words rather than the dirigible. No women had come with the Cofah. Maybe Zirkander's father had been wrong. Dragon or not, maybe this wasn't the right place. If Tylie had never been here, then where was she?

CHAPTER 4

C AS SAGGED WITH RELIEF WHEN she and Tolemek walked into the small second-story room above the drinking and disk-sliding establishment below. They had privacy. Of a sort. Laughter and shouts rose up through the thin bamboo floor every time someone's clay disk slammed into an appropriately large number of pins at the end of the lane. Every sound was audible in the room.

"At least it's more private than a tent," Tolemek said. "Slightly."

He walked over to a door on a side wall and rapped a knuckle against it. Given that it appeared to be made from sturdy paper rather than wood, Cas was surprised his knuckle didn't go through. If either Sardelle and Zirkander or Duck and Moe had a good time that night, the former being more likely than the latter, she and Tolemek would hear about it, especially if the noise from the gaming room died down later. The same went for her and Tolemek, she supposed, though he was still wearing his grim, determined face, the one that suggested he was thinking of his mission rather than sex. It was just as well. Cas was thinking of that dirigible. The fact that it wasn't a military craft relieved her somewhat, but it was possible that a squad of soldiers, along with an officer who outranked Colonel Zirkander, had been sent on a civilian transport to come find them. Kaika and Apex would have made it home by now, and they would have reported to the general, if not the king. Neither person was likely to be happy with Zirkander at the moment. Still, how could they have known where the squadron would go? Zirkander hadn't even known until he had spoken with his father.

That ship's appearance was likely a coincidence and nothing more. Maybe Cas would go out later and see who came off when it docked. *If* it docked. She hadn't seen any elevated platforms or other landing accoutrements for aircraft—their bumpy touchdown among the pineapples attested to the lack—but the dirigible had definitely been heading toward the bay when last she had seen it.

Cas strode past the room's small bed and opened double doors that looked like they led to a balcony, thinking it might have a view of the bay. They did have a view, but there was no balcony. The opening simply fell away into the alley below, an alley that smelled of urine and mold. Lovely. Higher buildings blocked much of the view of the water, but she made out the tip of the dirigible balloon around the end of one. Yes, it had definitely come in.

"Cas?" Tolemek was sitting on the edge of the bed. "Can we talk for a moment?"

She was reluctant to close the door, but the odor wafting up from below encouraged it. Besides, looking at the balloon wouldn't tell her anything. She would need to be closer to see if the craft sent people down.

"What is it?" Cas joined him on the side of the bed, wondering if he might have sex in mind, after all. She had been tense all day and wouldn't mind a release. Or a massage. Or a bath. Perhaps all three. Their room lacked washing facilities, but there might be something off the hallway. Maybe. Her previous time spent as a prisoner on a pirate ship had not suggested that such luxuries were important to them.

"The port master hadn't seen Tylie." Tolemek gripped the edge of the narrow mattress with both hands, fingers curling around it.

"So? From the glimpse I saw of that man, he would be lucky to find his prick with both hands."

"Yes, but—" Tolemek blinked and looked at her. "Did you call it his prick? I haven't heard you use… uhm, call it that."

As if she wasn't in the army and hadn't used much worse language. Granted, she usually did her cursing in her mind, but still. Had she truly not spoken of genitals with him before? Maybe she had been on good behavior, subconsciously trying to convince him she was a lady worth wooing. She snorted. Or maybe her agitation was showing. She should definitely bring up massages.

"It was on my mind," she said.

"The port master's prick?"

"No, yours. Though I thought we might wash it first."

"Ah." A hint of a smile touched his lips, one of the first he had shared in a while. Good. "Hold that thought, please. I wanted to ask…" The smile faded, replaced by a frown. "Maybe I shouldn't bring it up."

"The prick?"

"*No.*" He looked like he might elbow her in the ribs, but he wrapped an arm around her shoulders instead. "Listen, Cas. I appreciate having you here. I've kept my quest to help Tylie a secret for so long, afraid nobody would understand, that nobody else would care." His tone turned bitter. "My father certainly didn't."

"I know. I understand. I'll be glad when you find her, and I hope Sardelle can help her."

"Yes." Tolemek dropped his hands into his lap and stared at them. "Cas, have I… been too focused on finding my sister? I'm glad that you understand how much finding her and fixing the wrongs I've done, at least *this* wrong, means to me. But I don't want you to feel neglected. I care for you very much. I think…" He looked at her face, his dark eyes like pools of uncertainty, almost vulnerability, their expression at odds with his rugged visage. "I *know*. And I want *you* to know. I love you."

The naked statement caught Cas off guard, especially after they had been joking. She hadn't expected such a serious conversation, such a serious subject. "I… was just looking for a massage tonight."

Tolemek's mouth twisted, and he looked away.

"No, sorry," she blurted, grabbing his hand, even as she winced. Women were supposed to know how to handle the sharing of feelings, weren't they? But she had no idea.

Cas might have felt a childish adoration for Zirkander when she had been younger, but she had never professed her love for anyone, and she didn't know if she was ready to do so now. She cared about Tolemek, certainly. When she had thought that pit trap in the Cofahre lab had killed him, an intense feeling of loss had swept over her. Was that love? She tended to equate love with wanting to marry a man, birth his children, and spend all of eternity with him. So many female soldiers she had known had left the service soon after they had gone starry-eyed and proclaimed love for this or that man. Those women had traded their careers for staying at home and being mothers, and Cas couldn't *imagine* wanting that, not at this point in her life and maybe not ever. Was that something Tolemek wanted? Was he thinking they should marry eventually? And have children? And that she should quit the squadron? No, he had never hinted of such a thing. She should not make assumptions. Even though she had the distinct impression he would be happier if she didn't work for Zirkander.

She pushed her hand through her short hair, probably tearing a few pieces out. Tolemek shifted beside her on the bed.

"Sorry," she mumbled again, realizing she had been silent for a while. "I didn't mean to make light. I'm just—I don't know if I'm ready... I mean, I like you, Tolemek. More than like. You're very..." Seven gods, she was mangling this. Why hadn't he warned her first, so she could rehearse something?

"Never mind. I shouldn't have brought it up." Tolemek stood up, and her hand fell away. He took a couple of paces and stopped, facing the door, his chin to his chest.

Cas swallowed, knowing she had hurt him by not having the right words, by not saying his words back to him. But she did not want to lie or utter something she did not fully mean.

"Cas?" He lifted his head, but continued to face the door instead of her. "If you have to choose between going with Zirkander to find the dragon and going with me to find Tylie..." He finally turned back toward her, his dark eyes intent. "Which will you choose?"

She held back a grimace. It had occurred to her that this question might come up over the course of this mission, and she didn't want to have to make that choice. "I don't understand," she said, more to buy time to think than because she didn't. "Don't we still believe that your sister and the dragon are in the same place?"

"I hope they are. I'm not certain of it, especially after talking to the port master. I thought I would ask around more tomorrow, see if anyone recognizes her."

"The colonel wants to leave tomorrow."

Tolemek's jaw tightened. She shouldn't have mentioned Zirkander.

"But I think your answers are going to be where this dragon is," Cas hurried to add. "Why the Cofah took your sister and how she ties in with the creature. It makes sense to stick with the, uh, the others. Besides, we might need your help. If there's another big Cofah research facility..."

"We." Tolemek gazed at her, as if she had inadvertently given her answer, and it did not sit well with him.

She didn't know what else to say. She was on the clock, not out here on some personal quest. It wasn't about picking Zirkander over him. Her duty was to follow her superior officer. That was it. If she ran off on some side trip with Tolemek, she would be absent without leave. She would be risking her career. Maybe he *did* expect her to choose him over her career.

"It won't take us *that* long to get there and look around," Cas said, afraid Tolemek truly thought he needed to go off on his own and search elsewhere. "It's less than forty miles from here to the base of the mountain. Granted, if there's not a path, that'll be slow going, but I can't imagine it taking more than three days each way. We'll be back in a week. You'll either have your answers, or you'll have more of a clue as to where to go to find them. To find her."

"Yes, of course." Tolemek turned back toward the door. "If we're leaving tomorrow, I better go back out tonight and ask around." He touched his vest pocket, where he kept the pictures of the flowers and one of his sister, as well.

Cas stood. "Do you want me to go with you?"

"No. Stay here. Get some rest. The bath you've been wanting." He gave her a quick smile over his shoulder before opening the door. It didn't reach his eyes.

"I've been wanting that bath for you, too, you know," she called after him.

He lifted a hand in parting, then was gone.

"Men," Cas grumbled, then wished she had turned that same question on Tolemek. If the situation demanded it, would he choose her over his sister? No, she was glad she hadn't asked. She didn't want to get angry and say something she would regret. She would find the washroom, clean up, then go back out again and see what that dirigible was doing here. The number of pirate ships in port didn't suggest this would be a popular tourist area.

* * *

Finding the washroom proved more difficult than Cas expected. She had to go back downstairs, then push past sweaty natives mingling with sweaty pirates of various ethnicities, most shouting at each other in broken Cofah. She found a hallway and started checking doors. None of them had pictures or words or even graffiti that might have identified the contents. The second door she opened revealed a man peeing in a hole in the ground. He smiled over his shoulder at her, too drunk to be embarrassed, at least she hoped that was the explanation for why most of the stream was splashing off the tiles. Grimacing, Cas backed out, deciding to try the rest of the doors before resigning herself to the men's latrine.

The next door held a storage room full of casks of rum, but behind the fourth, she found Sardelle. She was standing with her chin in her hand, considering a hole similar to the one the drunk man had been defiling.

"Sorry," Cas said when she looked up. "There don't seem to be locks. I'll wait."

"No, no. I believe it's a communal lavatory and washroom. There's a second hole, you see." Sardelle stepped back, extending a hand. There wasn't any sort of divider for privacy. At this point, Cas was glad she wasn't supposed to pee out the door and into the alley from her room. Men might be able to handle such feats, but it sounded messy to her.

"Not quite up to the standards of the Iskandian capital." Not that Cas cared. She had peed in more uncomfortable places during her army training. "Did you say washroom?"

"Apparently. There's a hose, and that bucket has a sponge in it. I was just debating if one put the water down here when one was done or..." Sardelle sighed and lowered her hand. "It's not that I haven't roughed it in the past, but I was hoping for a warm bath after nearly being annihilated by that volcano."

"It's warm out. We could go dip ourselves in the bay." Cas was mostly joking—she hadn't planned to take anyone with her to spy on the dirigible—but Sardelle's brows rose thoughtfully.

"That might be more hygienic."

"I don't know. I'm guessing the sewer dumps out over there somewhere." If there *was* a sewer. For all Cas knew, the holes in the ground might simply drain into a pit in the alley.

"You didn't see the sponge, did you?"

Cas peered into the bucket and made a face. "When you said communal, you did mean communal, didn't you? And, uhm, used."

Sardelle smiled. "Let's check out the bay. I'm curious about that dirigible."

"You *are*? I mean, I was going to investigate it myself, because I'm concerned trouble may be following us, but I thought you and the colonel might, ah..." Cas rocked her hand, deciding to keep the gesture vague instead of employing one of the cruder ones to suggest coitus.

"He's having his beer with his father. I thought I should let them bond. Besides, I don't think Moe is that enthused about me."

"Because you saved our lives and our fliers?"

"Because I knocked him unconscious and he woke five thousand feet up in the sky."

"Ah." Cas pushed open the door. "To the bay then."

After she retrieved her pistol and rifle—Sardelle already had her sword belted around her waist, having perhaps had an inkling of how scary the washroom experience might be—they pushed their way back through the crowd. They passed the wooden lanes stretched out for the disk-pushing game and noticed Zirkander and Moe were standing at a small, high table, one lacking chairs.

Zirkander wore a goofy sun hat that kept his face in the shadows while sipping from a mug of beer. A second one rested in front of his father, who was trying to read something in his journal by the light of a candle. Sardelle walked over to the table, rested a hand on Zirkander's shoulder for a moment, said something in his ear, then kissed him on the cheek.

After Cas's uncomfortable discussion with Tolemek, she couldn't help but envy their ease. *Sardelle* probably hadn't hesitated to proclaim her love.

Zirkander clasped her hand, then turned the gesture into a farewell salute. Despite her earlier words, Moe didn't glower at Sardelle. He didn't seem to notice her at all. Cas wondered if he was noticing his son.

"I have a theory as to why Ridge became such a daring hero," Sardelle said with a wink when she returned to Cas's side and they were heading for the door.

Cas glanced back at Moe. "To try and impress his dad?"

"Or maybe just in the hope of being noticed."

It was strange to think of Zirkander that way. Like Duck had said, he was the big hero in the hangar. To imagine him as a reckless boy craving his father's approval was indeed odd.

Relief flowed into Cas when she stepped outside. Even though the city was alive with raucous crowds and noisy from the drums and zithers flowing out of pubs along with the howls of animals in the jungle, it felt peaceful after the smoky, loud interior of the building. She felt better as soon as the night air wrapped around her. The humid, sticky air clung to their bodies, but the heat was not as intense as it had been earlier.

"Ridge promised me he would also bathe in the bay later," Sardelle said as they walked down the main street toward the beach. Several men lounging on porches or leaning against street posts eyed them as they passed, but Cas had her rifle, and Sardelle had her sword, and nobody approached. "Sitting behind him and then Lieutenant Duck on the way here was… an olfactory experience."

"I suppose it's worse in the back." Cas wondered if Tolemek had been noticing her own odor. She doubted she could attribute that to his reason for leaving to scout.

"I don't think your engineers were thinking of comfort when they designed those fliers."

"No, fighting off pirates and Cofah mostly, I imagine."

"Ridge said he and his father were waiting to meet with someone who knows a guide who might take us to the mountain," Sardelle said. "The first people Moe tried laughed and walked the other way."

"Oh? I hadn't heard about that."

"Apparently, the Cofah have been through here, hiring guides, and those guides never came back, so nobody's eager to take the risk." Sardelle lowered her voice. "There are some stories about things going on out in the jungle."

"I heard about the cannibals."

"That's always been going on—I remember those stories from three hundred years ago."

"You've been here before?"

"Not this island, but others nearby. I used to work on a naval ship."

Cas realized she knew very little about Sardelle. Even though they had spent some time together now, it had always been with the men around, and Cas hadn't naturally been drawn to her, being put off by the sorcery. Even if it had come in handy numerous times now, she had a hard time not seeing Sardelle as something strange, something not quite human. And if she was honest with herself, it bothered her that Sardelle was with Zirkander, too, that *she* was the one who got to call him Ridge. Cas had long since gotten past the idea of having a romantic relationship with Zirkander, but she couldn't help but feel that she had known him much longer than Sardelle and that *she* ought to be the one on a first-name basis with him. It was petty, and she knew it, and she was trying to bury that resentment, or at least not let herself act on it in any way, but she did wonder if Tolemek sensed how much Zirkander meant to her and if that was why he had asked that question. She couldn't help it if she had known him for years and that he had been a mentor and, yes, a friend to her—first-name basis notwithstanding—since long before Tolemek had been in her life. But maybe she could make it clearer that *Tolemek* was the one she wanted to go to bed with and that he was the one she imagined being a bigger part of her future. Yes, and why couldn't she have told him that when he had brought up love?

She sighed.

"Everything all right with Tolemek?" Sardelle asked as they turned onto the sandy street paralleling the waterfront.

"You're not reading my mind, are you?" Cas asked in jest, though she wondered. Tolemek had said something about telepaths being able to do that and had also mentioned that the sword poked into his head now and then.

"No. You just seem glum, lost in thought. I hope nothing's wrong. This mission has been trying so far."

"Yes," Cas murmured. "No, Tolemek's fine. He's looking for information on his sister. The port master hadn't seen her."

"Ah."

That "ah" sounded too knowing for Cas's tastes. Time to put thoughts of romance aside.

The moon was higher in the sky now, shining a silvery beam onto the calm bay and onto the side of the dirigible too. Cas stopped, her back to a wall, to study it more closely. Lights burned behind the windows in the cabin, but the craft was too far out in the bay to make out people or anything inside.

"That's odd," she said. "They're anchored out there, but they're closer to that ridge on the other side of the bay than the docks. Nobody will be able to come to town. Do you think they're waiting, making sure they're out of range of the pirates? Maybe they're here to pick someone up?"

Sardelle had joined her against the wall, but she didn't respond. She merely gazed thoughtfully at the dirigible.

"...went this way," a man whispered nearby, from around the corner of the street Cas and Sardelle had turned off. "Two women. No men."

"...get them for us?"

Not likely. Cas lifted her rifle, her finger finding the trigger. Four shaggy-haired men lumbered around the corner and looked up and down the beach. Cas judged their distance. She could fire up to six rounds in fairly rapid succession, but she did need to pull the lever to chamber the next bullet between the shots. She ought to be able to hit three men before the fourth reached them. Sardelle would have to deal with the last one. It made Cas twitch to realize she would have to rely on someone else, but Sardelle could handle herself in a fight.

The men hadn't yet looked toward the shadows along the wall. A hand came to rest on Cas's forearm.

Her first instinct was to shake it off, but Sardelle leaned close and whispered, "They won't see us."

As if to make a joke of her words, the men turned toward Cas and Sardelle, walking straight down the packed sand street. Cas's finger tightened on the trigger, but she hesitated. She had no idea what passed for the law on this island, but she had already shot a pirate in the hand. Granted, that had been self-defense, but there hadn't been anything but pirate witnesses, and his buddy might lie. She couldn't preemptively shoot people, as much as she wanted to. The men weren't looking at her, anyway. Their gazes and pointing fingers were toward the end of the beach rather than Cas's spot on the wall.

"That one of 'em?" one asked, waving at a distant figure silhouetted by the moon.

"Might be. Come on."

The men passed Cas and Sardelle so closely that they could have touched them. The scents of alcohol, sweat, and smoke wafted off them in repugnant waves. Cas wrinkled her nose but didn't otherwise move.

She waited until the men had shuffled a couple dozen meters down the beach before whispering, "That's a handy skill."

"Yes, against humans, anyway. Animals sometimes see through it, and..."

"What?" Cas asked, surprised by the uncertainty in Sardelle's voice.

"Let's just say that I've been concerned that the dragon is working for the Cofah and won't take kindly to our intrusion. I certainly can't fool him. As far as magical power goes, Jaxi and

I would be like fleas in comparison to such a creature." Sardelle snorted. "Especially me, Jaxi points out. She thinks she may rate closer to a mosquito in her ability to harry a dragon."

"Oh." Maybe Cas shouldn't have asked. Even though the Cofah had the dragon blood, it hadn't occurred to Cas that the dragon might be a true ally of theirs. She winced at the thought of it flying through Iskandian skies, burning the countryside— and the cities.

"We're concerned that the dragon didn't talk to us. Jaxi reached out to him, and he should have been aware of her presence, but he neither welcomed us nor warned us away."

"Maybe it's—he's—unconscious," Cas said. "The Cofah have been taking all that blood…"

"Based on what we've seen, a relatively small amount has been taken, given the size of a dragon, and it seems like it's being done over time. That shouldn't affect the health of a dragon. I had the thought that the creature might be staying silent to lure us into a trap."

"Heartening."

"Yes, I know. Sorry, I'll try to be more optimistic about our mission. I—" Sardelle had been looking at Cas, but her gaze shifted toward the bay again, toward the dirigible.

As far as Cas could see, nothing had changed, but her vision, as sharp as it was, was limited at night. Presumably, a sorceress had more senses than eyesight to employ. "Can you tell how many people are on there?" she asked.

"Forty or fifty. I don't sense anyone with otherworldly power, nor do the people seem to be here for a military purpose. The ship has weapons, for defense, I assume, but the people inside are having dinner and drinking. They seem like civilians, tourists, maybe."

"You can tell all that from here?"

"Jaxi can, yes. But one of the hatches on the opposite side opened. I'm trying to see—let's go down to the water for a better view."

The woman-hungry brutes had disappeared around a bend in the terrain, so Cas didn't hesitate to follow her. A breeze came up to help them—or maybe Sardelle was responsible for that—and turned the end of the dirigible, so that open hatch became visible. Lights may have been burning behind the windows, but the room or luggage compartment or whatever they were looking at was dark. Cas couldn't see into the interior, but some quick hint of movement caught her eye, flying out like an arrow. But if it *was* an arrow, she lost sight of it against the dark sky.

"Is that..." Cas checked her pockets, not sure if she had left her collapsible spyglass in her pack. Ah, there it was. She slipped it out, extended it, and located the open hatch. "A thin rope or cable is coming out of it. Do you see that? It's taut." She followed it with the spyglass, but even with the enhanced distance vision, she had a hard time seeing where the rope ended. It had attached to something on land, though, on the far side of the bay from the city, in what looked like an uninhabited rocky ridge. The terrain thrusting out into the ocean was part of what protected the harbor. "Do you want to see?" Cas held out the spyglass.

"I see enough," Sardelle said. "Look." She pointed.

A dark figure leaped out of the hatch. He hung from a belt or something similar that he had looped over the rope, and sped down the taut line toward the landmass. Dark clothing, gloves, and a hood shrouded his body, so Cas couldn't tell anything about the figure, other than that the breadth of the shoulders and overall size meant it was probably a man. He sped down the rope at an impressive speed, then let go when he reached the ridge. He dropped ten or fifteen feet, but landed lightly, absorbing the impact without trouble. The darkness of the rocks soon swallowed him, and he was lost from view. Back on the dirigible, the rope was cut and the hatch shut.

"I guess he didn't want to pay the dock fees," Sardelle said.

Cas lowered her spyglass. "What are the odds that he doesn't have anything to do with us? Want to bet?"

"I don't know how anyone could know we're here."

"That doesn't answer my question."

Sardelle sighed. "No, I don't think I want to try and answer it. Or take your bet."

"We better make our wash session quick and report back to the colonel."

"I've already told him. No need to rush too much. I'd prefer to find a private spot where pirates won't amble past and leer."

"Can't you just make us invisible?"

"I suppose, but I don't want to have to smell pirates ambling past, either."

"Sounds reasonable." Cas trailed after Sardelle, though she couldn't help but gaze back toward the ridge and wonder who that ship had deposited.

* * *

Tolemek was in a poor mood by the time he turned down the street leading back to their lodgings above the Tethered Tentacle. Not only had his skulking around and questioning people amounted to nothing, but he regretted his entire conversation with Cas. She had been in a playful mood, and he had ruined it. And why? Because of his pathetic insecurities? What had he expected when he confessed that he loved her? That she would fling her arms around him and cry, "Me too!" in return? She had looked more like a cornered animal. If that hadn't been enough of a crime, he had pushed her with that stupid question about who she would choose if he and Zirkander went separate ways.

She had been right, in that there was no reason for him to worry about that possibility, not yet. So why had he asked? Because he had wanted her to answer that she would *of course* go with him instead of with the colonel? Yes, he had, even though he knew that was... wanting too much. And it wasn't fair to foist that question on her unless he had to. If the time did come, he had to understand that Zirkander was tied in with her career and her duty to her nation. If she chose to stay with her squadron, it wasn't as if she was choosing Zirkander over Tolemek. It just felt that way.

He took some solace in the fact that she had still offered to come with him to hunt for information. He shouldn't have rejected that offer. That had been petty. Like if he couldn't have all of her, heart and soul, he didn't want anything to do with her? No, that wasn't true at all. He needed to be more mature about this. Wasn't he supposed to be the older and wiser one? The older and wiser one who had spent far too many nights in his lab instead of experiencing meaningful relationships with women, relationships that might have taught him to be less of an...

"Idiot," he grumbled.

At least you acknowledge it, came a cheerful and unwelcome voice in his head. *Not all men are so percipient.*

What do you want, Jaxi?

To give you advice. You should return to your room, remove your shirt, and flex your muscles in a manly way as you recite a poem of penitence for your lady.

Tolemek grimaced. *I don't think Cas is the kind of woman who gets weak-kneed at the notion of poetry.*

All women get weak-kneed if it's heartfelt. Trust me, this works.

Didn't Sardelle say that you've been in that sword since you were a teenager? How much personal experience could you have on this matter? And why was he having this conversation with a sentient sword who was butting into his head?

I've been around for hundreds of years. I've witnessed countless relationships. And I've read thousands of books.

Tolemek imagined the sword lying across the open pages of a relationship manual. *So, basically you have* no *personal experience in this arena.*

I'm closely linked to my handlers, some of whom have been quite virile. Occasionally promiscuous. Not Sardelle. She was disappointingly chaste before meeting her soul snozzle. Now, she's making up for the celibate years. It seems repetitive to me, but they don't enjoy interruptions. Or suggestions. Or comments on form. It doesn't leave me with a lot to do while they're rutting like bonobos.

Tolemek's grimace deepened. *I... don't want to have these images in my head.*

No? For a freewheeling pirate, you're a bit of a stodgy stick, Tolemek.

Yes, I am. It occurred to him that Jaxi might be talking to him now out of boredom due to... an occupied handler.

You're a smart boy, aren't you? You're about to have visitors, so I'll let you get on with that.

What?

Several dark figures stepped out of the alley beside the Tethered Tentacle. They were all armed and wore a scruffy assortment of stolen gewgaws, flamboyant hats, and tacky jewelry. Two of the men gripped pistols in their hands, and they were all facing him.

"Evening, Deathmaker," one with a gravelly voice rumbled, tipping a hat with a brim wide enough that parrots could have nested on it.

"What do you want?" Tolemek asked, turning his torso away from the nearest streetlight and slipping a hand into his vest. He slid out one of his smoke grenades, as well as something more potent that would knock the men unconscious if they inhaled enough fumes. "And who are you?"

"Captain Moravian," the man drawled. "And crew. Part of it, anyhow."

The name was vaguely familiar, an Iskandian buccaneer if Tolemek recalled correctly. He had a sailing ship rather than an air-worthy craft, and the Roaming Curse hadn't encountered him before.

"We were just out for a stroll," the captain said, "and saw that you were out for a stroll too. On an island not many airship pirates have occasion to visit."

"Not many people at all have occasion to visit," one of his followers said with a snicker.

"I'm retired," Tolemek said bluntly, thumbing the pull-tab on the smoke grenade, debating whether he should throw it and run into the building. But nobody had raised a pistol yet. Maybe he could get some information from the pirates.

"Heard that. That you up and killed Captain Slaughter but didn't bother to take his ship. Funny, that."

"The Iskandians had blasted the ship full of holes."

"Ships can be fixed. Crews acquired. Unless you had something more lucrative waiting for you somewhere…"

"Like here," the snickerer said with another laugh.

"Here?" Tolemek asked. What in all the levels of hell could be lucrative here? They couldn't know about the dragon blood, could they?

"Whilst we were out strolling, we noticed you ambling into yon lodgings." The captain jerked a thumb at the building behind him. "And we noticed the treasure hunter ambling at your side."

"The treasure hunter?" Tolemek asked.

"Old Man Zirkander."

Huh, Tolemek hadn't realized Colonel Zirkander's father had a reputation independent of his son's. Moe would probably be upset to hear himself labeled as "Old Man" instead of Rock Cheetah. Did these pirates even know *Colonel* Zirkander was here?

"Man's known to have found some baubles in his time," Moravian said. "And to have mapped and researched a whole lot of wild lands. He's written about a lot of treasures, too, sharing information about those he wasn't interested in hunting for, on account of them being in territories unfriendly to Iskandians."

"I had no idea you had such an interest in treasures. How long have you been here, Moravian? You seen the Cofah ships coming and going?"

"All pirates are interested in treasures. In money. Keeps a crew fed and a man in baubles and women," Moravian said, ignoring his other questions. "My first ship came by way of snooping around in a forgotten cove that pirates from the olden days once used. Pays to read up on treasures, you know."

"I'm sorry to disappoint you, but I'm not here to hunt treasures. I'm looking for someone." Tolemek thought about asking after Tylie, but decided he didn't want to risk letting these people know he was hunting for kin. They might find a way to use that against him. "An old enemy," he tacked on.

"Of course you are, Deathmaker. We believe you."

More snickers came, this time from the whole group. They didn't seem interested in anything but treasure. Just as well.

"I believe this conversation is over," Tolemek said. "Unless you fellows want to buy me a drink, I'm going to bed." He took a step forward, watching them, testing them to see if they would let him pass.

The captain glanced down at Tolemek's hand. The shadows should hide the grenade, but maybe Moravian knew his reputation well enough to know he would have something ready. He tipped his big hat again, then stepped back into the shadows.

Tolemek walked past the group. When he reached the door, he glanced back. The pirates had disappeared. Tolemek hoped that would be the last he saw of them, but he wouldn't bet on it.

CHAPTER 5

THE RAFT SHUDDERED AND WOBBLED, stones scraping the bottoms of the logs as the four porters steered it into the center of the river, pushing off the rocky bottom with long poles. Even the middle of the waterway scarcely appeared deep enough to accommodate the dubious craft. As far as Cas could tell, nothing except vines held it together, and more than a few boulders protruded from the shallow water.

"They promised we could go ten miles upstream this way," Zirkander said, perhaps noticing her doubtful expression. He stood near the front, holding a pole of his own. He had already been called upon to use it, pushing the raft away from one of those sharp boulders. "And as slow as we're going, it's apparently even slower to travel on foot. Roads are non-existent on the island, and none of the trails stray far from the coast. The city doesn't like to encourage the cannibals to visit, it seems."

"You would expect criminals to have a greater sense of adventure," Sardelle said from her seat on the gear and backpacks of supplies piled in the middle. She smiled warmly at Zirkander.

Thanks to the thin door, Cas knew *they* had enjoyed their night together. For herself, she had kept her back to Tolemek when he came to bed, afraid he would ask more awkward questions she did not feel capable of answering, not in a way that would please him. He had slipped into the other side of the bed without anything more than a soft sigh. When morning had come, they had each done an impressive job of pretending the previous night's conversation had never happened.

Cas paced around the short raft, telling herself to pay attention to the present, not the past.

She had been asked to sit down and stay out of the way—at least, that was what she guessed the terse words and gesticulations from the porters had been about—but she couldn't relax on this deathtrap. Besides, the closeness of the brush on either side of the river, not to mention branches stretching over their heads—and sometimes so low they had to duck—made her uneasy. Between the denseness of the vegetation and the perpetual twilight caused by the thick canopy overhead, someone could approach very close to the group without their noticing. She hadn't forgotten the man from the dirigible.

Tolemek was sitting on the back of the equipment pile and facing the rear, in the direction of the town that had already disappeared, but he was tinkering with some gadget in his hands, and she didn't know if she could trust him to watch their surroundings. Duck was busy poling along with the porters, though he hadn't quite gotten the hang of it yet, and the men kept snapping at him in their own language or in broken Cofah. Even though Iskandian and Cofah were basically the same language, the dialect and accent made it hard for Cas to understand their version of it.

Zirkander was making a valiant stab at communicating with the men, though. At the least, they had figured out how to rate the drinking establishments in town, valuable intelligence, no doubt.

"Do you think the fliers will be all right, sir?" Cas asked during a lapse in the conversation. She leaned away from a vine dangling out of a tree branch, then grimaced when a lizard scampered up it. She had no idea what was venomous out here. The caws, squawks, and yips that drifted out of the dense foliage reminded her too much of the jungle on the first island, the one that had proven most inhospitable to their team.

"My father said he would look in on the men we hired to watch them," Zirkander said. "That library he found isn't open that many hours a day, so I shouldn't have to worry about him getting too distracted by his research to handle that task." His mouth twisted. Maybe he wasn't that confident in that assessment.

"I wish he had come along with us." Cas wasn't usually one to quail at the dark or the wilds, but she had been raised a city girl, and the primordial jungle made her uneasy. Moe might not have been to this island before, but he must have explored all manner of wildernesses like this.

"My father is nearly seventy," Zirkander said. "Claims of being a Rock Cheetah notwithstanding, this would be a taxing journey for him. Besides, he wasn't that interested in it."

That being the real reason he wasn't coming, Cas gathered. "I'm concerned the toilet paper wrapped around the fliers this morning was a sign that we're not welcome here," she said. Sardelle had admitted her ability to protect the craft would fade once they moved more than a couple of miles from them.

"I'm still puzzled as to where the nocturnal miscreants got that paper to start with. It's not as if there was any by that hole in the ground in the lavatory."

"We decided that was what the sponge was for," Sardelle said.

"There wasn't a sponge in the men's room. I had to use the hose."

"Chilly water."

"Tell me about it. You know, Sardelle, when I imagined traveling the world with you, this wasn't quite what I had in mind." Zirkander lifted his pole to push away from a boulder threatening to clip the corner of the raft.

"Nobody's tried to kill me yet on this island," Sardelle said. "That's something I can't say for Iskandia."

"Just wait. Things will change."

"In Iskandia?"

"Either that, or someone will try to kill you here." He smirked at her.

Cas walked the three steps to the back of the raft. Tolemek had stopped one of the porters and was showing him the picture he had drawn of his sister.

"No. No see girls," the man said. The other three porters had brown skin and short straight black hair, but this fellow had some mixed blood, with lighter skin and a few freckles on his cheeks. His Iskandian wasn't any better than the others, though. "You ask guides who go with soldiers. They know."

"I was told those guides haven't come back yet," Tolemek said.

"No, no back. Ever." The porter drew a circle on his chest and bowed his head. Some prayer for the deceased?

A rock scraped the bottom of a log, and the raft shuddered. The porter returned to work.

"Zirkander said his father is going to watch after the fliers," Cas told Tolemek when they were alone—as alone as one could be on a raft with nine people on it. She, Duck, and Tolemek had been discussing the how-do-we-get-home-if-the-fliers-are-sabotaged problem that morning while Cas had been setting booby traps in the cockpit of her craft. She had ensured nobody would *steal* her flier, but there were other things that could be done to harm it.

"Judging by Moe's tendency toward distraction, I don't know that I'm bolstered by that knowledge," Tolemek said.

"I know *you're* not talking about tendencies toward distraction. I once brought lunch to your lab, made tea, warmed up the food over a burner, and ate my half before you noticed I was there."

"I was too deep in thought over a perplexing problem to speak. I noticed you were there."

"Sure, you did," Cas said. "At the very least, Moe should notice if the fliers are wrapped in toilet paper again, and he can take it down."

"I'm not positive he would notice toilet paper wrapped around *himself*."

Cas snorted and thumped him on the arm. It was a natural action for her, usually, but as soon as she did it this time, she wondered if he would prefer a more feminine acknowledgment of his humor. Except that she didn't know what that would be. A kiss? Or a coy smile and batting of the eyelashes? Ugh. Anyway, this wasn't a private spot. He should have stayed in their room last night if he had wanted kisses.

"Did you find out anything about Tylie last night?" she asked, though she guessed he hadn't. He had not mentioned anything this morning.

"No. And I'm sorry I stormed out on you," Tolemek murmured, his voice low. "I shouldn't have picked a fight."

She appreciated the apology, but was reluctant to discuss the topic again, not when she hadn't resolved her feelings on the issue. She opted for a light response. "You call that a fight? There weren't even any bullets exchanged."

"Does that often happen when you squabble with lovers?"

"Not lovers, but I tried to shoot my father a couple of times."

"Does that mean I shouldn't hold my breath, waiting for an invitation to a family dinner?" Tolemek asked.

"If you were invited, it would probably be a trap, so he could kill you more easily."

"Yeah." Tolemek stared down at the logs of their raft, looking so glum that it made her heart ache. She wished she could do something—say something—to improve his mood, but apparently, making jokes wasn't the answer, not this time.

"My father never..." Cas lowered her voice, wanting the words to be for him alone. "Feelings were never discussed in my family, not after my mother died. You were supposed to be strong and independent, and it was a weakness to confess that you cared, I guess because that represented a vulnerability that could be exploited. My father never said he loved me, and I don't think I ever said it to him." Cas shrugged. This wasn't a point of pain for her, not anymore, and she didn't want to blame her father for who she was today, but she hoped Tolemek would understand that it might take her some time before she could say such a charged word to him, if ever. She did not want it to be a lie or a half-truth.

Tolemek grasped her hand in one of his and stroked the back of it with his thumb. "You don't have to explain anything to me, Cas. I just said what I said because I wanted you to know. In case I had given you reason to doubt. That's all."

And because he had hoped she felt the same. The fact that she didn't, or at least was not sure if she did, made her feel miserable, disappointed that there was something wrong with her. She had not known Tolemek for long, but after all the life-or-death situations they had been in, shouldn't she know?

"Got a log tangle coming down the river at us," Zirkander said. "Might need help."

A couple of the porters joined Zirkander at the front, ready to push aside the island-sized snarl of wood, grass, and debris. A few rusty food tins floated along with the snarl. The sides of the cans were too muddy to read, but the garbage might be evidence that the Cofah had gone up this river too.

"Is that one of the missing porters?" Sardelle asked, a strange note in her voice.

"What? Where?" Zirkander looked to either side of the river, to the walls of green choking the waterway.

"In the tangle." Sardelle pointed.

Cas placed her hand over Tolemek's for a second, then broke the clasp and stood up. She couldn't see anything past the three men in the front. Rifle in hand, she climbed atop the gear pile for a better look.

A male body was tangled up with the logs and grass, the brown skin waterlogged, the eyes closed in death. What remained of the clothing was similar to what their own porters were wearing, coarsely spun cotton shirts and trousers held up with ropes. Large flies hovered in the air above the body, but it didn't show signs of having been chewed on by scavengers. Cas couldn't tell what had killed the man, not seeing any sign of a bullet wound or other trauma. The mud and grass hid much, though, and only the front side of the corpse lay visible.

As soon as the porters saw the figure, they bowed their heads, muttering in their own language and making that circle over their chests again. When the clump of debris came close to the raft, Zirkander caught it with his pole, but he didn't angle it off to the side right away.

"Do we want to stop and bury or burn the body?" he asked the porters. "I don't know what the custom is here."

"No, no," the men said, more than one speaking at once. Their other words were indistinguishable, but they rushed forward with their poles, pushing the logs away from the raft.

"Guess that one goes out to sea," Zirkander said.

Foliage stirred at the edge of the river. A long, reptilian shape slithered off the embankment and undulated through the water toward the log tangle. An alligator. A big one. Its giant maw opened, its fences of pointed teeth silhouetted against the background, then snapped shut around the body. Alligator and man disappeared beneath the surface of the water.

"Or not," Zirkander amended soberly. "Looks like it's not healthy to work for the Cofah military."

Tolemek frowned. "It's no less healthy than working for the Iskandian military. There's no reason to kill one's porters, especially if one has heavy crates to carry back through the jungle. Whatever killed that man, I doubt it was a Cofah bullet."

"Was that supposed to be comforting?" Zirkander asked.

"Just an observation."

Sardelle gazed thoughtfully back down the river as the rest of the debris floated away, finally disappearing around a bend. The porters were still looking that way, too, and exchanging long looks with each other. It took the bump of another boulder against the raft before the men returned to their work. Cas went back to her vigil, watching the route ahead and to either side for threats. The body was a reminder that whatever lay ahead was at least as dangerous as whoever had come off that dirigible, if not more so.

* * *

By the time the porters steered the raft into an inlet choked with reeds, Tolemek was more than ready to escape the river. Around noon, they had passed a second body in a similar state as the first, and who knew if they had missed spotting others? Given the way the vegetation choked the waterway, more might have been hidden near the banks.

He had been kneeling for the last half hour and ducking to avoid branches scraping at his hair. The waterway had narrowed as the miles passed, with trees and plants thrusting farther inward and encroaching from above, as well. In the last hour, they had been forced to stop every few minutes to cut away vines and branches so they could continue.

Any relief Tolemek might have felt at the end of their water voyage was dampened by the discovery of a third body, another deceased porter, this one tangled in the reeds of their inlet. As with the others, there weren't any bullet or sword wounds that would have suggested the cause of death. A number of gashes had been taken out of the flesh—indeed, two big scavenger birds had flown up when the group approached—but he didn't think they had been what killed the man.

"Duck, want to help me set an alarm with some of those tin cans?" Cas pointed at the muddy shore ahead of them. Branches had been cut or burned back, creating enough room for a small campsite, and litter scattered the area.

"An alarm?" Duck asked.

"I've got this hunch that someone may be following us. I want to be warned if that's the case."

"I'm more concerned about what's ahead of us," Duck grumbled, waving toward the body. Nobody had missed it.

The porters hopped off the raft, hustling to drag it to shore, but they kept glancing at the corpse and making gestures over their chests.

"Help me, anyway," Cas said, slogging through the knee-deep water and ducking vines. She had shouldered her rifle and gripped one of the machetes the group had picked up along with their supplies.

"Let a person have *one* month of seniority, and she thinks she can order you around," Duck grumbled but splashed into the water and followed her.

Tolemek slid off the raft and into the water, as well, not liking that it was too murky to see the bottom. Something brushed past his leg, making him glad for his long trousers and boots, not that either would be much protection if another alligator appeared.

"Let's get the gear off," Zirkander said, already removing backpacks from the raft and tossing them to the bank. "Don't take long, Ahn. I want to see if we can cover a few more miles before night falls."

Sardelle and the porters helped him unload the gear, but Tolemek wanted a closer look at the body. He withdrew his utility knife and cut into the reeds, trying to free it.

"I don't think that one wants to come with us, Tee," Zirkander said.

"It might be conducive to our future health to figure out what's been killing these people."

"I find it telling that there aren't any Cofah soldiers wrapped up in the weeds."

"You think the Cofah were the ones killing their porters?" Sardelle asked.

"They might not want anyone to survive to blab about their secret."

Tolemek put away his knife and tried to drag the body toward the bank, but the reeds proved reluctant to give up their prize. Soft clanks came from the brush, Duck and Cas setting their alarms. He pulled harder, worried he wouldn't have time for as much of an inspection as he might need. Something slid past his leg again.

Duck let out a startled squawk. Everyone spun in his direction, a weapon of one kind or another in hand. Even the porters had bone cudgels and daggers that they brandished. Tolemek couldn't see Duck from his spot, but he found his own hand on one of the pistols holstered at his waist. Everyone was on edge; they would be lucky if they didn't shoot each other.

"Leeches out here," Cas said, a distasteful note in her voice. "Check under your clothes."

"And in your trousers," Duck added, his voice far more distressed than hers.

Tolemek frowned down at his leg. He was fairly certain that whatever had brushed past him had been larger than a leech, but he would have to check when he reached shore. He cut at a few more reeds, trying to figure out what had hold of the body.

Something clasped his ankle.

Before Tolemek could react, his leg was yanked toward the center of the river with such force that his other leg flew up, as well. He landed flat on his back, muddy water flying everywhere. He scrabbled for the knife at his waist, but something wrapped around his torso and pulled him under the water. He hit the rocky bottom so hard, he almost lost all of his air—and the knife. Dark water swallowed him, and he couldn't see a thing. He managed to keep his grip on the blade and grabbed at his chest, finding a rubbery limb—or tentacle?—as large around as his forearm.

He sawed at it, not sure what he was attacking. Not that it mattered. He was being pulled farther away from shore and deeper into the water. The seven gods only knew where he was being taken. He hacked at the limb harder, his slashes wild. He scarcely cared if he cut his own clothes—or skin—so long as he freed himself.

Distant yells reached his ears, muffled by the water, but he barely heard them over his own thrashing. He hadn't had a chance to suck in a big breath of air, and his lungs already burned. It didn't help that the tentacle was tightening around his chest, squeezing him with the strength of a python.

Tolemek kept sawing, but his blade slipped, struggling to bite into the rubbery flesh. He tried stabbing behind him as far as he could reach, thinking there might be a head or body he could connect with. Maybe that would do more damage, or at least convince the creature to release him. His blade bounced off something squishy, but all that happened was the tentacle tightened even further around his chest. Precious air bubbled from his lips, and his ribcage creaked in protest. Something snapped in his vest. One of his vials. Fresh fear rushed through his body. What if it was one of his acids? Even under water, that could eat through his clothing and into his flesh.

Calculation replaced the fear in his mind as he realized an acid might eat through a tentacle too.

Gunshots fired somewhere nearby. Tolemek winced. As much as he would appreciate help, he did not want the others to accidentally shoot *him*.

He struggled to pry his way into his vest. To add to his misery, something in the water was stinging his eyes. The vial that had broken—it must have been one of his compounds for forming caustic gases. He hoped the water diluted it quickly.

Almost breaking his fingers in the effort, Tolemek finally managed to grip the vial he wanted—he *hoped* it was the one he wanted—and yank it out. His lungs were screaming for air. He tried to get his feet under him even as he worked off the cap. The water hadn't been very deep the entire way up the river. If he could just stand, his head should break the surface.

But the cursed tentacle had him pinned and would not let him adjust. He tried to extricate the viscous acid in the vial without touching his own skin. He dabbed it against the tentacle. Would the creature feel it? Was there enough to make a difference? Or would the water simply wash it away?

More gunshots sounded, along with splashes all around him. Something hard thudded into his rib cage. Someone's boot? Great, his comrades were going to trample him in their eagerness to help.

Abruptly the tentacle released him. The tip of it thudded him in the temple as it whipped away. His head was snapped back, dazing him. The vial tumbled from his fingers.

Bullets fired right above him. He blinked a few times and gathered himself, pushing away the pain. He had to get out of there.

He had been spun around and had no idea which way the bank was, but he didn't care. All that mattered was putting distance between that creature and himself—and finding some air.

Before he could do so, he was halted with an abruptness that jolted his knee. The tentacle around his ankle—he had forgotten about that one. He slashed at it with his knife even as he lunged toward the surface with his upper body. His lips finally broke out of the water. He gulped in air before the tentacle pulled him below again. He hacked at it in anger and frustration. Whether he cut through it or not, he wasn't sure, but its grip lessened. He yanked his leg free and scrambled away. His knees banged on rocks, a sign of the water growing shallower. He raced out as quickly as he could, mud sucking at his boots every step of the way, the diabolical river reluctant to let him go. Finally, he collapsed on the bank, sucking in deep breaths as his oxygen-starved muscles trembled.

A shot fired again, and he pushed his hair out of his eyes. He questioned whether he had the strength to fight further, but if the others had gotten into trouble on his behalf, he had to help.

Out in the river, Cas, Duck, Sardelle, and Zirkander were hacking with machetes and shooting into the water. They stood more than waist deep—for Cas, the water was closer to chest deep—and no less than six dark purplish tentacles flailed in the air all around them. Sardelle lopped them off easily with her sword, which was glowing fiercely, leaving golden streaks in the dim air as it slashed about. But the creature continued to fight. Judging by the way Zirkander's short hair was plastered to his head, he had been pulled under at least once too.

Tolemek forced himself to stand. The porters were staying on the bank, their eyes huge as they watched the battle—or maybe it was Sardelle's sword that had surprised them. Either way, they were not inclined to risk themselves. Tolemek grabbed a machete from one of their hands. Though it was the last thing he wanted to do, he waded into the water again to help.

Before he had gone more than a couple of feet, Sardelle jumped into the middle of the team's circle, plunging her soulblade into the water. The wavering tentacles all around the group halted, hung in the air for a moment, then slumped to the surface with defeated splashes.

"Is that it?" Zirkander asked, wiping water off his face without lowering the machete in his other hand.

"I think so," Sardelle said wearily. She slumped against his side.

Cas found Tolemek's eyes. "Are you all right?" She lowered her rifle and slogged through the water toward him.

Tolemek looked down at himself, not entirely certain yet. A blue stain marked his vest, thanks to one or more broken vials, but all of his limbs appeared to be attached. Sucking in a deep breath hurt his ribcage, but he did not think any bones had been broken.

"I think so." He lifted an arm toward Cas, but realized he was still standing in a few inches of water and scrambled backward, finding solid ground before pausing for anything so indolent as an embrace.

Cas must have approved, because she smiled and nodded, joining him there.

"Thanks for the help," Tolemek said, enveloping her in a heartfelt hug. He resisted the urge to pick her up—the one time he had done that during an embrace, she had glared bullets at him—but he squeezed her nearly as hard as that tentacle had squeezed him.

"You're welcome," came Zirkander's sarcastic response as he, Sardelle, and Duck climbed out of the water. Blood was dripping from a cut at Zirkander's temple, and he looked like he had taken the most abuse after Tolemek.

"Thank you, as well, Sardelle," Tolemek said, deciding to ignore Zirkander rather than give him a response that probably would have been equally sarcastic. "And please give my gratitude to Jaxi, as well." He was surprised the soulblade hadn't echoed Zirkander's "You're welcome" in his head.

"Jaxi and I are feeling contrite," Sardelle said, "since we couldn't figure out how to help earlier. That octopus had dragon blood. It was highly resistant to magic, so we had to do it the old-fashioned way." She made a face at the pulverized purple flesh sticking to her sword and dug out a soggy rag to clean off the blade.

"*Octopus?*" Tolemek said, at the same time as Zirkander said, "*Dragon* blood?"

"I thought octopuses were strictly seawater creatures." Tolemek stared at the remains of their foe. "And rather smaller than that."

"And that they didn't have *dragon* blood," Zirkander said. "Didn't we agree that people—and animals, er, whatever—can only have dragon blood if some predecessor of theirs *mated* with a dragon?"

"That's generally how it worked," Sardelle said.

"Are you telling me that something as mighty as a dragon got bored one night, flew into the ocean, and explored the creative uses for tentacles? Do octopuses even have brains? Do they even mate? Like we do? Like dragons do?" Zirkander shoved his hand through his hair. "Why didn't I bring Apex? I feel the need to consult him on this."

"I think Apex is lucky he's *not* here," Duck grumbled. "He

thinks dragons were noble. This might disturb him."

"Jaxi says she recalls stories of a few blood-swapping experiments that didn't actually involve sex. Science experiments, if you will. An attempt to create worthy pets. Octopuses do have brains, by the way. They're considered quite clever compared to other water-dwelling creatures."

Zirkander's mouth opened and closed a few times, but he seemed to have run out of words.

A splash came from the water. Tolemek half expected the octopus to be rising for a second battle, but another alligator had appeared from the brush. It swam across the murky inlet toward the reeds and chomped down on the body Tolemek had been attempting to free.

He lifted a hand, as if he might yell or slap his leg and scare it away, but the creature was nearly fifteen feet long. It tore its prize free, then swam downstream, soon disappearing from sight.

"You're welcome," Zirkander called after it in the same tone he had used on Tolemek.

Sardelle raised an eyebrow at him. "You think it wasn't going after the body because it knew about the octopus?"

"Yes, it's smarter than us apparently."

"The jungle doesn't want to let me examine these bodies," Tolemek murmured.

"Do you think the octopus is what killed them?" Duck asked.

Tolemek spread his arms. Until he could examine one, he would only be guessing.

A roar came from the opposite side of the river. A spotted jaguar crouched atop a thick branch, its yellow eyes watching them. Maybe he was happy about the destruction of the octopus too.

Zirkander picked up his backpack and waved toward the jungle. "Let's get moving, people. I do *not* want to camp here tonight. I want—" He looked around. "Where did our porters go?"

Surprised, Tolemek spun a circle. He hadn't heard a sound, but all four men had disappeared.

Sardelle sighed. "I believe that was my fault. Jaxi was glowing vigorously for a while there. I didn't think to mute her—she's tough to mute, regardless."

"No kidding," Zirkander said.

"I think she might have scared the men away."

"How is a glowing sword scarier than a five-hundred-pound octopus?" Tolemek asked.

"Any chance of getting them back? Can you tell how far they've gone?" Zirkander asked Sardelle.

"I'm not sure. The jungle is so dense with life that it's lighting up my senses. It's hard to distinguish person from animal when they're layered like they are here."

"I was hoping we would keep our guides longer than half a day. We were getting along so well." Zirkander sighed and pointed at the heavy packs the men had left in the mud. "Any chance Jaxi is willing to carry our extra cargo? Since her ferocity is what scared off our porters?"

"We're discussing it," Sardelle said. "The word demeaning has come up."

"It wasn't too demeaning for the porters. Or for us." Zirkander adjusted the straps on his own pack.

"Yes, but you're not a former world-renowned sorceresses. Her words, not mine. Actually, I may have edited her words for social considerations."

"Anyone else hoping the dragon uses Sardelle's sword for a toothpick?" Zirkander asked.

Despite his resolve to stay on Jaxi's good side, Tolemek found his hand drifting upward. Cas and Duck simply offered raised eyebrows. They probably hadn't experienced the joy of having the soulblade romp through their minds.

Not everyone is so special.

Tolemek grunted and raised his hand higher.

"Jaxi says that she might be willing to lighten our loads," Sardelle said. "For those who recognize and are properly appreciative of her virtues."

With great reluctance, Tolemek lowered his hand. He had his microscope case, as well as a box full of testing equipment.

Carrying all of that, along with his share of food and water, would be a daunting load.

Good lad.

"I'm not real sure what to think about talking swords, but I'll take the lead. This wilderness is a mite more crowded than my woods back home, but I'm not afraid of it. Much. I'm a brave feller." Duck waved his machete overhead, looked around, and said, "Anyone seen a trail?"

"I think you just volunteered to make it, brave feller," Zirkander said. "The plants probably grow so fast that trails get swallowed up in a few days. It's a good thing you're young, strong, and bold."

"Not quite sure about his boldness after that incident with the leech," Cas murmured.

Duck glowered at her. "We'll see how bold you are when you're the one being plucked instead of the one doing the plucking."

"I'm not quite sure what that meant," Zirkander said, "but I don't want to know, either."

"Nope. Some details shouldn't be shared with one's commanding officer." Duck pushed aside some thick leaves, cut through a vine, and climbed over a log, choosing a route that would very slowly take them toward Mount Demise.

The jaguar roared one more time. Tolemek didn't know if it was a farewell roar or an I'll-see-you-people-tonight-for-dinner roar.

CHAPTER 6

A DISTANT JANGLE WOKE CAS FROM a light sleep, and she sat upright, cracking her head on a branch before she remembered where she was. She crawled out from under the leafy tree "skirt" the entire group had collapsed under the night before. It had been pouring, and Cas was amazed that the thin tarp they had laid on the muddy ground to keep them and their gear dry had worked. As soon as she slipped out from underneath the branches, a river of rain funneling off a broad leaf splashed her in the face, and she decided that more than the tarp might have been keeping them dry. Perhaps Sardelle or her sword had provided some protection.

She squinted into the gloom around the campsite, searching for whoever was on guard. She thought morning might be approaching, but it wasn't much brighter than it had been during her shift in the middle of the night, so she wasn't positive.

"I heard it," came Zirkander's soft voice from the shadows of a tree.

"My alarm?"

"Either that or the monkeys found a few tin cans to practice their drumming on."

"Maybe Duck and I should go back and have a look." Even as she made the suggestion, she hoped Zirkander didn't take her up on it. She wasn't afraid of the predators—animal and otherwise—but the thought of backtracking wearied her. It had taken them four hours the afternoon before to slog this far; it was depressing to think that they were still close enough to hear her trap go off. Granted, she had designed it to be loud, but she feared they had only come about a mile, even if they had traveled four times as far on foot, circling gullies and ravines, not to mention impenetrable stands of cane plants that grew in dense clumps all through the area.

"I don't want to split up the group," Zirkander said.

Snarling yips arose nearby, followed by a yelp of pain.

"We'll need to move soon, anyway," he added. "Duck shot something on his shift, and it died over there. It's drawing scavengers, large scavengers by the sound of it."

"I heard." In the middle of the night, the gunshot had woken her, making her bolt upright. That had been the *first* time she bonked her head on a branch. Duck had assured everyone that he had taken care of it, and the camp had gone back to sleep, but Cas had only dozed for most of the night.

"Maybe we can find a place to set a trap for our pursuer," Cas said. "With us breaking the trail, he'll likely reach us today."

"*Pursuers.*"

"Sir?" Cas thought of the single man from the dirigible.

"Jaxi says there are several people back there, several armed people."

"Jaxi? It—she, uh, talks to you too?" In the hopes of finding shelter from the rain, Cas pressed her back to the smooth bark of the tree next to Zirkander—the thick bole was wide enough that the entire group could have stood shoulder-to-shoulder around it and maybe the porters too, if they had still been there. If anything, this new position was damper, with rain running down the tree's bark in sheets. "Sir, aren't you getting soaked?"

"I haven't been dry since we got off that raft, so I don't think it matters at this point. Yes, Jaxi talks to me. And yes, you'd better call her a she if you don't want to irk her."

"What happens if you irk her?"

"At the least, you probably won't experience the dry zone that everyone else slept in last night."

Cas had nothing to say to that. She would have liked to do some quick maintenance on her rifle, but if the powder inside the bullets wasn't already damp, she didn't want to risk causing it to become so. Between the rain and the muggy warmth, the air was as humid as soup.

"There are people out there," Zirkander said softly.

"Out there? In the trees?" Cas hadn't seen anything moving, but the foliage dropped visibility to a few meters in any given direction, if that.

"Literally, yes." He shifted, fishing something out of his pocket. Was that his lucky dragon figurine? For a moment, he seemed like he might say more, but colonels didn't confide in lieutenants. Apparently, they confided in sentient swords instead. He walked over to the tarp and tapped the boots sticking out of the shelter with his own boot. "Wake up, troops. We may have company coming."

The squawks and chirps of the jungle stopped abruptly. Cas shifted uneasily, keeping her back to the tree. What predator did those animals sense that had alarmed them into silence? Neither carnivorous octopuses nor yipping coyotes—or whatever that was tearing into the animal Duck had shot—had caused a stilling of the ambient noises before. Soon, only the sound of the pattering rain filtering down from the canopy remained.

A faint *zzzippt* came from the trees. Something thudded into the bark above Cas's head. An arrow.

She returned fire, almost on instinct. She couldn't see her attacker, but she judged the angle of the arrow and made a guess as to its point of origin. A scream erupted from the jungle, not a scream of pain, but a high-pitched *yi-yi-yi-aye-yi* that sounded human, but barely.

Her back still to the tree, Cas readied another round. She considered ducking beneath the skirt of leaves they had slept under, but the foliage wouldn't stop arrows. Besides, Sardelle, Tolemek, and Duck were in the middle of scrambling out from under the trees.

Brilliant light appeared over their heads, a miniature sun pushing back the gloom of the jungle and stealing the shadows from the trees. Sardelle crouched beneath it, her sword in hand. Another arrow sped out of the trees, this time toward her. She cleaved it in half before it could strike her.

Cas fired back in the direction of the attacker, though she had yet to see anyone out there. Leaves rustled, and twigs snapped, the sounds coming from numerous spots around their tiny camp.

"Ridge," Sardelle said, "do you want a shield around us, or do you want to be able to fire back?"

Another high-pitched scream erupted, this time from less than twenty feet behind Cas's tree.

"Nobody asked for your opinion," Zirkander grumbled, then replied, "Shield us," to Sardelle. "Cas, Duck, don't fire."

"Wasn't going to, sir," Duck said. "Can't see through these trees enough to spit and hit the ground. Hate to waste my rounds too."

Cas's cheeks warmed. She shouldn't be wasting ammunition, either. They didn't have an unlimited supply. But she was used to her instinct-driven shots working much of the time.

More arrows shot out of the jungle, all zooming toward Sardelle's light, but they bounced off an invisible barrier before striking it. Cas lowered her rifle, lest she be tempted to shoot. The last thing she wanted was for some bullet to ricochet off the shield and hit one of them.

Tolemek strode to her side, putting his back to the tree next to her. "What are we dealing with?"

Cas plucked the arrow out of the tree and held it up to his face.

"So not the jaguar, eh? I thought that cat was considering me for dinner."

"Maybe he was jealous that your mane is bigger and fluffier than his."

"You're thinking of lions," Tolemek said. "And my mane isn't fluffy."

"No argument with big?"

Tolemek pushed his ropes of hair away from his face and glowered at her. "Any chance our ammo is dry enough to use? I tipped my pistol upside down earlier, and river water and bits of octopus dripped out of the barrel." He dug the weapon out of his holster.

"Should be fine. Those are Iskandian bullets."

"I'll ignore the implication that Cofah bullets are inferior."

"Good." Cas smiled and bumped her shoulder against his arm.

"Can you keep that around us while we travel?" Zirkander waved to indicate Sardelle's barrier. "In case we need to—"

A scream burst out from the branches overhead, and a figure leaped down toward them, arms and legs outstretched, bone daggers gripped in both hands. Cas jerked her rifle up and almost fired before remembering the shield. She released the trigger a split second before the man landed. He thudded chest first onto the invisible barrier, bounced back up a couple of feet, then dropped down again, appearing to hang suspended, flat on his bare stomach, ten feet above the ground.

"That's bizarre," Duck said.

The man must not have been injured, because he jumped to his feet, the pads of his moccasins visible from Cas's spot almost directly under him. He didn't wear a shirt, but he fortunately wore a breechclout that kept his nether regions from displaying themselves. Black and ochre paint swirled across his body in waves and circles that appeared more random than significant. He glowered down at the team, jumping a few times to test the barrier, then he screamed again, a long undulating cry that hurt Cas's ears. Other cries came from the surrounding trees, and she felt like a fighter in some old-fashioned gladiatorial event, part of a show to entertain the elite. Or in this case, the crazy.

"There's another one." Zirkander pointed toward a high branch a few trees away.

A second man crouched up there. As soon as Zirkander pointed at him, he leaped from his perch. He landed on the barrier a few feet away from the first man, dropped to his knees, and tried to drive a dagger into the barrier. Cas had assumed they were allies—they wore the same skimpy clothing and were painted in similar manners—but the first man saw the second, pointed with his daggers, and launched himself at the newcomer. They smashed together, grasping and slashing, then tumbled off the rounded edge of Sardelle's barrier, leaving a smear of blood hanging in the air. Leaves shook and rattled, raindrops flying from them as the men wrestled and thrashed around the edge of the barrier.

"I'm beginning to see why tourism isn't a big industry here," Zirkander said. "This jungle is..."

"Bizarre, sir," Duck said. "Most certainly bizarre."

A great cat roared somewhere nearby. The jaguar from earlier? Even with Sardelle's light brightening their surroundings, the plants were still too dense to see far.

Whatever it was, the roar caused the thrashing to halt. The cries coming from the trees also stopped. A twig snapped, someone retreating at top speed, and then silence descended on the jungle, only the patter of rain continuing.

"Cross out that idea," Zirkander muttered.

"Ridge?" Sardelle asked, her face tight with concentration.

"While I was on watch, I was thinking that if we could befriend some of the natives, we could hire them to be our new porters."

"Their actions were not normal," Sardelle said.

"Whatever gave you that idea?" Zirkander pointed at the blood smearing the barrier. "Aside from the fact that they started out attacking us, then turned on each other?"

"Those men were highly agitated, scared, and confused." Sardelle took a breath and lowered her arms. The light faded, leaving that dim grayness of dawn. The barrier must have dropped, too, because the rain resumed pattering onto Cas's head. "Tolemek," Sardelle said, "do you have any thoughts as to what might cause that?"

"Some drug perhaps?" Tolemek said. "A hallucinogenic compound ingested as part of a ceremony? Perhaps they were on some hunt and stumbled across us instead."

"Is it hard to engage in a group hunt when you're trying to stab your buddy at the same time?" Duck asked.

"What if it's something else?" Cas asked. "Could it be related to the dead men in the river?"

"Without examining those bodies, we have no way of knowing if the natives in the river were killed by trauma, by something they ingested, or by some illness," Tolemek said. "Nor can we guess at their state of mind before their deaths. I don't believe there's any evidence yet to suggest these two incidents are related. Granted, there might have been plenty of evidence that we were unable to gather. My studies were admittedly brief."

"Can you really call it a study when an alligator steals your subject before you've gotten close enough to touch it?" Cas asked.

"A valid point. If we come across another body, one that's not guarded by a malevolent octopus, I'll perform an autopsy."

"I'll take a closer look too," Sardelle said, "to see if I can detect anything. I had assumed the Cofah had simply cracked those porters on the backs of the heads and left them to die, so their secrets wouldn't be spilled, but that may have been a premature assumption."

"What I'd like to know," Zirkander said, waving to the jungle, "is if we're in any danger of catching the crazy."

"Catching the crazy?" Tolemek arched his brows. "Not if they ingested something."

"What if it's a disease?"

"That causes craziness?"

From the way Tolemek scratched his head, Cas assumed this wasn't a common thing, but her own unscientific mind couldn't help but think of the way he had described his sister as being mentally unstable. He might have believed it had something to do with the dragon blood in her veins and the magic she had never been properly instructed to use, but what if it was something more than that? Something related to all of this? She shook her head. It was probably an illogical stretch. The sister was from Cofahre, not this remote jungle, and had presumably spent years in that asylum without giving anyone else the disease—or whatever it was—that she held within her.

"I wouldn't guess that we're in any danger," Tolemek said, "but I wouldn't necessarily want to share a handkerchief with those boys in loincloths until we learn more."

"I think it's a good policy not to ever share handkerchiefs with boys in loincloths," Zirkander said.

"True."

"Now that we've all been so politely roused from sleep, I believe it's time to continue on," Zirkander said. "Cas, at least we know who triggered your alarms."

Cas offered a noncommittal, "Hm."

The attack had come so shortly after the jangling of cans that she doubted the crazy natives could have covered the intervening ground so quickly. It was possible there were two groups of natives out there, but it was also possible they still had someone following them. She would watch the terrain as they walked and try to find another place to set a trap, maybe one that would do more than make noise this time.

* * *

Mid-afternoon found Tolemek walking behind Duck on a muddy trail, a small notepad open in one hand. It was the first man-made route they had stumbled across in their trek, and even though the footing wasn't smooth, he managed to scribble a couple of notes. He had two columns, one labeled "crazy natives" and the other "dead porters," and he was listing the meager observations that he had made on the appropriate sides. Thus far, he was inclined to think the events were unrelated, but a good scientist did not rely on hunches or assumptions. If some new danger out here might keep him from reaching his sister, he intended to be prepared for it.

"Add dilated pupils to both," Sardelle said from behind him.

Tolemek tripped over a root. "What?"

"That man who landed face-first on my barrier had dilated pupils, abnormally so, considering my nearby light source, and Jaxi and I have been discussing what we remember of the bodies in the river. Two had closed eyes, so we couldn't tell, but one's eyes were open. He almost looked like he had been scared to death."

"I didn't announce that I was working on this list," Tolemek said mildly. He hadn't started it until they had come out on the trail. "And you're too short to see over my shoulder."

"Jaxi is not restricted by shoulders."

"In other words, she's the one who was spying on my work, not you?"

"Indeed so," Sardelle said, sounding amused, but maybe embarrassed too. "I have more respect for people's privacy."

"Mydriasis is typical after death, so I don't know if I should put it in the dead-porters list, but I'll put it in the other column."

Tolemek was impressed that Sardelle—or Jaxi—had been that observant.

"Ah, I guess that's true," Sardelle said. "Maybe I'm looking for links that aren't there."

"Sardelle?" Zirkander called softly from the head of the group. He and Duck had stopped.

Sardelle slipped past Tolemek to join them. Cas came up from behind, her face mud-spattered and her short, damp hair hugging her head in a way that made her impish features more prominent. The rain had stopped an hour earlier, but the air remained muggier than a steam room, and none of their clothes had dried.

"Doing all right?" Tolemek asked, lifting an arm, even though she was probably fitter than he and more used to long hikes. He didn't know if she would accept the offering of support.

She looked at it, hesitating, but then stepped close and let him put his arm around her shoulders. "Yes. You?"

"Fine. Making a list." Tolemek showed it to her. Aware of how keen her eyes were, he added, "Did you notice anything about the dead bodies or about the belligerent natives that would be worth putting on it?"

"I didn't get close enough to notice anything special about the bodies, except that they didn't have obviously lethal wounds. Or any wounds, for that matter."

Tolemek nodded.

"The natives…" She peered at his list. "It may just be a result of adrenaline, but the first man's hands were shaking."

"Ah?" Tolemek didn't know if it would prove significant, but he wrote it down.

"They're looking at something." Cas tilted her head toward Sardelle and Zirkander and walked up to join them.

Zirkander was pointing toward a jumble of mossy boulders off to the side of the trail. "Should we consider them interesting jungle decorations and continue on, or is it possible there's some significance? Like maybe they have something to do with why this trail is here? Not that I mind, but I've been wondering who's been maintaining it and why."

Tolemek stepped on a log for a better look and realized they weren't boulders but the foundations of a building and the remains of some walls. In addition to the moss, plant leaves stretched all over the area, nearly covering the evidence. Now that he was looking for it, Tolemek spotted the remains of a few more structures, including a stout black post that rose from the mud. Its top had long ago been lopped off, but the moss didn't quite hide numerous carvings on the surface.

"They're probably a thousand years old, or more," Sardelle said.

"Jungle decoration it is."

"Wait a moment." Sardelle stepped over branches and around trees, heading toward the post.

Curious, Tolemek trailed after her. Cas remained on the trail, her gaze shifting back and forth from the route ahead to the route behind. He had caught her watching the route behind them numerous times during the day. He would have to ask her if she was simply being alert or if she believed someone might be on their trail, someone aside from those crazy natives. The group hadn't seen them again after that initial attack.

"It's a dragon." Sardelle had stopped in front of the post, and she wiped away some of the moss and grime to show more of the carvings. "Several of them. You can't see the colors, but from the size and facial features, I'd guess we have a bronze, a silver, and those are perhaps the feet of a gold on top, where it was cut off."

"You say the ruins are a thousand years old?" Zirkander asked from the trail.

"At least. Some of the histories suggest dragons originally evolved in the jungles. Others claim they came from another world altogether, but either way, they've been documented— if only by pictographs and petroglyphs—in this part of the world dating further back than anywhere else. They're also still worshiped in a lot of the cultures out here—or at least that was the case three hundred years ago. I haven't brushed up on recent history yet." She gave Zirkander an apologetic shrug, then walked around to the other side of the post.

"Half of our Iskandian gods have dragon bodies," Zirkander pointed out dryly. "The aborigines aren't the only ones who found them powerful enough to worship."

"Yes, but it's been many centuries since anyone back home did more than make lucky charms out of the dragon gods, considering them whimsical spirits who might or might not help with life's problems."

Zirkander cleared his throat and touched his pocket. "Yes, I suppose that's true."

"Those with human form have replaced... now this is interesting." Sardelle leaned closer to squint at a carving.

Tolemek stepped past a patch of mushrooms as big as his head to join her on the back side of the post. Sardelle was still wiping away mud and moss, but he sucked in a startled breath, recognition striking him like a hammer.

"It's the dragon. Tylie's dragon."

"*Tylie's* dragon?" Zirkander asked.

Tolemek scarcely heard him. The dragons on the front of the post had possessed different faces. This one was distinctly similar to the one his sister had painted all over her asylum room. Not similar. The *same*. A pointed snout, angular reptile-like features, closed eyes, a high brow that made him look interested, or perhaps amused, by the world around him, diamond-shaped scales visible in the rock even after all this time.

Tolemek rubbed his face. How could it make sense that Tylie would have drawn this dragon from two thousand miles away? Without ever having seen it? Maybe the resemblance meant little beyond a similarity shared across many members of the species. Or maybe this was some distant ancestor to the one Tylie had drawn. It couldn't be the *same* dragon after all these centuries. All of the histories said that dragons were long-lived, but not *that* long-lived. They could see a couple of centuries at the most, wasn't that what he had read?

"Sardelle?" he whispered, though he didn't know what he meant to ask.

"It's definitely similar." She raised her voice. "We found a dragon carving that looks like the image Tolemek's sister painted on her wall."

"That's a thousand years old?" Zirkander asked.

"Hm, maybe not." Sardelle ran her finger along the ancient black stone. "Judging by the wear, this carving isn't as old as the ones on the front of the post." She lifted her gaze toward the branches and leaves above them. "It's possible this side is slightly more protected from the elements, but I think it may be more like five hundred years old."

"Oh, is that all?"

Tolemek touched the carving. "Its eyes are closed. The ones on the front have open eyes."

"I noticed that," Sardelle said.

He lowered his hand and walked toward the ruins, wondering if they might yield more clues. Of course, he didn't know if he had truly *found* a clue, if the resemblance meant anything. It wasn't as if he had seen hundreds of dragons or could trust every picture in the text books. For all he knew, every third dragon looked exactly the same.

The murmur of a quiet conversation came from the trail. Zirkander's head was bent as he listened to Cas. Had she explored farther up the path? She was pointing in the direction the group had been heading.

Afraid he would be called back to the trail soon, Tolemek walked quickly, searching the ruins for other carvings. Some held smaller etchings, but of hieroglyphs rather than anything as big and sophisticated as a dragon. He couldn't tell what the buildings had been for, either, whether they indicated a gathering place for religious ceremonies or if there were enough of them to signify an entire village. The dense shrubs and thick, flowering vines hid too much.

"Tolemek?" Zirkander said.

"I'm coming."

"No hurry, but it sounds like you might have the opportunity to examine some bodies after all."

When Tolemek looked toward the trail, Cas nodded at him, her face bleak.

"A village?" Sardelle guessed, picking her way back to the

trail.

"What remains of it," Cas said. "The people are dead or missing. It looks like something happened recently."

"How far ahead?" Tolemek asked as he returned to the trail. "Did the people die from wounds or in the same manner as the porters in the river?"

"I didn't get that close," Cas said. "I smelled... the smell of death, rotting meat, and went to look, but I wasn't sure if it was safe. Aside from the bodies, it looks like most of the people left, and I thought they might have ordered the area quarantined. The trail goes right into the village, but I didn't know if we wanted to investigate or... make a wide circle around it."

Tolemek wanted to investigate, but he understood her reasoning. If there was something contagious, something that might affect their group, as well...

"Sardelle?" Zirkander asked softly. "My thought would be to avoid it so we don't risk catching anything ourselves, but is it inevitable that we'll continue to encounter people out here? People who may or may not be dead? Maybe we need to do our best to figure out what's going on."

"I'll go," Sardelle said. "I won't be so presumptuous as to say I'll be unaffected, but those with more dragon blood in their veins tend to have higher immunity from common pathogens that affect humans. Also, I can usually go into a meditative state and speed up my recovery if I'm ill or injured."

Zirkander's expression grew grim. He was doubtlessly reluctant to let her go—Tolemek wouldn't want to let Cas risk herself, either—but all he said was, "Oh? You think we're going to stop and let you meditate if you get sick? We're on a quest here, you know."

Sardelle smiled. "I assumed you would carry me while I meditated."

"I'm already carrying two bags' worth of gear, and I'm not at all convinced that Jaxi is making my load lighter. I think she's teasing me, making it weigh something different from hour to hour."

"I'd like to tell you that Jaxi wouldn't do that, but... you've met her. I don't think you would believe me." Sardelle lifted a hand and headed up the trail. "Give me twenty minutes, and I'll come back."

"Wait." Tolemek removed his pack and started untying his microscope case and tool bag. "I have dragon blood, too, right? I'm going in."

Cas frowned at him. "Isn't yours more diluted?"

"I don't know, but someone needs to perform an autopsy on one of these dead people, try to figure out why they're dead."

Sardelle gazed back at him, her lips turned downward, too, but she didn't object. Tolemek took his case and jogged after her.

"What do we do while we wait, sir?" Duck asked. "Have lunch?"

"Have lunch?" Zirkander asked. "When there's a village of dead people over the next hill?"

"You think they'll mind?"

That was the last Tolemek heard of the conversation, but he did give Cas a long look over his shoulder before rounding a bend in the trail. He was fully aware that by going into the village, he risked not only becoming a victim of some illness but also becoming a carrier. Sardelle may have been trained as a healer, but he didn't know whether that had anything to do with diseases, or if she merely doctored wounds.

The smell of decaying meat left out in hot weather touched his nostrils. He could tell even before the village came into sight that these people had died days ago, and he feared the bodies would have already been mauled by predators.

A monkey jabbered from a treetop, but the jungle was otherwise quiet. Maybe it knew that death lurked here.

Two ancient, black stone obelisks marked the entrance of the village, but these didn't carry any carvings. They simply reached up to the sky, their tops disappearing into the leaves and fronds. Beyond them, the trail widened into a cleared area where stone houses provided more permanent—and architecturally sound— structures than Tolemek would have imagined from the primitive people who had attacked them that morning. But perhaps this was another tribe, one more advanced than the others. In addition to the houses, there were elevated platforms in the trees, some open and empty, but some with wooden dwellings built atop them. The doors to many of the houses stood open, and here and there abandoned projects—baskets half filled and hides partially scraped—suggested people had left in a hurry.

Despite the smell of death, Tolemek's first thought was that everyone *had* left, because he didn't see anyone, dead or otherwise. If Cas hadn't said something, he might have been stumped, but Sardelle walked up to one of the elevated platforms, this one built on a wooden scaffolding rather than around the trunk of a tree. She climbed to the top of a ladder and frowned sadly over the edge.

"The bodies?" Tolemek guessed.

"Yes. They were painted and carried up here, probably as protection from predators. Maybe this is what the funeral ceremony consists of here." She dropped her chin to her fist and closed her eyes.

At first, Tolemek thought she might be praying, but she must be using her magical senses to examine the bodies. He took his bag of tools and walked toward the base of a ladder leading to a similar platform. There were five in total. The entire village looked like it might house sixty or eighty people, so this wasn't representative of an epidemic, but there were more dead than could easily be explained by a hunting accident or people succumbing to old age. Besides, those things wouldn't have caused the rest of the people to abandon their village in a hurry. Still, someone had stayed and taken the time to build these platforms and lay the dead to rest.

Tolemek passed a toy, a doll lying forlornly in the mud, and a wave of sadness came over him as he wondered if the owner would ever be able to return to collect it. He struggled to find the emotional distance he needed to assume the role of scientist, to analyze the data here, no matter how gruesome it might be.

He climbed to the top of the platform he had chosen and found a pair of children, brother and sister their similar features implied. Their hands were linked, as they lay on their backs, their closed eyes tilted toward the jungle canopy. The bodies were in good shape still, and his nose caught a scent of some alcohol-like substance. He doubted they had been preserved in any way—the smell of decomposing tissue promised that—but maybe something had been applied to keep the aerial predators away. The bodies hadn't been disturbed yet.

Not liking the idea of performing an autopsy on a child, he checked the other platforms. Sardelle's head was still bowed as she considered the body of a woman. A man with graying hair rested on the next closest platform, his face gaunt in death, gravity pulling the skin down. His hands had been folded across his chest, and he wore a white funeral robe. These people were wearing more clothing—more neatly stitched clothing—than the crazies in the breechclouts. It definitely appeared to be a different tribe.

Tolemek climbed to the man's platform and knelt next to the figure. The wood shivered beneath his weight, but the scaffolding had been assembled well enough to support two people. He touched and probed with his hands before pulling out any tools. Rigor mortis had long since passed, and putrefaction had set in. He breathed through his mouth to keep his stomach calm.

"There's skin under this one's nails," he said, not certain whether Sardelle would hear him or was too lost in her own mind, but he tended to talk out loud when he researched and examined, especially when dealing with corpses. The undeniable nearness of death always made him want to hear voices, if only his own, since they promised life. Those who knew him as the Deathmaker would doubtlessly laugh to learn of his discomfort. "Bruises on his knuckles. Looks like he was in a fight before he died, or that he started one." Tolemek unfastened the funeral robe. "He doesn't seem to have taken damage of his own." He pushed back the sleeves. "Oh, wait. There are a few bruises on his wrists. Someone might have been grabbing him, or these might be rope marks too. Yes, they're more consistent than damage from someone's grip would be. Perhaps the villagers tied him up to keep him from harming others?" Tolemek shouldn't speculate at this point; he should only record evidence, but he couldn't keep his mind from spinning hypotheses as to what had happened.

"But what caused him to act thusly?" He searched for lesions and other skin disfigurations that might hint of diseases he was familiar with, but found nothing. He pulled a scalpel out of his bag, apologizing to the dead man's spirit, because he would have to check his organs and tissues in hope of finding the answers he sought. He told himself the jungle would take back the body eventually, anyway, but that never made this easier.

"There's some swelling in the brain," Sardelle said, almost startling him into dropping the tool. "I can't tell the cause, but maybe you want to start your search there."

"A tumor?"

"I don't see one. Your man has the same swelling. The other organs look fine to me, aside from the usual decomposition you would expect to be taking place approximately three days after death."

"I understand," Tolemek said, glad for her calm, academic tone. He wasn't glad she had told Zirkander they would be done in twenty minutes. He pulled out a handsaw, but his examination would take more time. "Sardelle, do you want to ask—"

Ssh, came a whisper into his mind.

He wasn't sure if it had been Jaxi or Sardelle, but Sardelle was looking intently into the jungle to the left of them.

How often does Sardelle *speak into your mind?* The sarcasm that accompanied those words definitely belonged to Jaxi. *We've got visitors again.*

More of the disturbed natives from this morning? Tolemek looked down at his handsaw, wondering if he had time to extricate brain matter and make a few slides, and wondering, too, how much the people out in the jungle would object to it.

You'll be able to judge by the number of arrows they pierce your chest with. Better hurry up. There are a lot more than this morning. I think the villagers may have come home.

CHAPTER 7

THE JUNGLE HAD GROWN QUIET again. Cas watched the trail in both directions, but kept glancing into the brush, as well, unable to shake the feeling of being watched.

"It's been twenty minutes, hasn't it?" she asked. "Maybe we should check on the others."

"I'm told Tolemek just pulled out a handsaw," Zirkander said. He was leaning against a mossy stump so he could see both ways, up and down the trail, and his hand never strayed far from the hilt of his pistol. Maybe he felt the same uneasiness that Cas felt. "I don't think you want to see what he's doing in there." He met Cas's eyes. "Then again, you're unflappable when it comes to shooting people, so maybe it wouldn't bother you."

"It would bother *me*," Duck said. "I don't want to see the Deathmaker cutting open anyone's spleen."

"Apparently it's a brain."

"Oh, even better."

Leaves stirred at the edge of Cas's vision. She frowned back down the trail and caught sight of something brown and hairy through the brush. An animal? No, too tall. That was someone's head.

"Off the trail," Zirkander whispered, pointing at the ruins. "Someone's coming."

Cas led the way between the plants, heading for one of the low walls, careful not to step on any twigs or branches. Duck moved soundlessly, too, and reached the remains of the building first. Zirkander came more slowly, walking backward, his pistol raised toward the trail. He reached the broken wall at the same time as someone spoke.

"Getting close," a man said. "Fresh tracks."

Zirkander ducked behind the wall. "I'm trying to warn

Sardelle," he whispered. "Unfortunately, I can only receive, not send." He stared in the direction of the village, even though the foliage and a hundred meters or more separated it from them. "I should have run ahead to warn her," he whispered. "They might be distracted." He shifted his weight, as if he meant to do so now.

Cas laid a hand on his forearm and pointed between a gap in the crumbling wall. "Too late."

The brown-haired person had come into view, along with four others, including an older man wearing a hat with a brim so wide a python could have coiled its entire body around the crown. Judging by the voices and the squishing of boots into mud, there were a couple more men farther back.

"Pirates?" Zirkander mouthed.

Cas thought of her alarm and nodded. This was the group that had likely triggered it.

The brown-haired pirate in front had his gaze to the ground, watching the tracks as he walked. Cas rested the barrel of her rifle between the gap in the rocks. If he was good, he would notice that the group had veered in this direction and that only a couple of people had continued onward. Getting into a firefight when the other side had more than twice the numbers wasn't usually a good idea, but she, Duck, and Zirkander had cover. This might be the best place to ambush their pursuers. She glanced at Zirkander for permission to fire, but found him looking behind them instead of at the trail.

He held a finger to his mouth. Cas hated to look away from the known threat, but she glanced back too. For a moment, she didn't see anything except the trees and leaves, but then she spotted a brown-skinned man crouching ten feet up in a tree. He held a bow, with an arrow nocked. Zirkander pointed past Cas's shoulder, and she followed his gaze, grimacing when she spotted a second man. These people weren't painted and nearly naked the way the other ones had been, but they had shaven heads and grim faces that made them seem all the more dangerous. More deadly.

A scream of pain came from the trail. One of the pirates clutched at an arrow sticking out of his shoulder.

War cries erupted from the trees on either side of the path. The cries didn't have the tinge of madness that had come from the lips of the attackers that morning, but they did sound determined— and angry. Several men leaped out of the branches, using vines to swing toward the pirates, daggers clenched between their teeth. Pistols fired, even as men cried, "Look out," and, "Take cover!"

Cas put her back to the crumbling wall, expecting some of the natives would angle toward her team, as well. A man on a vine swung right over her head on his way to the trail.

Zirkander touched her shoulder and pointed toward the other side of the ruins. "That way. We'll grab the others and get out of here while the natives are distracted."

He didn't give Cas time to argue, not that lieutenants were supposed to argue with colonels, anyway. Using the low walls for cover, he weaved through the ruins, paralleling the trail. Duck ran after him without hesitation. Cas followed, but kept an eye on the trail and the trees. If they hadn't been attacked yet, it was probably only because they hadn't been noticed—or because the noisy group of pirates offered a more obvious threat. There was no reason to think the natives would be less irritated with Iskandian intruders.

As soon as Zirkander reached the end of the ruins and pushed his way into the brush, Cas spotted another man swinging down from the trees. This one's vine wouldn't take him all the way to the trail; his eyes were locked on Zirkander. Not sure her commander saw him, Cas brought her rifle up to fire. Zirkander's pistol arm whipped up, and he shot at the same time. Their bullets slammed into the man's bare chest. The native released his vine, tumbling ten feet to the ground.

"Guns to our right," someone near the trail called.

"Just worry about these damned—" The speaker's words switched to curses.

"Arrows?" someone suggested.

Cas rushed to catch up with Zirkander and Duck. There was little point in stealth now. Anyone paying attention would know there were people out here.

More war cries came from the trees, and blue-feathered

arrows sailed from the branches. One whizzed past, not two feet in front of Cas. She lowered her head further, but kept running, jumping logs, squishing through mud, and nearly pitching into a sinkhole. Zirkander must have heard her startled squawk at the last, because he paused, turning back toward her. She waved him on and yanked her boot free, almost losing it in the process. He waited for her, then gestured for her to go ahead.

"We should be even with the village," she said and pointed to the left, where the trees were thinner. "We should—"

Another barrage of arrows flew from the trees.

"Duck," Zirkander barked.

Cas dropped to her knees, more because her foot slipped in the mud than because she wanted to be that low. She didn't see any arrows that time, but heard a few zip past over her head. There had to be dozens of warriors out there, firing at her team and at the pirates. This was madness; it would be pure luck if they didn't get hit. She much preferred being the one in the trees, sniping at targets.

"Sardelle and Tee are up ahead." Zirkander helped her up, his words barely audible above the war cries ringing from the trees.

Cas scrambled through the brush, catching up with Duck. She spotted Tolemek beside a tree, as well as Sardelle, her arm raised and hand extended. They were surrounded by six men, banging knives and fists at an invisible barrier. Tolemek, scrambling to stuff tools into one of his cases, looked like he had been interrupted in the middle of his work. Two of the natives were pointing at his case and yelling as they banged their fists against the barrier.

Duck tripped on something and made a noise as he bumped into a tree. Half of the irate natives turned in his direction. Cas shot one in the knee before he knew what was happening. Zirkander's and Duck's pistols fired too. Two men pitched backward. The others surrounding Sardelle's barrier hesitated, then ran, disappearing into the leaves in a blink.

"My lady," Zirkander said, throwing Sardelle a salute as he ran up. "I've missed you terribly."

"It *has* been agony being parted." Sardelle lowered her arm—

and presumably the barrier.

"Got your brains collected, Tee? This seems a particularly fine time to depart."

"Did you not miss me terribly as well, Zirkander?" Tolemek stuffed his case back into his pack and slung both over his shoulder.

"You're grumpy, gloomy, and have hair one could hide knives in. What's not to miss?" Zirkander touched Sardelle on the shoulder as he passed but didn't slow down for long. Still paralleling the main trail, he led the way.

An arrow sped through the trees, landing in a trunk a few feet from Duck's head. That spurred him into motion, as well, and he sprinted after Zirkander.

Cas jogged up to Tolemek, making sure he didn't need help with his gear before continuing on.

"I'm not gloomy, am I?" He adjusted his pack on his shoulders and nodded that they could go.

"Pensive is the word that comes to my mind."

"Cogitative?"

"If you want to be cogitative, I won't argue with it." Cas spotted one of the natives running through the brush, but the man seemed to be heading for the pirate gathering instead of her team, so she didn't fire. She already felt bad for shooting people who might have been doing nothing more than defending their village.

The sounds of the fighting faded, and Zirkander slowed down and veered to the left, probably hoping to pick up the trail again. The jungle hadn't been quite as dense around the village, but it had grown wilder again, and he and Duck had been forced to trade pistols for machetes.

"Tolemek?" Zirkander sliced a few vines away from his face and ducked a branch a foot thick. "Any idea why pirates have been following us into the jungle? There might be a bounty on my head, but I have a hard time believing it's high enough to warrant the kind of risk those fellows back there are enduring."

Cas chewed on the side of her cheek, trying to decide if any suspicion lurked in his voice. He didn't think Tolemek had something to do with the appearance of those pirates, did he?

"I don't know for certain," Tolemek said, "but my guess is that they're treasure hunters."

Treasure? Cas took a wide step around a tree that had a large snake draped across the lowest branch. What kind of treasure could be out here?

"Hunting for a treasure more impressive than my head?" Zirkander asked.

"That wouldn't take much," Tolemek muttered, then he raised his voice to add, "A group of pirates stopped me outside of our lodgings the night before we left. They seemed to think that the appearance of your father signified treasure in the area."

Zirkander paused, his machete raised for a stroke that he didn't make. "That would be the kind of information that would be useful to relay to your expedition leader." His jaw tightened in a rare sign of irritation.

"I'll keep that in mind."

"Is he going to be in danger from them?" Zirkander finished the stroke with his machete, cleaving a branch with more force than usual. "Damn it, I should have dragged him along, whether he wanted to come or not."

"That didn't go well with the flier," Sardelle murmured.

"If something happens to him, after *I* was the one to bring him here…"

"The pirates followed us," Cas said. "Maybe that means they think we're the more promising target."

"I hope so." Zirkander lowered his machete. "Sardelle, can you tell if they're still following us? The pirates? Or the natives?"

"They're still fighting back there. The villagers are focused on the pirates." Her voice held a strange note, as if she was confused.

"That's a good thing, right?" Zirkander pushed past a clump of fronds, each one as tall as he, and muttered a, "Hah. There's the trail." They had come out on the other side of the village.

"Maybe," Sardelle said. "I believe those people came back because of us, because we were disturbing their dead."

"Oh."

"At least they didn't seem as addled as the ones from this

morning," Cas said. "That must mean that not everybody out here is being affected by this… whatever it is." She looked at Tolemek. Had he discovered anything yet?

"Or they could be infected and simply aren't displaying symptoms yet," he said.

"See, Tee, that's gloomy thinking there," Zirkander said.

"Pensively gloomy," Cas said at Tolemek's frown.

"Do you now believe it's a disease?" Zirkander asked. "Not some psychedelic berries they licked?"

Tolemek hesitated. "I only have guesses now. But I gathered samples to examine later."

Duck's lip curled at the word samples.

"Uh oh." Zirkander stopped.

Cas hustled to slip past Duck and Sardelle so she could see. "New problem?"

"Just that we've reached the end of the trail." Zirkander pointed at a reed-clogged pool that lay ahead of them. The path stopped, rather than going around it. "This must be where they collect their water. No need to explore inland farther." He raised a hand to his eyes, sheltering them from afternoon sun beaming down through a rare gap in the canopy. "The ground rises on the other side. Maybe we're getting close to the mountain."

"I would settle for a place where I can make some slides and take a look at them," Tolemek said. "Preferably not near this pond. I see an alligator over there. And those reeds might be hiding some creature that likes to eat scientists."

Cas poked him in the side. "That's even gloomier."

"I told you." Zirkander winked back at her. "All right, who's going to lead at breaking the trail this time? Sardelle, isn't it Jaxi's turn?"

"You want me to use her as a machete?"

"I was thinking she could add her fiery flare to clearing the way, burn a nice path for us. Or is that also demeaning?"

"You'll find out if your pack doubles in weight soon." Sardelle squeezed his hand and walked past him, pulling out her sword. The sleek blade pulsed a few times, then a beam shot out, incinerating a toadstool next to Zirkander's muddy boot.

"That accuracy is fairly impressive," Zirkander said without batting an eye, "but I'd like to see a further demonstration. With the trail."

"Sometimes I feel left out," Cas admitted to Tolemek, "because I can't hear any of this interplay with the sword."

"Don't," he said. "Consider it a boon."

* * *

Tolemek scowled at the slide and fiddled with the knobs, trying to coax more magnification out of the sturdy but limited field microscope. He had seen evidence of the swelling in the brain tissue that Sardelle had mentioned, but he couldn't detect anything foreign in the samples he had taken. Not with his eyes, anyway. He sensed... Maybe it was his imagination, but he sensed something was there, something too small for his microscope to reveal.

"Sardelle?" he called, lifting his head.

To his surprise, Zirkander, Sardelle, and Duck had already packed and were leaning against trees, waiting. The last Tolemek had noticed, they had been eating breakfast, with Duck still snoozing. He didn't even see Cas. Had she gone ahead to start cutting a trail?

"Yes?" Sardelle asked.

"Are you all waiting on me?" Tolemek was sitting on a rock with his microscope set up on another rock. He hadn't started packing yet.

"Nah," Zirkander said. "We're waiting on Cas. She's climbing a tree to see if there's any sign that those pirates made it through and are still following us."

"So you wouldn't have waited if it was just me?" Tolemek asked dryly. It would have been somewhat alarming to look up from his microscope and find the rest of the group gone.

"I wouldn't leave anyone," Zirkander said. "I might have taken Sardelle's sword and seen how many chunks of your hair I could cut off before you noticed, but I wouldn't have left."

"Don't give Jaxi any ideas."

Sardelle walked over and crouched beside Tolemek. "Did you find something?"

"No, but I have this niggling sense that something's there." Tolemek was still struggling to accept the idea that he had latent magical power, but had to admit that his senses—what he had always considered intuition—rarely failed him, especially in regard to science. "I thought my examination might reveal some type of bacteria we're not familiar with, but I'm wondering if this might be some non-bacterial pathogen, something too small for my microscope to detect."

"A virus," Sardelle said.

"Yes." He lifted his brows. "I thought you might be able to see more than the microscope can."

"That would be a useful skill."

"Oh," he said, assuming her comment meant she didn't possess it.

"There is—*was*—a small branch of our healing school that studied microbiology, but we had even more primitive microscopes back then, so it was difficult to garner more than a very basic understanding of disease theory. In order to help people, we healers enhance the power of a person's immune system by channeling our energy into their bodies. This allows them to fight off diseases and to heal wounds at a much greater speed than usual, and it's often possible to cure someone who might have otherwise succumbed to a potent virus."

"So if we were to capture one of these crazy people, you could cure him?" Zirkander asked from his tree. He and Duck were playing some game that involved bumping hands and making finger gestures.

"Possibly," Sardelle said. "There are cases of diseases being too potent or too far along. In the end, sorcerers aren't gods, or even dragons."

"I wonder," Tolemek said, his eyes losing focus as he considered the symptom list he had put together so far. "No, probably not. A human would either succumb to a virus or fight it off eventually, right?"

"Are you thinking of your sister?"

"Are you reading my mind again?"

"Just guessing this time." Sardelle smiled gently. "Did she show symptoms similar to the people we've seen?"

"Just in her spurts of... wildness." He resisted the temptation to use the word "craziness." Tylie had been lucid and normal for much of the time. But she had always complained about the voices, and sometimes, she had snapped in front of him, going from normal to wild, harming others, harming herself. He sighed. "Her eyes were never dilated though. And she's had this... whatever *this* is for years."

"We'll figure it out. I suspect the answers are somewhere on this mountain." She waved toward the way ahead. Though the dense foliage continued to smother the landscape, blocking the view of the volcano, they had started climbing as soon as they had left the pool the day before, and Tolemek believed they had risen several hundred feet from sea level. If they ever found a break in the jungle—or climbed a particularly high tree—they might be able to see the sea in the distance.

Cas strolled into view from the direction Sardelle had been pointing. She smiled at Tolemek, the expression warming him and driving away some of the malaise that had him down. Or gloominess, as Zirkander would call it. Not for the first time, he wished he hadn't been a dolt that night in town, that he had spent it with Cas instead of wandering the streets and bumping into treasure-hunting pirates. They had laid next to each other during their nights in the jungle, when one of them wasn't on watch, but even after dark, the air remained muggy and sticky, not conducive to snuggling—or even wanting to be touched. He was actually starting to miss Iskandia's gray winter skies.

"I brought you something," Cas said, her eyes bright as she strolled toward him, her hand behind her back.

"Is it a rifle, pistol, or other weapon?" Tolemek asked.

"That would usually be a safe guess," Zirkander told Sardelle as she rejoined him. She swatted him on the chest.

"Not this time." Cas withdrew her arm and revealed a vibrant red flower, its rounded petals forming a bulbous body almost as large as her hand. The tip reminded him of a belly button.

Belly? Tolemek stood, his gaze riveted. "That's the blood belly. From the mural."

"I thought so." Cas handed it to him.

"Huh," Duck said. "Usually boys bring girls flowers, not the other way around."

"There's a pond over in that direction," Cas said, ignoring him, "and they were growing all around it."

The warmth in his chest grew, gratitude toward Cas for keeping an eye out for him and for being with him on this journey. He touched a hand to her cheek, the other coming to rest on her hip, and leaned down to kiss her. He knew he shouldn't—not with the others looking on—but he needed her to know how much he appreciated her help, how much he appreciated *her*.

To his delight, Cas did not stiffen or pull away. She stepped closer to him, rising on her tiptoes to return the kiss, smiling as their lips touched. Maybe she wanted to alleviate his gloominess, or maybe she was simply glad they had found a clue. Either way, the sweetness of her touch made him lament once again that he had wasted their private night together.

"Is that allowed?" Duck asked. "During the mission?"

"I think so," Zirkander said. "We can call this a rest break."

"He's smooshing his flower."

Though Tolemek did not want the moment to end, the commentary stole some of the romance. He stepped back, letting his hand linger to brush his fingers across Cas's dirt-smudged cheek. The grime did nothing to diminish her appeal.

"Thank you," he murmured, holding her gaze.

"You're welcome." She pressed the flower into his hands.

Tolemek rotated it, examining it from all sides, impressed by its vibrant color. He could see why it would stand out to his sister.

"I've seen the *marsoothimums* here too," Sardelle said. "If we find the blue flowers, we'll know we're in the right area."

"I'll watch for them," Cas said. "They're at a higher elevation, right? That's what the colonel's dad said."

Sardelle nodded.

"Lieutenant Ahn," Zirkander said. "While I'm glad that your

scouting mission was so fruitful—" he wriggled his eyebrows, "—did you see any pirates, cannibals, or other threats while you were out there?"

"No, sir. I did climb a tree—" Cas wiped her hands on her trousers, grimacing at the sap, "—but I didn't see any cooking fires or anything that would indicate there were people behind us. I did see a snake larger than I am. It hissed at me, and I left the tree. This place is… Let's just say that I would like to request a nice, flat desert for our next mission. Or perhaps even a city. With cozy inns. Baths."

Sardelle shared a wistful smile with Cas.

"I'll let the king know of your preferences," Zirkander said. "If he's still talking to me when we get back."

Cas grabbed her pack. Figuring the group was ready to press on, Tolemek put away his slides and his microscope.

Tolemek?

The mental call startled him, and he dropped the microscope case. *Jaxi?* he asked. It didn't *sound* like Jaxi, but nobody else had ever spoken into his mind. The voice seemed distant, almost as if the speaker was calling to him from a mountaintop.

Tolemek, are you coming?

He leaned forward, using a rock for support. It couldn't be. She had never spoken to him.

Tylie? he asked.

Tolie, be careful. Don't get sick.

He gulped. It *was* her. He'd had numerous nicknames in his life, but nobody except for his sister had ever called him Tolie. And that had been years ago, when she had been too young to pronounce his whole name. *Sick? Tylie, what do you mean?*

Nothing except silence answered him. Could she hear him? No, probably not. He had no idea how to send out his thoughts.

Tylie? he asked again, hoping she might be monitoring his mind somehow, the way Jaxi sometimes did. But could she know how to do that? When she had never been trained? *Tylie? Are you there? Can you hear me?*

Silence.

Someone touched his shoulder. Tolemek straightened,

reluctantly accepting that his sister wasn't going to contact him again, not now. Maybe if they got closer, she would be able to.

"Are you all right?" Cas lowered her hand to his forearm, resting it there.

"Did anyone else hear that?" Tolemek met Sardelle's eyes, assuming she would be the other person who might have heard a telepathic communication. Or if not her, Jaxi.

She shook her head. She wore the same concerned expression as Cas.

Tolemek tried to smooth his features. "I thought I heard—no, I *did* hear Tylie."

"Your sister?" Zirkander asked. "I didn't know she could do that."

"Neither did I."

"You haven't seen her for a while," Sardelle said. "Those with the gift do often figure some things out for themselves, even without training." She tilted her head. "What did she say?"

"Don't get sick." Tolemek eyed the case with the slides in it.

"Ah."

"Good advice for all," Zirkander said. "Let's go find that third flower, eh?"

Chapter 8

The blue flowers were everywhere. They blossomed on vines that snaked up the trunk of every other tree as the group climbed higher. Cas had seen a few more of the blood bellies and *marsoothimums*, as well. At first, Tolemek had seemed pleased by the discovery, but he was wearing his pensive—gloomy—expression again, staring at the trail ahead of him instead of admiring the landscape.

Granted, Cas wasn't admiring the landscape, either. She kept trotting off to the side or up ahead, searching for spots where she might look out behind them. Even though they had stumbled onto a trail and the trees they were walking through had thinned out, she hadn't spotted anything more malevolent than birds and monkeys.

"Sardelle?" she asked after scampering down a tree and returning to the group. "Can you sense anyone back there? That's a thing you can do, isn't it? You have before."

"Usually I can," Sardelle said, "but as I was telling Ridge, the density of life in the jungle makes it difficult to pick out individuals. Also..." Her gaze drifted up the slope.

"Yes?"

"I feel the dragon. Strongly. He's such a presence that he blots out my ability to detect lesser life forms. Sort of the way you have trouble hearing someone sneaking up on you when you're in the middle of a room full of talking people."

"Oh."

Sardelle tapped the hilt of her sword thoughtfully. "Jaxi and I did both think there was something familiar about that person who left the dirigible. I didn't say anything because even then, the dragon's presence was affecting my ability to discern different entities. I also thought it might just be that the ship was full of Iskandians and that they would seem more familiar to me than the pirates and natives in town."

"I've wondered about that person myself," Cas said. "I also believe it's possible some of those pirates got away and may still be after us."

"If they are, I don't think they'll find a treasure up here. Unless they want the dragon blood."

"There *are* some who would pay a great deal for those vials."

"Perhaps so."

"Sardelle?" Zirkander called softly from his spot at the head of the column.

She and Cas jogged to catch up with him. Their trail had intersected a second perpendicular one, and the colonel had stopped, looking down at something.

"Don't get too close," Tolemek said.

Probably good advice, but as usual, Cas's height meant that she had to push past the others to see what they were looking at. Tolemek's hand dropped onto her shoulder, halting her, but she had already spotted the large dead animal slumped against a tree on the opposite side of the trail. She had never seen a tiger before, but recognized the black stripes on the orange fur. The black feathers were more confusing. The fact that the carcass had been gnawed on and pecked at made it difficult to figure out what she was seeing, but it looked like a giant bird had crashed into the creature. And then died. No, that didn't make sense. She tried to take a step closer, but Tolemek's hand tightened.

"Are those *wings?*" Duck asked.

"It's a winged tiger," Sardelle said. "I've read about them but never seen one. Remarkable."

"It would be more remarkable if it wasn't dead." Zirkander shuffled back. "Look at the size of him. The muscles. That is— was—a top-level predator right there. And in the prime of his life. Things like that don't just pitch over and die."

Tolemek looked at him sharply. "Are you suggesting this is related to the dead humans?"

"You tell me, scientist."

"I don't know. I would have assumed it got in the way of some other top-level predator and lost the fight."

"There's not much sign of that." Cas pointed. "No claw or tooth marks on its face or neck. Something's been munching on its organs, but small creatures. Scavengers."

"Munching on its organs, Raptor?" Duck asked. "Sometimes it's a little chilling the way you talk about death. But maybe that just means you two—" he waved his fingers at Tolemek, "—are meant for each other."

"Er." It was such a random place for such a comment that Cas didn't know how to respond.

Tolemek lowered his hand from her shoulder. He didn't look like he knew how to respond, either.

"I don't sense that it died of physical trauma," Sardelle said, then looked at Tolemek, her eyes solemn. "It's displaying the same swelling of brain tissue that the humans we examined did."

Zirkander pushed his fingers through his hair a few times. "Does this mean... *everything* can catch this... whatever it is?"

"Viruses, if that's what this is, usually have a limited range of hosts they can infect." Tolemek shrugged down at the dead tiger. "But perhaps this one can affect all mammals."

"Including those with dragon blood," Sardelle whispered.

"What?" Zirkander asked.

"Unicorns, winged tigers, soaring lizards... some of the other near-mythological creatures. We've discussed this before. It's believed they have dragon blood, the same as that fresh-water octopus. I don't know if that creature was affected by the virus, but this one was." Sardelle met Tolemek's eyes again. "My theory that we may have more immunity to a virus, if that's what this is, may not be worth much."

"I knew the risks when I went into the village," Tolemek said.

Cas frowned up at him. She didn't know a damned thing about diseases or viruses or whatever they were dealing with and had no idea if Tolemek and Sardelle were in more danger than any of the rest of them, but the idea that he might have put himself at risk to learn more for everyone else's sake gave her a sense of discomfort she didn't quite know how to interpret. Guilt? Concern for him? Both?

"We've probably all been exposed at this point," Zirkander

said. "Sardelle, any thoughts on where we might find the dragon? I've been angling toward the top of the mountain, but that's a vague destination. There are more trails up here than I expected too."

"That way, I think." Sardelle pointed at the corner of the intersection between the two trails, where a solid knot of trees made travel unlikely.

"Helpful." Zirkander quirked his brows at her. "Will Jaxi be sarcastically carving the way again?"

"Duck and I will look for tracks," Cas said. "Given how quickly the brush grows over the trails here, someone's been maintaining these, and recently too."

"Sir," Duck said, "is she allowed to volunteer me to scrounge around in the dirt near diseased corpses?"

"Just the other day, you were remarking on how I have seniority over you," Cas said.

"Remarking on it? I was lamenting it."

"Just don't get close to the body," Zirkander said. "We're leaving that for Tolemek."

"Really," he said.

"Don't you want to get your microscope out and look at some brain bits?"

"Brain bits, Zirkander? How is it your people consider you a national hero?"

"We have low standards for heroism in Iskandia."

"Obviously."

Cas turned up the side trail while Duck walked farther on the one they had been following. Neither would qualify as a road, but this one appeared to have seen more use of late, though not since the heavy rains of the day before. Most of the prints were washed out, leaving her to judge the traffic by the compactness of the earth and the recently hewn branches on either side. She crouched to examine a rut that cut through the mud, running down the center of the trail. It was too deep and narrow to have come from a wheeled vehicle, but perhaps from a runner on a sledge or travois? Such as might hold a crate full of vials?

She squinted down the slope, then up the other direction. As

Zirkander had said, the top was a vague destination since they didn't have a map with an X marking the dragon spot. They had already reached an area that looked like the one in the mural, but the entire top of the mountain might house those flowers. At least if they headed to higher ground, they might find better views of the surrounding land.

"I think this is the most likely route," Cas said.

Zirkander had been walking along the same trail as she, except heading downhill. He touched the ground and looked back. "You have the runner mark up there?"

"Yes. I was thinking it might have carried a crate."

"Me too. Up it is, unless you've found something over there, Duck."

"A few old footprints," Duck said. "They were made by boots, not those hide shoes the natives wear."

"Evidence of the same here." Cas pointed to a two- or three-day-old print that had survived the rain.

Zirkander joined her, nodding up the slope. "We'll see if we can follow that rut back to where it came from."

This trail was wide enough for two people to walk side by side. Zirkander stayed up with Cas while Tolemek and the others stretched out behind them. She caught Sardelle giving the dead tiger a long frown before following. Usually, Cas would stay in the back, to watch the route behind them, but she wanted to ask Zirkander something, something that it might be better if Sardelle and Tolemek didn't hear. Sardelle, especially. The notion that she might hear Cas's question, anyway, through Zirkander's thoughts or however that worked, made her uncomfortable, but she was concerned that nobody had brought the subject up.

"Sir," she said quietly, "about the dragon…"

"Yes?" He responded quietly too. Maybe he knew what she was going to ask and already shared her concerns.

"We're here to get rid of the source of the dragon blood, right?" She might want to help Tolemek, as well, but it was her duty—being a part of Zirkander's squadron—that had brought her here. "What happens if the dragon is truly an ally to the Cofah and voluntarily giving his blood? Do we… try to, uhm."

She wouldn't normally hesitate to speak her mind, but the fact that everyone from Sardelle to her sword to Tolemek's sister might be able to monitor her made her nervous. "Do we try to kill it?"

His face had gone grim before she had spoken the final question, and there wasn't a hint of surprise in his eyes now. Yes, he had been pondering this question too.

"We have to eliminate the threat to Iskandia," Zirkander said. "To have come all this way and to have... broken so many rules, to do anything less would be unacceptable. I don't want to see the capital destroyed someday because the Cofah have unmanned fliers that can bomb the city without ever risking a Cofah life. And that's only a hint to what they might be able to do with that blood. We have to assume that there are other labs out there and that the one we destroyed will be rebuilt."

Cas nodded. Good, he *had* been thinking about this. "Two questions then. How does one kill a dragon? I know they didn't have bullets back then, but from all the stories I've read, arrows and javelins didn't do much. It was usually dragons that killed other dragons, wasn't it? Some of them sided with humans, with specific nations, and fought with them, right? But if they're as powerful as they sound, I'm not sure why they would have bothered."

"We'll have to ask our dragon expert about that." He pointed a thumb over his shoulder, toward Sardelle presumably.

Cas wished Apex hadn't been sent back to Iskandia. For this conversation, she would rather talk to him than Sardelle.

"I'll admit I'm hoping for a non-violent solution," Zirkander said. "Like maybe we can use our pretty smiles and charisma to talk the dragon over to our side, or to at least convince it to leave the Cofah and become a neutral party."

"Do pretty smiles affect dragons?"

"I don't know, but the old songs claim the bard Frontier Festyr had the ability to tame a wild horse with a grin. They didn't even take care of their teeth back then, so I ought to have the advantage." He clapped her on the shoulder. "I want to see what the exact situation is before plotting dragon slayings.

What's your second question?"

"It's tied in with the first. I get the sense that for Sardelle, the dragon, whoever he's working for, is a relative of sorts. Or that she feels that way toward it. Will she allow us to… do what needs to be done?"

"I don't think it's likely it's a relative, given that she's from Iskandia and he's… from *here* apparently." Zirkander waved toward the top of the mountain. "Part of some long lost clan of dragons that's been hiding out in this remote area, maybe. It's more likely he's related to that tiger back there."

Cas grunted.

"But Sardelle is practical. I think if a peaceful solution can't be reached, she'll understand. And help us."

Cas hoped that was true. She wasn't as certain that Sardelle would be able to be objective about the dragon.

"Either way, you might not want to think about the possibility overmuch," Zirkander said.

"Because Sardelle's sword might hear?" The possibility of having it or Sardelle reading her mind made Cas uncomfortable.

"Because the *dragon* might hear. I figure if Jaxi can get in my head and root around, a dragon would have even less trouble. Just because it didn't respond to whatever mental message Jaxi and Sardelle sent, that doesn't mean it's not aware of us coming. And if it's aware of us coming, the Cofah might be too."

"Comforting."

A faint odor reached Cas's nose. She held up her hand, stepped on a log, and peered into the brush to the side of the trail. In the thick shadows beneath the trees, it took her a moment to see anything besides leaves, but then she spotted another carcass, a deer-like creature this time. More of it had been devoured than of the tiger. Tastier meat perhaps.

"Another dead animal," she said when she hopped down. The others had caught up.

"A lot of them here," Duck said.

"I'm not sure two is a *lot*," Zirkander said. "This is the wilderness. Animals kill and eat each other."

Something plummeted from the sky and landed on the trail

twenty meters ahead. Cas had her rifle pointing at it before she knew what it was, but she didn't fire. There was no point. It was a big bird, a type of falcon, and it was already dead.

Duck cleared his throat. "Is *three* a lot?"

"Maybe," Zirkander said.

"Does anyone worry that it might not be right healthy to keep heading up this mountain?"

"Trust me," Zirkander said, "it's on my mind. Every time I cough, I'm sure it's going to end with me keeling over, after I go crazy and try to pummel everyone in the party." He smiled, but it didn't reach his eyes. *Had* he been coughing?

Tolemek lifted his chin. "You could try, Zirkander."

While the men exchanged speculative stares, Cas headed toward a stream trickling past, parallel to the path. She had to clamber over a log, push past a thorny bush that wanted her rifle for a souvenir, and slip down the side of a mossy rock, nearly landing in the creek, but she made it. "Everything is a fight here," she muttered.

She unslung her nearly empty canteen and dipped it toward the clear rippling water, but froze with its mouth an inch away. She looked up and down the stream, half-expecting more carcasses to be littering the area. They weren't, but a new thought had jumped into her mind, chilling her. What if the water was the problem? What if it was the way the disease was being transmitted? Or what if it wasn't a disease at all, but some poison or toxin that the Cofah were dumping into the streams as part of an experiment? An experiment that they wouldn't undertake on their own soil, but one they might try on a remote island, assuming nobody would report their vile work here?

"Cas?" Zirkander called. "Are you coming back, or did you decide it was time for a bath?"

"No…" She stared down at her canteen, afraid now to fill it. But she had already filled it from water sources in the jungle. They all had. It might have looked clear, but Tolemek had said whatever was affecting those people's brains was too small to see, even with his microscope.

"No, you're not coming back, or no you're not bathing?"

Foliage crunched behind her, and Duck and Zirkander came into sight. Cas stood slowly, facing them with her canteen.

"The water, sir. I realized we might have a problem." Cas shared her thoughts, half hoping one of them would tell her that she was being silly, that diseases—or manmade poisons—couldn't be transmitted that way.

Zirkander studied the stream and rubbed his jaw—he, Tolemek, and Duck hadn't shaved for a few days, and Cas thought the scruff looked scratchy and grimy. "I would have expected Tolemek or Sardelle to mention something if we had to worry about the water, but maybe that was an incorrect assumption."

"Where did they go?"

"They're crouching over that dead raven, head to head, pointing and discussing it. I'm trying not to find their newfound interest in corpses alarming."

"Scientists are strange," Duck said. "Sorceresses, too, I suppose. But maybe they'll save our lives."

"I would be amenable to my life not needing saving."

Cas frowned down at her canteen, puzzling over how to top off her supply without risking more exposure. Or did it not matter at this point? Had they already been exposed to what was making the rest of the jungle sick?

Duck took her canteen, stepped across the stream, and stopped in front of a bush with broad leaves. He folded one, held the mouth underneath it, and captured an impressive amount of water that ran off. "As long as it keeps raining every day, we gather water this way."

"Did you lick the leaf first?" Zirkander asked. "You're sure that's not a poisonous bush?"

"I've actually been testing a number of shrubs along the way here—you can start out rubbing a leaf against your skin to see if there's a reaction. And I've eaten some of the fruit. We have supplies for a few more days, but you never know when they'll run out." Duck nodded at the big-leafed shrub. "I wouldn't eat this fellow, but the leaves aren't toxic to humans."

"I knew there was a reason I brought you along," Zirkander said. "Those keen wilderness survival skills."

"Yes, sir. They're what keep me in high demand with the ladies back in the capital." His mouth twisted wryly.

Back in the barracks, Cas had heard stories of Pimples' dating woes, but Duck didn't usually talk about his personal life. Or maybe she didn't pay attention. She'd always had that tendency to focus on work instead of romance—especially the romantic lives of others—until a certain pirate had fallen into her cockpit.

Zirkander clapped him on the shoulder, filled his own canteen with the water from the leaves of an identical bush, then headed back to the path. Cas accepted her canteen from Duck, thanked him, and returned to find Tolemek and Sardelle standing up. Tolemek tucked something into an inside vest pocket. Some sample he had taken? Cas didn't look too closely. Whatever Duck thought, she wasn't interested in studying brain bits up close.

"Have you two tested the water?" Zirkander asked. "Cas was wondering if the streams might be responsible for spreading the disease."

"I haven't tested it," Tolemek said. "Given my experience with the brain tissue, a negative result under the microscope wouldn't prove anything one way or another."

"Hm." Zirkander leaned his head toward Cas. "I think that means we better continue to gather water from the leaves."

"Agreed, sir."

Tolemek frowned at Zirkander. Cas didn't know if it had anything to do with their easy camaraderie, but she stepped away from her commander just in case.

"I haven't sensed anything off with the water," Sardelle said, wiping her hands on her leather trousers, "but I will also agree that a negative doesn't mean much in this instance. It *does* seem that there has to be some common element that's causing the animals and the humans to become affected. While there are examples of airborne diseases, there's usually a sharing of bodily fluids or other close contact. *If* we're dealing with a disease."

"I hope the animals and the people aren't sharing bodily fluids." Zirkander grabbed his pack and canteen, waved toward the trail, and headed up, glancing at the permanently grounded raven.

"Likely not, but people do sometimes live in close quarters with domesticated animals," Sardelle said.

"That winged tiger wasn't domesticated. I've heard those like to munch on people."

"I know." She fell in beside him. "I'm sorry, Ridge. I don't have any answers for you yet."

He wrapped an arm around her shoulder for a moment before letting it drop. "It's all right. We'll figure it out."

Cas shouldered her own canteen, trying not to think about the number of times she had filled it from the ground water already on this trip.

CHAPTER 9

TOLEMEK STOPPED COUNTING DEAD ANIMALS after they passed the twentieth one. Every instinct inside his body was crying out for him to get out of this place before it was too late. Like Zirkander, he kept worrying that he was experiencing the first symptom of the illness; he kept catching himself touching his forehead, trying to determine if the beginnings of a fever burned beneath his skin. Cas's idea to avoid the groundwater was a good one, and he wished he had thought of it earlier.

"I think we're going to have to camp on the trail, sir," Duck said. "There aren't any clearings. If anything, the jungle has gotten denser again." Denser and darker. A strange mist had rolled out of the undergrowth as twilight approached, one that seemed unlikely on a mountainside. "We—"

A shot fired in the distance, from somewhere behind them. Tolemek tried to meet Cas's eyes, but she was staring back down the trail, her expression knowing rather than surprised.

"Our pirate friends?" Zirkander asked.

"Possibly." Cas didn't sound convinced.

"I'd hoped the crazy natives had taken care of them."

"Ridge?" Sardelle asked, facing the jungle instead of the trail behind them.

"Yes?" Zirkander asked.

"I think we're close."

Tolemek's heart thumped behind his ribcage. He hadn't heard again from Tylie, and he kept worrying that he was too late, that the Cofah had somehow sensed him coming and had stolen her away again.

Sardelle stepped off the trail, slipping between two towering fern-like plants, and disappearing into the gloom. Zirkander frowned back toward the gunshot, his hand on his pistol.

Tolemek pushed into the ferns. He probably *should* be concerned about threats behind him, but it was what lay ahead that held his heart.

"We'll follow her," Zirkander said. "Duck, do your best to hide our trail."

"Sir," Cas said, "should I wait here? See if someone comes up behind us?"

Tolemek froze, his foot halfway over a mushroom-bedecked log. Even though he knew Cas was capable of a great deal, he didn't want to break up the group. No, he silently urged Zirkander. Order her along.

"Let's stay together, in case Sardelle gets us irrevocably lost. I'll let you set a nice trap outside of whatever mud hole we end up camping in tonight."

For the first time since he had met the man, Tolemek wanted to hug Zirkander. Not enough to actually turn around and do it, but he was relieved to see Cas stepping off the trail behind him.

Tolemek hurried to catch up with Sardelle, who was already disappearing into a dense thicket of reeds. She had worn a distracted expression as she had walked off the trail, and he wasn't entirely positive she was going to wait for them.

Don't worry, pirate boy. You and your microscope are important to us.

I had no idea my fate mattered to you. He jumped around a lichen-covered boulder and slipped into the reeds, having to walk sideways to squeeze through. Mud squished beneath his boots.

It's more the microscope than you, Jaxi replied.

You have a fondness for inanimate objects? I suppose that makes sense.

What is that supposed to mean? Does someone want his pack to increase to its actual weight?

You better not do that unless you want Sardelle to deal with that dragon alone. Which might happen anyway if Tolemek couldn't keep up with her. The reeds poked and pushed at him, some too thick to easily be pushed aside.

The dragon isn't the next problem.

What is?

Jaxi didn't reply. Wonderful. Another mystery. Just what he needed.

Tolemek pushed out of the reeds, only to step in deeper mud. Mosquitoes nipped at his exposed flesh. He hesitated, wondering if he should pull out a light. Twilight had grown so thick beneath the canopy that it might as well be night, and he didn't want to step into a sink hole.

"Sardelle?" he called softly.

Crunches came from behind him, along with a grunt that sounded like it belonged to Zirkander. Tolemek planned to wait for him until a faint yellow light reached his eyes. Jaxi's golden glow? If so, it was quite a ways ahead.

He risked walking farther into the mud, keeping his hands on branches in case the dubious ground gave away. As he moved along, the light grew more pronounced. Now he could see the silhouettes of the mosquitoes buzzing in front of his face. He wasn't sure if that was an improvement or not.

"Over here," came Sardelle's soft call from the side.

Tolemek jumped, realization sending a hot tingle through his limbs. If she was to the side, that wasn't Jaxi's glow he had been following. No, the more he considered it, the more it appeared natural. He couldn't see flames, but it seemed like the glow from some lantern. Or given the distance, a campfire or bonfire was more likely.

Though he wanted to push ahead and see who was up there burning wood, he veered over to Sardelle. He winced with each step, since the mud sucked at his boots noisily.

"It's drier over here," Sardelle whispered as a further incentive.

He climbed onto higher ground and joined her behind a gnarled tree. She did have Jaxi in her hand, but the sword wasn't glowing. A good idea, if there was someone up ahead.

"Is that a campfire?" he whispered. "Are there people up there?"

Duck and Zirkander joined them, their heavy breathing suggesting they had been fighting reeds and mud, as well. Tolemek peered past them, searching for Cas's slight form. She hadn't disobeyed orders and stayed behind, had she?

"A fire, yes," Sardelle said. "And people."

"And a dragon?" Zirkander asked.

Sardelle hesitated. "Yes."

"Still not talking to you?" When she didn't answer, Zirkander shifted his weight, his clothing rustling. "Or is it?"

"It didn't say anything, but I—Jaxi—had a sense of it warning us away with its mind. Ordering us away, was actually what she said."

"How did it warn or order without words?" Tolemek gazed toward the distant yellow glow, torn between wanting to wait for Cas and wanting to see what lay ahead.

"There were images. Of death. Unpleasant death."

He wished he hadn't asked.

Cas slipped past Duck and Zirkander.

"Nice of you to join us," Zirkander said.

"Did you hear the scream?" she asked.

"No."

"It came from the same direction as the gunshot. There are definitely two parties out there."

"Pirates and crazies?" Zirkander asked.

"I don't know."

"We haven't seen any signs of other natives since starting the climb up the mountain," Duck said.

Zirkander sighed. Tolemek pushed past Sardelle, heading for the glow.

"Watch out for the drop," she said.

He halted, eyeing the mist curling around his legs. "Drop?"

"Twenty feet ahead."

Tolemek inched forward, keeping his hands on the branches again. After the mud, he expected a sinkhole, but Sardelle's "drop" was much, much grander. The trees thinned, then fell away, and he found himself gaping into a giant circular depression. A crater. There was a place back home that his father had taken him to as a child, where an asteroid had slammed into the earth, leaving a mile-wide depression. This was a much greener and more lush version of something the same size. He looked skyward, surprised they hadn't seen it when they had flown over the area, but the stars weren't visible. A latticework of vines and leaves arched over the crater in a dome that extended to the trees along the rim, blending seamlessly with the canopy.

"That should not be possible without supports beams," Tolemek said slowly, wrestling with the engineering aspect. "Support trees, anyway."

"It's magical," Sardelle said as she approached, as if she were stating the most obvious thing in the world. "Very old magic that's been here for a long time. Centuries. If not millennia." She waved toward the center of the grassy crater at an ancient stone structure. It resembled a mix between a pyramid and a ziggurat, with its tiered levels worn at the edges and coated with thick moss. The ruins rose at least fifteen stories, the top even with the rim Tolemek and the others stood upon. A dirt road meandered up to a rectangular opening in the base—an entrance to the structure. Two large bonfires burned in giant stone braziers on either side. Another brightened the inside of the fang-filled maw of a dragon head statue at the top of the ziggurat. "There's magic coming from the pyramid too," Sardelle added. "Some old artifacts, perhaps. I'm sure I would have sensed all of this when we flew over the area if not for the dragon's overwhelming presence." She sighed. "I've been using that for an excuse often, it seems. It's just… This makes it hard for me to imagine a world where dragons were once the norm. Or at least were only moderately rare."

"Should we be standing here with that man on guard down there?" Cas whispered from behind them.

Tolemek hadn't noticed anyone, but he stepped back behind a tree, trusting her eyesight. He stared into the shadows of the recessed doorway, finally picking out an armed man standing against the wall inside. A man armed with a rifle, not a bow or bone knife. The gloom hid the details, but Tolemek thought he made out trousers, boots, and a long-sleeve shirt, such as a Cofah soldier might wear.

"Let's follow the edge of this pit around to the side," Zirkander murmured, also tucked behind a tree. "See if we can approach without being seen. Maybe there's another way in. Assuming we want to go in." He glanced at Sardelle.

"The dragon is inside," she said.

"Funny how that doesn't answer the question as decisively as one would hope," Zirkander said.

"How would a dragon get inside a pyramid like that?" Duck asked. He was crouching behind them, his face and clothes so spattered with mud that he almost looked like he had attempted to camouflage himself. Maybe he had. "That door is more human-sized."

Sardelle only shrugged.

"We'll go around the top for a ways," Zirkander said. "But don't think I'm not noticing that if we had stayed on the trail, it would have wound around and come out right over there." He pointed along the rim, about fifty meters to their left where a trail led out of the jungle and down the sloped side of the crater in switchbacks. Zirkander made a show of plucking a broken reed out of his hair, then scraping a sticky web off his shoulder.

"The guard is looking in that direction." Sardelle smiled gently. "You were wise to follow me."

"Uh huh. Ten nucros says he's looking at his feet and wondering what superior officer he irked to get stationed in this remote hole."

"Actually, he's looking up the road, sir," Cas said. "Attentively."

"He seems concerned," Sardelle said.

"About his lack of career prospects." Zirkander pointed. "Back away from the edge. We'll see if we can find another way down without resorting to machetes."

Sardelle followed last, and Tolemek wondered what she sensed from the man, or if she was merely guessing at his thoughts. He couldn't even see the guard's face in the shadows. Cas's nickname of Raptor apparently had as much to do with her eyesight as her aim. Sardelle had never mentioned it, but maybe Cas had a smidgen of dragon blood in her family line somewhere too.

A low, throaty growl came from the brush ahead.

"Now what?" Zirkander touched his pistol, glanced toward

the crater, then pulled out his machete instead.

Another growl came from ahead and to the right of the first one. A pack of wolves or coyotes? Between the darkness, the trees, and the mist, Tolemek couldn't see more than a few feet ahead.

"If we have to fight, that guard's going to hear it," Duck whispered.

"I know," Zirkander said.

"Sardelle, can you convince them to go away?"

"Trying," she said softly. "There are eight, and their minds aren't normal. They're not hungry, and they know we're a threat, but they're experiencing... something hard to describe. Anger? Madness?"

"The same craziness as everything else around here is experiencing?"

"Probably."

A third growl came from ahead and to the left, followed by the panting of other animals. The creatures seemed to be standing close together so far. Tolemek reached for his vest. He hated to waste his formulas on wildlife—who knew how heavily guarded that ziggurat would be?—but they had to get in.

"Hold your breath," he said, then flung a glass bulb of liquid at a tree ahead of them.

It shattered, and he winced at the sound, but he didn't think it would carry to the bottom of that crater. Had it been daylight, he would have seen the chemicals turn to smoke and vapor, but all he could tell now was that the glass shards tinkled to the forest floor. And the animals reacted.

A growl turned into a startled yip, then a snarl. The branches shuddered, then something charged at them. Zirkander was still in the lead, and he raised his machete, readying himself. The tangled overgrowth and close branches scarcely left room for defense. Certain he would need help, Tolemek drew a dagger and stepped forward. But the first beast, a great shaggy black wolf, was already leaping through the air, fangs snapping toward Zirkander's throat. He swung the machete, striking it in the side of the head at the same time as the creature burst into flames.

Zirkander stumbled back, nearly crashing into Tolemek. The wolf cried out, but its pain was short-lived. Within seconds, all that remained were charred flakes of ash that wafted to the ground.

Zirkander faced the brush, ready for another attack. But no more movement stirred the foliage.

"The rest seem to be sleeping," Sardelle said, stepping up to his shoulder.

"I see." Zirkander nodded to Tolemek, then told her, "I thank you for the help, but in the future, you needn't react quite so quickly. Give me a chance to impress you with my fighting prowess before you incinerate my enemies."

"That was Jaxi. She was concerned."

"Not about the proximity of my arm hair to her inferno, apparently."

"She thought you might become infected if it managed to bite you," Sardelle said.

"Ah, in that case, I applaud her initiative."

Tolemek pushed his way forward through the brush. With his sister so close—he *hoped*—he didn't have patience for chitchat. He stepped past several slumbering wolves, glad the tranquilizer had worked quickly. Jaxi might have set the jungle on fire if her inferno had been any larger. The guard would surely have noticed that.

Please, I have pinpoint accuracy.

Tolemek shook away the intrusion. He just wanted to get to the side of that ziggurat so the guard wouldn't be able to see them descend, then find a way inside. If he had to plow through that soldier to get to Tylie, he would do so, but he hoped there might be another door that wasn't guarded. If nothing else, he might be able to climb up to that dragon head on top and find a way in from there—someone had to be coming out to keep that fire lit.

Actually, the fires are magical.

Tolemek sighed.

You might want to talk to me, Jaxi pressed. *I have news.*

What?

I believe I've located your sister inside.

Tolemek paused, resting his hand on the damp bark of the nearest tree. *Is she... Can you tell if she's all right?* He had heard her voice, so he knew she was alive, or at least had been the day before. But he had no idea what she was doing here or what state she was in.

I can't tell much with that dragon blowing his big, scaly aura all over the place, but she's alive.

At this point, Jaxi's lack of reverence didn't surprise him, but Tolemek did wonder at her wisdom of speaking of a dragon thusly, a dragon that might have big ears.

Actually, dragons are like snakes—no external ears. They hear with their minds.

Maybe they have big minds then. Can you tell where Tylie is in the ziggurat? If he could find that back door in, maybe he could find a way to get to her without ever having to deal with the dragon. He could leave that to Zirkander. He would be willing to help, but a lot more willing once he knew Tylie was somewhere safe and unlikely to get caught in the middle of a Cofah-Iskandian battle.

She seems to be right in the core of that pyramid, Jaxi thought. *Next to the dragon.*

Damn it. Why? He didn't expect Jaxi to have the answer, but couldn't help but blurt out the frustrated words in his mind.

Why? Isn't that obvious? She's linked to the dragon.

"Does anyone smell something?" Duck asked from behind him. "Something *bad*?"

"Yes," Cas said.

What do you mean linked? Tolemek demanded, barely aware of the conversation. Or the presence of the others. He kept stumbling forward in the growing darkness, not willing to pause until he reached a spot where he could go down the side of the crater.

She's a Receiver. It's probably why they brought her here. To communicate with the dragon.

Tolemek stumbled to a stop, stunned. What in all the layers of hell was a Receiver?

A natural telepath with the ability to hear other people's thoughts. With training, she would be able to hear other telepaths calling from great distances. In the army unit Sardelle worked with, there was a man who could relay messages across the entire continent.

A cold chill that had nothing to do with the mist wrapping around his legs came over Tolemek. Duck and Cas brushed past him, using their rifles to push away ground cover, as if they were looking for something. Again, he barely noticed. *What happens, if these people* aren't *trained, Jaxi?*

Depending on how strong their natural aptitude is, it could cause some issues. She can probably hear at least some of the thoughts of others, and it can be difficult, especially for a child, to figure out why people aren't thinking the same things as they're saying.

Seven gods, is that why she's... He resisted the urge to say crazy. He had always hated thinking of his sister that way.

Not showing similar qualms, Jaxi suggested, *Missing a few paddles on her waterwheel? It might be.*

Just how long have you known about this? Are there any other secrets about my family you'd like to tell me about? Remembering the way Jaxi had bluntly told him *he* had magical powers, Tolemek tried not to let his exasperation into his thoughts, but he didn't quite manage to sublimate the image of strangling a sword that came to mind.

You act like it's my fault you and your kin are so oblivious about what you are. I'm not sure today's generation deserves dragon blood.

Jaxi...

I haven't had any idea who or what she is. This is the first time I've been close enough to sense the presence of another sorceress.

She's not a sorceress.

She could be. Isn't that what we're here for? To find her and teach her to be one?

Tolemek closed his eyes. *I just want her to be safe. To have a chance at a normal life. To not be... shunned for being different.*

"Sir?" Cas called back. "You're going to want to see this."

"I really doubt that's the case." Duck made a throat-strangling noise, as if he was trying to keep from throwing up.

"That may be true," Cas said softly.

"What now?" Zirkander sighed from behind Tolemek. He sounded weary.

"Nothing pleasant," Sardelle said.

"Tolemek?" Cas asked. She didn't say anything else.

He put the conversation with Jaxi aside and walked ahead. The smell he had been trying not to notice increased: the stench of rotting meat. It was like the odor of the dead from the village but even worse. Whatever carcasses the team had discovered had been out here much longer.

"Over here," Cas called softly.

He continued until he found her and Duck, only their heights allowing him to tell them apart in the vestiges of twilight. They were standing still, staring down at ground that was more open than that around it, as if it had been cleared for a bonfire.

"Can we risk a light?" Cas asked.

"Here." Sardelle came up beside Tolemek, her soulblade out. It glowed so softly, it illuminated only the ground and the brush for a couple of feet around.

Congratulations, Jaxi, Tolemek thought, though he had no idea if she was still listening to him. *I wouldn't have guessed subtlety was in your repertoire.*

My repertoire is overflowing. And you might want to keep your sarcasm to yourself. This is going to disturb you. It disturbs me. I'm glad I don't have a nose anymore.

The soulblade's soft glow revealed recently churned earth, with a few branches and roots sticking up from the dirt.

Look again.

Tolemek stepped closer, then wished he hadn't. They weren't branches. That was a human arm, what remained of one. It had been torn from its body and chewed on. It wasn't the only one. Sardelle shifted the blade around, revealing everything from ribs to femurs and skulls littering the earth around the surrounding shrubs and trees. Some had been scraped clean by teeth and claw; others still had meat on them.

"It's a mass grave," Cas said, standing on the far side. More ground had been dug up over there.

Duck stood beside her, pinching his nostrils shut as he stared down at a hole.

Tolemek forced himself to walk over, careful not to step on bones. The soft, damp earth sunk beneath his boots. Nobody would notice, not with all the paw prints in the dirt.

The hole held corpses that hadn't been devoured yet, but the worms and other decomposers had gone to work, destroying facial features and making the people unrecognizable. Still, much of the clothing remained. Some of the people wore the garb of natives or the roughhewn clothing common in the city, but others were clad in Cofah uniforms.

"Why?" Tolemek whispered. "Why are they doing it to our own people?" He had assumed the deaths of the porters and the natives had been deliberate, some callous testing of a new toxin or disease on people deemed subhuman or inconsequential. Or perhaps it had been accidental, the fallout from a scientist's creation. But there were as many Cofah bodies in the grave as there were natives. Maybe more.

"Let's discuss this upwind," Zirkander said, his voice calm, though his eyes had a haunted looked to them.

"Or we could *not* discuss it," Duck croaked and hustled into the brush on the far side.

The rest of the group started after him, but something in the open grave caught Tolemek's eye. "Wait," he rasped, stretching out a hand toward Sardelle's sword. He waved her closer, needing more light.

"What is it?" She didn't sound like she *wanted* to come closer. Understandable.

Tolemek picked up the skull that had drawn his attention, shreds of flesh still attached to the bone. A hole had been cut into one temple, a hole large enough to allow someone to access the brain matter. He turned it toward the light, though he already had his suspicions. The edges were straight, neat. It wasn't a hole an animal could have made with tooth or claw. A saw had scored those lines, then someone had carefully extracted the bone.

"Someone else has been performing autopsies," he said.

He looked up at Sardelle, as if she might have the answers. Her eyes were wide, and she only shook her head.

Tolemek returned the skull to its resting place, not that this mass grave appeared restful. "They should have burned the bodies." He wiped his hands on his trousers and looked down at them, the uneasy feeling coming over him again that they had all been contaminated, that it was only a matter of time before someone started showing symptoms.

His legs felt numb as he followed Sardelle another hundred meters to where the rest of the group had stopped. Insects hummed and buzzed, but the jungle was otherwise quiet.

Tolemek leaned against a tree next to Cas. Sardelle sheathed her sword, and darkness overtook them. He had no idea what the expression on his face had been before she extinguished the light, but Cas took his hand. For his reassurance? Or hers? Maybe both. Either way, he clasped her hand back, then pulled her into a hug. So little fazed her, especially when it came to death, but she wrapped her arms around his waist and buried her face in his chest.

"So, what's the verdict, scientist?" Zirkander asked.

Good question.

"I don't know what it is," Tolemek said, "but I no longer think my people know what they're dealing with. I'm wondering if some experiment got out of hand or took an unexpected turn."

"So, no chance of them having a cure or antidote in there?"

Tolemek looked back toward the grave, even though the darkness and distance now hid it from view. "There's a chance, I suppose."

"Do you think this is something they're making based on the dragon blood?" Zirkander asked. "Another potential weapon to use against Iskandia? Or whoever irritates them next?"

"I don't," Sardelle said. "Since humans and dragons can breed, it doesn't seem plausible that anything in the blood would be toxic."

Tolemek was reluctant to gainsay her, since she presumably knew more about dragons than he did, but after a moment, he said, "I'm less certain. If a tiny drop is potent enough to power an aircraft, it possesses properties we can't possibly understand. Mating doesn't involve exchanging *blood*, just the building blocks contained within, uh—" He would have waved at his genitals, but Cas was standing in front of them, and it was too dark for gestures, anyway. "The male's and female's baby-producing material."

Zirkander snorted.

Cas leaned back and swatted him on the chest. "Tactful."

"Blood is still important," Sardelle said. "If the blood types aren't compatible, the fetus will be aborted. There are humans who are different enough that they can't produce children with each other. Dragons are remarkable in their ability to mate with many different species. Some of the scholars of my time proposed that it was the magic itself or perhaps the fact that dragon-to-dragon offspring were so rare that they evolved other ways to continue their line. Others claimed it was simply because they were gods."

"That's all interesting," Zirkander said, "not that it explains the octopus, but I'm more concerned about what the Cofah are doing with that blood and how to stop them."

"Walking in and shooting them should work," Cas said.

"You have a knack for bluntness," Tolemek murmured.

"It's a useful trait for a soldier."

"We'll go in and assess the situation," Zirkander said. "Later tonight, when it's more likely people are sleeping. We'll still have to deal with the guard out front and any alarms he may have rigged, unless someone's aware of a back door."

Tolemek looked toward Sardelle, thinking of the way Jaxi had melted that vault entrance in the volcano laboratory. But nobody answered. The crickets hummed softly.

"You're all looking at me, aren't you?" Sardelle asked.

"I'm looking at your sword, actually," Zirkander said. "Do you think Jaxi could burn us a nice hole in a side wall, so we could slip in unobserved?"

"Jaxi says that stone wall is extremely thick—there's a lot more rock than open space in the pyramid."

"Does that mean she can or can't do it?" Tolemek said.

Can't you people just subdue the guard? You have more weapons than he does.

And he presumably wasn't the only guard in the place. *You burned down a one-foot-thick steel vault door. And a wolf.*

Yes, and now I'm tired.

"She thinks it'll be faster just going in the front and dealing with the guards," Sardelle said. "I can convince the man in the doorway to take a nap. I wouldn't think there would be a lot of soldiers patrolling the tunnels once we're inside. They've lost a lot of men, and they must be busy working on their mission."

"Unless they're expecting us," Zirkander said. "Didn't you say the dragon might know we're here? And Tolemek's sister apparently is talking to him, so she knows we're here."

Tolemek scowled at his dark form. "What are you saying? That she would tell her captors that we're coming?"

"We don't know for sure that it's a prisoner-captor relationship, do we? Maybe they offered her escape from that hospital in exchange for working for them, and she agreed."

"She wouldn't betray me," Tolemek said. As for the rest, he silently admitted that he couldn't know for certain. Hadn't *he* worked for the Cofah once, after all? They *were* his people, and perhaps he would still be in the military today if his disgrace in battle hadn't led to his discharge. And he knew so little of Tylie now. It had been so long since they had a normal relationship.

"All right," Zirkander said. His tone was neutral, but Tolemek got the impression that Zirkander was humoring him. "We'll still wait a couple hours, in the hope that most of the people inside will be asleep."

"We shouldn't delay further," Tolemek said. "Time could be more important now than ever." He waved in the direction of the mass grave, implying that they had all been exposed to whatever was killing people. In truth, he was more worried about Tylie, that she was in trouble in there, being tormented and forced to work for the military.

"We should be able to finish this one way or another tonight," Zirkander said. "A couple of hours shouldn't matter. Besides, I wouldn't mind if those pirates showed up again and made a distraction for us."

Cas stirred, stepping away from Tolemek's chest. But if she

had something to say, she kept it to herself.

Tolemek didn't want to wait. He didn't say as much out loud, but his fist balled of its own accord, and he stalked into the brush, thoughts of going in on his own filling his mind. Maybe that wasn't such a bad idea. He couldn't forget that Zirkander was here for the dragon, not for Tylie. If the group of Iskandians decided the dragon needed to be destroyed and if Tylie was caught in the middle of it...

He could *not* allow that to happen.

CHAPTER 10

AS FOUND TOLEMEK STANDING AT the edge of the crater, staring down at the ziggurat. Or maybe scowling down at it. The shadows hid his face, and she read his mood more by his stance and the sulky silence bleeding off him than anything else.

"Did they send you to make sure I didn't run off?" Tolemek asked.

"I'm sure Sardelle could monitor you without my help. But I'm going back to see if those pirates are indeed finding their way here. I wanted to make sure you're all right."

"You're leaving?" He shifted to face her.

"Not far. I'll be back to help you roll that snoring guard into a closet after Sardelle knocks him out."

Tolemek grunted. "I doubt thousand-year-old ancient pyramids come with closets."

"You don't think people needed to hang up their clothes back then?" Cas stepped forward and took his hand. "Will you wait to go in? Just a couple of hours? I don't think we should split up the group."

"Aren't you about to leave the group?"

"I'm scouting, not splitting."

"That's a relief." Tolemek squeezed her hand. "My concern is that the group and I are going to have different goals once we go inside." He took a deep breath. "Listen, it might be my father's fault that Tylie was in that asylum, but I broke her out and then… when I couldn't help her, I took her back. I thought I could more easily try to find a solution on my own, if I wasn't dragging her around with me and watching after her." He turned to face the crater again, but his chin drooped to his chest, and she doubted he was seeing anything. "If I had kept her with me, she wouldn't be in this situation now. She never would have been made into some tool for the government. If they've been hurting her, coercing her somehow—" He lifted a hand to rub his face. "This is my fault. Every delay..."

Cas shifted, not knowing what to say to alleviate his guilt. She had never been good at dealing with other people's emotions. She didn't know if she could blame her austere upbringing for that, or if it was just some failing in her blood. "We'll get her. Whatever's happened, it's *not* your fault, but you're going to fix it. We'll get her out of here, and Sardelle will know how to help her."

Tolemek sighed noisily. She didn't know if that meant her words had helped or not.

"I don't know what you're thinking," Cas said, "but if you believe the colonel's mission will endanger her, I don't think that's the case. He's not someone who's going to sacrifice a woman for some perceived greater good. He's more likely to get himself in trouble trying to be a hero."

"Glad to hear it." Tolemek sounded bitter.

Maybe she shouldn't have mentioned Zirkander. Every time she did, it seemed to grate at him. She didn't know whether she should apologize—and would she have to continue to apologize every time she mentioned her commander's name?—or accept that it was his problem that he needed to resolve on his own.

"I'm going to go check on our pursuers," she said, letting go of his hand.

"Cas?" he said softly as she stepped away.

She paused. "Yes?"

"Thank you."

She didn't know what she had actually done, but she said, "You're welcome."

She waited another moment, to see if he would say more, but he didn't. Hoping that meant he would stay put until she returned, she slipped into the brush, heading back toward the main trail. Zirkander thought she was going to check on pirates, and it was possible they were back there, but her senses had never relaxed, not since they had left town, and she couldn't shake that feeling that something more inimical than bumbling treasure hunters was following them.

Indeed, as she crept through the brush, the sense grew more profound. Maybe it was all her imagination, or the creepiness of this place getting to her. She wasn't superstitious, and dead bodies rarely bothered her, probably not as much as they should, but the mystery disease added a strange element.

After following the rim of the crater, she reached the trail that meandered down the hill toward the ziggurat. The close, humid air smelled of the fires burning in the braziers. The guard was still at his post. He must not have noticed any of the shots that Cas had heard in the distance, or he—or a team of soldiers— would have come out to investigate. None of the natives had guns, at least insofar as she had seen, so the sound of firearms would be a sure sign of intruders. She gazed down the trail and was on the verge of stepping out to follow it, but her instincts screamed a warning. She stepped into the shadows between two trees instead and found the trigger of her rifle with her finger. Reminding herself that she shouldn't fire so close to the Cofah guard, she lowered the weapon on its strap and slid out a dagger instead. She wasn't the most powerful person, but if she could sneak up on an enemy, she could cut a throat efficiently enough—her father had seen to that. But she had no idea where her enemy was. She must have heard some tiny noise or seen a shadow moving at the corner of her vision—what else could have set her senses to jangling so? But no matter how hard she strained her ears now, she couldn't hear anything above the buzz of insects and the soft rustles of nocturnal creatures scampering through the leaf litter. Nobody was walking up the trail, and the guard hadn't moved. So what—

"Over here, Caslin," came a soft voice from the trees behind her.

Cas spun in that direction, her knife ready. She recognized that voice, but hearing it didn't make any sense, not way out here. She had to be mistaken.

She waited for him to speak again, even as she tried to pick his figure out of the shadows. But the voice had come from too deep in the trees, and his dark clothing hid him too well. As sharp as her eyes were, she couldn't find his silhouette among the foliage.

"Yes, it's me," he said. "I must speak with you. Move away from the rim, so the guard won't hear us."

Cas swallowed and tried to sound calm when she answered. "What are you doing here, Father?"

She didn't move from her spot. She thought of the dirigible, the familiar look of that form sliding along that rope. She should have known. Even looking on from the distance, she should have known. And maybe, on some subconscious level, she *had* known. Maybe that was why she had been so wary, so alert all the way up here.

"I'm on assignment," Father said, his soft voice giving away nothing.

It was the most obvious thing he could have said and the most bewildering, as well. "On assignment for whom? And to do what? To spy on us? To follow us? How could you have even been *able* to follow us?" Or was it possible he was on some independent mission that had only by chance intersected with hers? It seemed so unlikely. This wasn't exactly a popular destination. Could someone else have learned of the dragon blood and been researching the source independently?

"That is my secret to keep until I'm done," he said. "Now, step away from the rim. I have a warning for you."

Cas warred with her natural instinct to obey his orders, as she had for so much of her life, and with her instinct to not trust the situation, to not trust *him* in the situation. She doubted he was a danger to her specifically, but she had no doubt that he would accept an assignment that would hurt her in emotional ways if not physical ways. Could Tolemek be his target? Or maybe even Zirkander? Since he had disobeyed orders and veered off on his own, someone back home might be irritated with him.

Finally, she picked her way toward her father, her shoulders tense, her knife still in hand. Could she strike at him if she found out he had come for someone on her team? For one of her friends? In Tolemek's case, *more* than a friend. Even though her father had molded her into the sniper he wanted to add to his business and treated her more like a son than a daughter, he had never been cruel, just distant. He had never caused her to loathe him in a way that made her want to hurt him. Oh, there had been times when she had imagined unpleasant fates for him, usually when he had been inflicting some training on her while the other girls her age had been playing games in the schoolyard. But surely other children had worse childhoods. She couldn't imagine shooting him, even if she hated him at times for trying to make her into his ideal progeny instead of letting her choose a life of her own.

Full night had long since fallen, and she had to feel her way deeper into the trees. She stopped when her boot encountered soft mud that might have signified a sinkhole. Figuring she had gone far enough, she put her back to a tree, sheathed the knife, and folded her arms over her chest.

"What is it, Father?" she whispered.

From far closer than she expected, he responded. "Find a reason not to go into the pyramid with the others." He clasped her arm, and she fought the urge to pull away. His voice was intense, an order, but it seemed to hold a plea, as well. Was he worried about her? Could he somehow know more than their team did about what lay in wait? "You'll be in danger," he added.

"I've been in danger all week." Her entire career, for that matter.

"I must complete my assignment," he said. "I don't wish you to be harmed."

"Does your assignment have anything to do with anyone in my party?"

He paused. "My assignment is confidential. As always."

Of course it was. "How did you find us?" She had already asked it and didn't know if he would answer, but maybe he would give her something, *want* to give her something. So long as it wasn't confidential. She wanted to snort at that idea, but it *was* consistent for him. He had never spoken of his missions to her when she had been growing up, and he had spoken of the need to remain trustworthy to clients when he had been teaching her the business.

He released her hand, stepping back. Cas had only the vaguest sense of his form in the darkness beside her; he was probably wearing a hood, as he often did, to hide his light brown hair. He might also have dark paint on his face. How long had he been following them? Had he been close enough to touch them—to shoot them—more than once, without her detecting it? Had he overheard private conversations? She grimaced to think of him listening to the chat she'd had with Tolemek in their room back in town.

"I can't speak of it with you," Father said. "I only revealed myself because of my concern for you. I implore you to find a reason to stay outside the pyramid. Tell your *commander*—" his voice took on a snide quality as he said the word, "—that someone should stay outside to remain on watch for the pirates."

"Are they still back there?" Cas wondered if the pirates had been shooting at him, or he at them for some reason. But it seemed unlikely that they would have noticed him if he didn't wish it.

"A handful of them have pressed on. They believe you are on a treasure hunt."

"Yes, I know."

"Be careful, Caslin."

She hadn't heard him move, not so much as a leaf rustling, but already his voice had grown more distant.

"I do not wish to see harm come to you, but I have accepted this mission, and I will not fail in carrying it out, even for you."

"If you kill any of my friends…" She bit her lip, not sure how to finish the threat, or if she even wanted to make one. She didn't *think* her father would turn on her, but was she entirely positive that was the case? Would he have needed to warn her to stay away if it were?

She let her head thunk back against the tree. It didn't matter now. He was gone. She might not have heard him leave, but she had sensed it. Maybe he was even now sneaking back to her team, intent on finishing his mission.

That thought almost made her sprint back to them, but the thickness of the brush impeded her, and her own spinning thoughts impeded her too. If her father wanted to kill Tolemek or Zirkander or even Sardelle, couldn't he have already done it? He had been stalking them for days. Surely, he'd had them within his rifle sights. Of course, if *Sardelle* was his target, maybe he hadn't been certain a bullet would be enough to kill her. If he had seen her shield the group from those arrows, he might think she had that capability to shield herself all the time. Maybe she did. Cas had no idea if the soulblade slept or if it was cognizant of dangers to its wielder all the time. Cas knew nothing about magic, beyond what she had learned in the last couple of months, and she doubted her father had any particular knowledge of it, either—it wasn't as if people were hiring him to assassinate witches every other week. He could be studying Sardelle from a distance, trying to get a feel for her abilities, before pouncing.

But what would Sardelle have to do with the ziggurat? If she was his assignment, why would he have to come all the way here to find her? He had warned Cas not to go *inside*. Could he know about the dragon? Maybe he had also been sent to ensure the Cofah had no more blood to use. Or for all she knew, he might be there to collect a few vials for a wealthy client back home.

Cas swiped a vine away from her face and pushed aside her thoughts. She was almost back to the others. Even though she knew it wouldn't be what her father wanted, she would have to warn Zirkander. And Tolemek too. In case she was wrong and he *was* a target. Her belly clenched at the idea of that. He would need every chance at defending himself.

She paused at the sound of voices.

"...what about *inside* the gate?" Zirkander asked. "Any idea how many people are in there? Or if there are any booby trapped doors in the ground that send a man plummeting a hundred feet into a room to be incinerated?"

"A *hundred* feet?" Sardelle asked lightly, her voice close to his. Cas hesitated, reluctant to walk up on them if they were embracing—or doing *more* than embracing. "Really? However did you survive the fall?"

"I landed on Tolemek's hair. It's cushy."

Sardelle snorted. "I'm sorry, but it's still a hazy blur in there to me. The dragon makes it like trying to find the stars in the sky when the sun is out. And the trying is giving me a headache. I shudder to think about what power he can wield when even his aura makes my brain hurt."

A twig snapped. Cas didn't know if they were shifting positions to kiss, or if someone had turned in her direction. Sardelle had mentioned she was struggling to sense people, but Cas was probably standing close enough for her to know she was there.

Cas cleared her throat before coming closer. "Sir? I have a... concern to report."

"Another one?" Zirkander sounded about as enthused as the pig on the spit about to be roasted over the fire.

"Sorry, sir."

More twigs snapped, and he stepped away from a tree, so she could see his outline facing her. She winced, knowing that her father would see his outline—all of their outlines—too, if he was in the area, watching this conversation. For now, she didn't have that feeling of being watched, as she had for so much of their journey, but that wasn't all that reassuring. It could mean he had gone inside the ziggurat already, that he was ahead of them, doing something that might be at odds with their mission.

"There's an assassin here," Cas said, "from back home. A sniper, really, but he's accurate with a knife and a garrote too."

Zirkander sighed. "And would you by chance happen to *know* this assassin-sniper?"

"Yes, sir."

A long silence followed.

"Do *I* know this assassin-sniper?" Sardelle asked.

"You've met briefly," Zirkander said. "He showed up after my house had been vandalized. At the time, I thought it was merely inconvenient timing. Now I'm wondering... Ahn, did you speak to him or just see him? Any idea who sent him or why he's here?"

"Or how he found this place?" Sardelle added.

Zirkander's words had set her mind to turning again, and Cas didn't answer right away. He had mentioned that he had seen her father before they left for the mission, but she hadn't realized it had been at his house or that Sardelle had been there.

"I did speak to him," she said slowly, mulling over the possibilities. "He wouldn't tell me anything, except he warned me not to go in the pyramid. Sir, what was he doing at your house? I haven't spoken to him in…" She couldn't even remember the last time. They had been avoiding each other since she joined the military.

"He gave the impression that he was there to pummel me—or worse—because I'd allowed you to cavort around with a certain pirate. Because, as you know, I had so much to do with that."

"Right. And he met Sardelle at the time?"

"Briefly. He also offered me his card, in case I wanted to hire him to deal with the vandals."

"Thoughtful," Cas said. "Did he also go into your house?"

"Not that we were aware of. Why do you ask?"

"I don't know. I guess I was just thinking he might have tracked us here somehow, but unless he's become a sorcerer in his spare time, I don't know how he could have followed us across the ocean, to multiple stops."

"I assume he's the one who came down on the dirigible?" Sardelle asked.

"I didn't ask, but it seems likely," Cas said. "And that was a civilian craft, wasn't it?"

"Perhaps someone else in the city is aware of the dragon blood and wants to make sure the possibility of the Cofah weaponizing it is eliminated," Sardelle said.

"Not many people should know about it," Zirkander said. "The king, General Ort, Colonel Therrik, and possibly other men on his team."

"Colonel Therrik," Sardelle mused. "Perhaps he didn't care for being left behind and took matters into his own hands."

"I doubt he makes enough to hire Cas's dad. If he does, I'm going to have a chat with the king about my own insufficient wages. Besides, how would he have known to send Cas's dad *here*? We had to do some figuring to learn where the dragon was."

"Others may have figured more efficiently."

"Really," Zirkander said, sounding slightly offended.

"Judging by what we've seen so far, this isn't a small operation. One of the Cofah who was stationed here might have blabbed at some point."

"Hm."

Cas shifted her weight, feeling the press of time on her shoulders. Maybe Tolemek had been right and they should have gone inside immediately.

"Would the king hire an assassin?" Sardelle asked.

"I suppose it's possible. We're not close drinking buddies. He doesn't confide his feelings about these things to me."

"Sir," Cas said, "I definitely got the feeling my father was planning to do something in the pyramid tonight. Maybe we should make sure we get in there right away. In case what he plans to do isn't what we plan to do."

"If someone in Iskandia hired him, it might just be to destroy the dragon blood," Zirkander said.

"Or the *source* of the dragon blood," Sardelle said.

"Er, how much does it cost to hire a sniper to kill a dragon?"

Cas didn't have an answer for that. It didn't sound like something that would be possible, even for her father.

"I'll get Duck and Tolemek," she said.

She slipped through the brush, hearing Zirkander grunt as he hefted his pack to his shoulders. Good, he was ready to go. Cas didn't want to delay any longer.

She found Duck snoring softly as he lay on a log. But Tolemek wasn't in the spot where she had left him. With an uneasy feeling dropping into the pit of her stomach, she circled the area, calling his name softly. Nothing except for a few frogs answered her.

* * *

Tolemek followed the wall of the ziggurat, staying close as he approached the entrance, so the guard wouldn't see him until it was too late. He trod softly through the tall grass swaying about his waist, placing each foot with care. With one hand, he followed the lumpy, moldy contours of the great rectangular stones that had been used to build the place. With the other, he held a small leather ball that could unfurl and deliver knock-out gas. Sardelle wasn't the only person who could convince people to take naps.

He glanced up the trail before creeping the last few steps to the entrance, making sure it remained empty. If there were any pirate treasure hunters descending on the ruins, they hadn't made an appearance yet. He couldn't see Zirkander and the others from down here, either. Good. Once he had Tylie out and some place safe, he could reunite with them.

A soft rain had started falling, sifting through the woven vines and leaves that comprised the ceiling far overhead. Tolemek crept to the recessed doorway, listened for a moment, and didn't hear so much as a rustling of clothing or a sigh of breath. He leaned around the corner, ready to throw his ball at the guard's feet.

But the guard lay crumpled on the ground, unmoving.

Tolemek glanced behind him again, expecting to see Zirkander and the others strolling down the trail, Sardelle with her hand held out, showing some indication that she had just slung her magic about. But the path remained empty, as did the entire crater.

Tolemek eased through the doorway, into a stone tunnel lit by hanging lamps that burned a stinky animal fat and left sooty stains on the walls. He knelt beside the guard, curious as to whether magic had felled him, or if something more mundane had been responsible. As soon as he touched the man's neck, he felt the stickiness of still-warm blood and had his answer. A small dart stuck out of the side of his throat. It didn't appear big enough to have punctured his jugular, but it might have delivered some fast-acting poison. Tolemek could name a number that might work, some that could be made from ingredients procured around here.

He pulled his hand back, wiping his fingers carefully before walking deeper into the ziggurat.

As Jaxi had mentioned, there was far more stone inside the structure than open air. The tunnel was tight, claustrophobic, and he wondered how a dragon could have found its way inside to start with. Surely, they couldn't suck in their bellies and fly through spaces this narrow. But he no longer found himself skeptical as to whether there truly was a dragon. He might not be as sensitive as Jaxi or Sardelle, but he could feel a presence now too. Something weighing on his mind, like an impending headache.

By now, it didn't surprise him that etchings of dragons had been carved into the walls. The edges had worn away, but many of them were still visible. Though he was determined to press ahead and find his sister, not take his time sightseeing, one block of images did make him pause. Unlike with the dragon carvings, these were paintings, the colors fairly vibrant, more recent perhaps. They were of people instead of dragons, of bare-chested warriors carrying spears and attacking other groups of warriors. The war scenes were normal enough, and wouldn't have made him slow down, but others featured men around a fire, eating from skulls as if they were bowls. Given the dead people he had seen in the grave, the skulls cut open for examination, the parallel made him uncomfortable.

He took a deep breath and forced himself onward. Another time, he could consider the cannibalistic nature of the local tribes. After he found Tylie.

When he came to the first intersection, a maze of options opened up to him, three tunnels that continued horizontally, two holes that led downward, into darkness, and two more that rose upward. A rope dangled from one of those. Interlocking stones formed the walls on all of the passages, even those dropping into the earth. He would have assumed nothing but dirt lay beneath the "ground floor" of this strange dwelling, but clearly, it had a basement of some sort and an extensive foundation.

He would have chosen to continue straight ahead—the horizontal passages were lit—but voices came from that direction. He considered his ball and the fact that it was the only one he had remaining, then stuck it in his pocket and jumped, catching the rope instead. He pulled himself up, not certain what he would find, but the darkness should hide him from view, even if he only climbed ten or fifteen feet.

"…so ready to leave this hell," came a muffled voice from the tunnel below. The speaker was drawing closer to the intersection, boots clomping ponderously as he walked, almost as if he was carrying something heavy.

"Think they'll let us?" another asked, his voice also sounded oddly muffled. "If we're not sick?"

A soft draft brushed Tolemek's cheek. He had reached a cross passage. He patted the cool wall around him with one hand, identifying a hole about three feet wide by three feet high. He thought about pulling himself in, but the conversation below made him pause. If he could learn more about the disease, he couldn't pass up that opportunity, especially when it might become painfully relevant soon.

"Dragon's spit, I hope so."

He stilled himself on the rope, hoping the men walking below wouldn't notice it twitching. But the two figures who plodded past probably wouldn't have noticed if the rope had hit them in the heads. They were wearing dark leather head coverings, like nothing Tolemek was familiar with. Helmets? He couldn't tell exactly from his brief view from ten feet above the men, but they wore similar suits, *heavy* suits if the tread of those boots was an indicator. He hadn't seen anything like them in the Cofah army.

Unfortunately, the men continued straight ahead, in the direction of the dead guard. They would know someone had infiltrated the structure before Tolemek had gone a hundred meters, before Zirkander's team even came down from the crater. He didn't know who had killed that guard, but it was going to make things inconvenient for everyone else.

He considered whether to go back down to the lit corridors, but decided to try the new tunnel instead. Though dark and tight, it was paralleling the one he had meant to check out below. Maybe it would end up in the same place and help him avoid the Cofah.

"Or maybe you'll get yourself hopelessly lost," he muttered.

Tolemek felt his way down the passage, resolving to turn around and go back to the ground level if it didn't take him anywhere within a few minutes.

The sound of voices and other life faded from hearing, and

he had the sense of being in a tomb. Every time his shoulders brushed the walls, he grew certain the tunnel was closing in on him. He was trying not to think too much about the architecture of this place and what such a small passage might have been used for, but he wondered, nonetheless. When the wall opened up to one side, he slipped out a match, wanting to make sure he wasn't bypassing a branch in the tunnel that he might want to use.

He scraped the bulbous head on the stone floor, and flame flared to life. The light showed the tunnel continuing on but also alcoves opening up to either side ahead of him. Oblong stone boxes about two feet high rested in those openings, the sides carved with people in robes and dragons flying over their heads. It wasn't until after his match went out that Tolemek realized he had been looking at sarcophagi. At least they weren't painted with cannibalistic imagery. That didn't make him any happier about crawling through the passage, but he pushed forward, anyway, hoping their presence suggested another way out. It would have been hard, if not impossible, for people to maneuver the big boxes in here via that vertical shaft.

As he crept along in the dark, he worried he had made a mistake in leaving the others. Would it have been easier to find Tylie with Sardelle's input? Or maybe he should have attacked those two men below and tried to subdue them for questioning. In those clunky uniforms, they wouldn't have reacted quickly. By leaving them ambulatory, so they could discover that dead entrance guard, he may have condemned Cas's team to walking in on an alarm. He sighed, again irritated with whoever had killed that guard. He would prefer to rely on stealth until he had Tylie.

After another fifty meters, the outline of the passage grew visible, and Tolemek no longer needed a match to see the sarcophagi-filled alcoves. The route took a ninety-degree turn, and even more light became apparent, a glow slightly different from that of a fire, a more reddish tint. Maybe it was his imagination. Or maybe he was approaching some room lit by magic. Anticipation made the nerves in his stomach twitch. The intensity of his headache increased. Did dragons glow? Maybe he was about to see the creature that had started all of this, that was somehow tied to his sister. He hastened forward, banging his elbows in his eagerness to get closer.

A square of reddish light appeared after another bend. The end of the tunnel. He crept closer, not spotting a floor or ceiling beyond the opening. He forced himself to slow down, in case he was about to poke his head out on some busy area.

A cavernous opening waited for him. He had reached the hollowed core of the ziggurat. Its walls stair-stepped upward toward the top, high above him. His first thought was to wonder how the architecture could support the weight of all those giant rocks. His second was to look down.

And stare.

For a long moment, thoughts refused to form in his mind. The prone figure of a silver dragon filled much of the space below, its sleek, scaled back rising at least ten feet, even though the creature rested on the ground, its legs hidden from view under its body. Its thick sinuous tail curved about its form, almost reminding Tolemek of a dog curled up on its side to sleep. The dragon wasn't moving, but large bunches of muscle lay beneath those scales, promising great power.

Yeah, dragons aren't known for their wimpy natures.

Jaxi, Tolemek blurted in his mind—he almost blurted it out loud, but he caught himself. More than the dragon might be down there.

Right below Tolemek's perch, the walls became vertical instead of following the exterior contours of the ziggurat, and one of those walls was made from glass instead of stone. A door was set into one side with an instrument panel embedded next to it emitting the red light he had seen. There was light coming from somewhere behind the glass wall too. From his viewpoint, he could not see far into the room, only glimpsing the ends of a few tables and counters, but one held a rack of vials and another a few beakers. Had he found the laboratory where they were extracting the blood? As far as he could tell, the dragon was asleep—or unconscious—so maybe they were simply walking up, sticking a needle between its scales, and extracting its blood.

Strange that the big creature would allow that, unless it was indeed working with them. Or maybe the Cofah had injured it somehow.

I don't think that's the case, Jaxi thought. *Also, did you know the others are worried about you and wondering why you ran off?*

Yes, I'm sure you can point them to this location, so they can do whatever it is they deem fit. He tilted his chin toward the dragon and the laboratory below. *Is there any chance you can tell where my sister is?*

I could barely tell where you *were. There's a lot of interference from Giant and Sleepy down there. Listen, you shouldn't have gone off alone. Cas's father is here, apparently with a mission to kill someone. Or something.*

What? How does that... even make sense?

Cas isn't real sure about that, either, from what I gather. But listen, we're having some trouble out here. Perhaps you'd like to come out and throw around some of your dreaded concoctions.

Tolemek winced. If they—Cas—needed help, he didn't want to leave the group to fend for itself, but he was so close. Tylie must be nearby. She *must*.

What's going on that you and Sardelle can't handle?

Jaxi didn't answer. Tolemek let his head thunk against the side of the wall. Would there be someone in the lab who could lead him to Tylie? He wished he could tell how many people might be working in there. He slipped his hand into his pocket and rubbed the leather ball. He considered dropping the twenty feet to the floor, running for that door, and trying to surprise those inside. But what if the dragon woke up? What if the door was locked? He would be stuck on the floor with a creature that might find him a tasty snack.

Reluctantly, he decided he needed to look for another way into that laboratory. On the way, he would check on the others. He wished he knew if they were still outside the ziggurat or had come in.

Jaxi?

Again, he didn't receive an answer. Tolemek pushed up to his elbows and was about to try and turn around when movement caught his eye below.

The clear wall shimmered, a strange ripple that plucked at his senses. If it was made from glass, there must be some magical element about it. The door opened, and something else shimmered, a barrier that stretched from wall to wall above the dragon. After the brief ripple, it disappeared again, leaving Tolemek glad he hadn't tried to jump down there, after all.

A man carrying a rifle walked out of the laboratory. At least, Tolemek thought it was a man. The figure wore the same bulky, form-obscuring garb as the other two men had, a head-to-toe leather ensemble that appeared about as comfortable as a thorn in the foot. A big helmet covered his entire head, with flaps extending to the shoulders. A glass face panel presumably allowed the wearer to see. The whole suit reminded him of what divers wore when trying to salvage wrecks from the ocean floor. It was slowly dawning on him what that might signify in this situation when a second figure walked out of the room.

His breath caught. Tylie.

She *wasn't* wearing a suit. She wasn't even wearing shoes. She padded forward on bare feet, a dirty dress hanging limply down to her calves. Her face and bare arms were dirty, too, and she looked cold. Unlike the hot, humid jungle outside, the tunnel passages were cool, like caves. Tolemek couldn't see her face well, looking down from above, but she walked forward slowly, her chin to her chest, her long, straight brown hair falling forward in curtains, shadowing her cheeks.

He wanted to yell out to her, to see her eyes, to know if she was sane, to know how badly she was being treated, to know how to pull her away from these people. But the guard had taken up a position beside the door, his back to the glass, and his rifle in his arms. He watched her through his clear faceplate.

Tylie didn't look back, didn't acknowledge him. She padded toward the dragon, carrying a small rack of empty vials in one hand and an oversized tool in the other with a needle so long and thick that Tolemek could see it from his perch.

Tylie! he tried calling with his mind, even though he knew he had never learned a mote of telepathy, hadn't even been aware that such a thing existed until a couple of months ago.

But she was the one who could call out, not he, and she didn't look up. Somehow, she had known he was on the mountainside earlier, but she must not be aware of him now. Maybe the dragon's presence blunted the effectiveness of her senses, the same way it affected Sardelle.

Tolemek gripped the edge of his hole with both hands, watching with horror as she walked closer to the dragon, its size dwarfing her. It hadn't moved yet, nor shown any hint that it might wake up, but he couldn't help but fear that it would. That its eyes would open, and its giant head would swing toward Tylie. The long, sword-like fangs in its mouth might not be visible from where he perched, but he had seen the skeletons in the museums. He knew they were there and that they could chomp a human in half easily.

When Tylie reached the dragon's side, she set down the vials, then reached out, not with the needle but with her hand, resting her palm against the silver scales. She bowed her head even further, as if offering a prayer. Or an apology? Everything about her stance, along with the presence of that guard, said she was a prisoner.

The man must have said something, because Tylie looked over her shoulder at him for a moment. Then she lowered her hand and moved the needle toward the dragon's hide. Those scales appeared hard enough to repel bullets, but she found a spot behind its arm—leg, whatever dragons had—and poked her needle between two scales. Tolemek held his breath, certain the creature would wake up, certain it would spin toward the one daring to prick it.

But it didn't move. Tylie plucked up one of the vials, fastening it to the back of the tool, and dark red blood flowed through the needle and into the receptacle.

While she was filling the second one, another man walked out of the room, this one also wearing the protective clothing and helmet. Judging by their bent heads, he spoke to the first. Whatever the barrier was that separated Tolemek from the dragon and that chamber, he couldn't hear a thing through it. But as he watched the men converse, his thoughts spun back to the purpose of those suits. He hadn't ever worn such a thing or even seen one, but if that apparatus on their backs was a filter or self-contained oxygen supply, the gear might have been designed to protect the wearer from bad air—from *infected* air. He didn't miss the fact that Tylie wasn't wearing one, and his fingers tightened further around the stone edge of the shaft. If that barrier hadn't been there, he might have risked injury to jump down and attack those men, to rip off their helmets and force them to breathe the air they were making Tylie breath. Whatever was causing the sicknesses—the deaths.

Was it the dragon itself? Its blood? Sardelle had objected to the idea, but she, too, had been born into a world that hadn't seen dragons for centuries. How much of an expert could she truly be? If it was the blood, had Tylie been infected because she was handling it? Or was it possible she had some immunity, and that was why they were using her? If so, why would that be? If that winged tiger had been infected, then possessing dragon blood alone didn't protect a creature.

Tylie was on the sixth and final vial. Tolemek forced his tight grip on the edge of the floor to loosen and slid his hands along the smooth rock, wondering if he might find some tiny pebble to toss down there, something that might alert her to his presence without drawing the guards from their conversation. All he found was a tiny fleck, scarcely a millimeter thick. He doubted it would make a noise when it landed, but he lofted it in Tylie's direction anyway.

It struck the translucent barrier and burst into flame. For a moment, it was as if a match burned above Tylie's head.

Tolemek stared down, willing her to notice the flame. But it burned out too quickly. He sighed and was about to withdraw, resolved that he would have to search for another way down, but his sister lifted her head. She looked straight at him. It was only for a second, then she dropped her face again, but they had made eye contact. It had been as if she knew he was there all along.

For the second time in his life, her voice sounded in his head.

The dragon is dying, she informed him solemnly.

Are you *all right?* The dragon's welfare wasn't high on his list of concerns. *I'm here to get you out of here. Can you help me? Tell me how to get down there? To reach you?*

We can't leave Phelistoth marooned here.

Phelistoth? Was that the dragon? It wasn't important now. *How many men are there, Tylie?*

We have to figure out how to help him, how to free him. This is my fault. Tylie didn't look up at him again—maybe she didn't want to draw the guard's attention in his direction—but she shook her head slowly, morosely, and he sensed her pain. *It's my fault, Tolie.*

You can tell me about it later. This place is a maze. I need your help. Actually, he was guessing that it was a maze. Maybe he should have gone straight down that passage from the front door, and it would have led him to this room. He would go back and try that if she didn't give him the information he needed. But it would be useful to get some inside intelligence, here. *Tylie—*

Don't you understand? They wouldn't know about him if it weren't for me. He would still be sleeping.

He looks like he's sleeping now. Tolemek kept his thoughts calm and patient—or tried to at least. Tylie had never been entirely there when he had spoken to her, not since she had been a child, and she might be nearly eighteen now, but it was as if her mind had gone backwards instead of growing up with her body.

No, he's unconscious now, Tylie responded, urgency in her words. *He's dying.*

Tolemek looked up at the tiered stone ceiling. Earlier, he had thought there might be an exit up there, that people would need to be able to climb up there and light that dragon head brazier, but there wasn't so much as a ladder or a dangling rope. He also didn't see anything that resembled a trapdoor. He couldn't imagine how the dragon had gotten in here in the first place, and he couldn't see a way to get him out. *Tylie, you're my primary concern. What's the best way down there? How do I get you out of here?*

I'm not going without him.

Tylie... Tolemek resisted the urge to let his forehead thunk to the stone floor. *We have to—*

Her head whipped around, and he stopped, as if they were

having a conversation out loud and might be overheard.

One of the guards was pointing at her. She picked up the small rack, now full of blood samples, and walked back toward the men, her head bowed.

Tylie? Tolemek called with his thoughts, in the hope she was still listening to him, or receiving him, whatever Jaxi had called her ability.

She didn't answer. She walked through the doorway and disappeared into the lab. One of the guards followed her. The other frowned at the dragon, then looked up. Tolemek hadn't made a noise and hadn't expected either of the men to glance upward, not now. He froze, afraid that movement would draw the guard's eye, but he knew he was in sight, that the red light on that panel illuminated enough of the core that the shadows wouldn't hide him. The guard looked right at him and grabbed his gun. Tolemek ducked back into the tunnel, cursing himself for lingering there. He half expected bullets to fly in his direction, but the guard must have remembered the barrier. He simply shouted something that, between the helmet and the barrier, Tolemek couldn't understand. It didn't matter. He got the gist. The Cofah knew he was here.

CHAPTER 11

CAS CROUCHED IN THE BRUSH at the top of the crater, her rifle across her thighs. Ten men in pirate clothing were shooting and creeping down the trail toward the ziggurat entrance, using crude wooden shields hacked from logs to protect themselves from gunfire that came from the guards. Yes, guards. Where there had been one before, six or eight men had gathered in the tunnel mouth, and they were returning fire. The stone walls protected them—and the fact that the intruders were busy dodging their fire. Cas couldn't imagine the pirates making it past the guards. Or anyone else making it past them, either. But the pirates pushed on, drawing closer to the braziers. Two in the back were readying grenades, while two others tried to sneak close from the sides.

"That's going to be a problem," Duck whispered from beside her. "Reckon we missed our chance to get in?"

"Unless we want to get shot," Cas said. "Or unless we shoot all of them."

"I suppose that's an option for you. How many rounds do you have in that rifle?"

"Enough for a few pirates." From the elevated position, Cas could pick off the closest men without too much trouble, but she couldn't see the guards in the tunnel, except when one leaned out to shoot at the pirates angling for the door from the side.

"Well," Zirkander said from behind a nearby tree. "We got our distraction."

The proper response to one's commanding officer was usually a polite, "Yes, sir," no matter what the situation. Cas couldn't help but point out, "Yes, but it's right in *front* of the only door."

"I did note that."

"Are you all right, Ridge?" Sardelle asked, coming up behind him. "You sound tired. And you're slumping unnaturally."

"I'm fine. Aside from realizing we should have made our incursion ten minutes ago. And slumping isn't unnatural when you've been traveling for days."

"It is for you. You're always full of vigor."

Cas would have snorted at the comment—shouldn't couples talk about vigor in private?—but Zirkander *did* sound tired.

"You keep rubbing your face," Sardelle said. "Your skin is warm."

Zirkander sighed. "I know."

Cas stared at the grass, her stomach sinking. They had been worried all along that they would become infected by whatever this disease was. Had it finally happened? Or had it happened to all of them long ago, and Zirkander was the first to show symptoms?

"Ridge…" Sardelle whispered, defeat in her voice. She leaned against him.

"Let's just get into the pyramid and finish this mission," Zirkander said. "We'll worry about the rest in the morning. Will you tell Jaxi that we really do need that back door?"

For a long moment, Sardelle didn't answer, and Cas thought she wouldn't, that she would refuse to look past Zirkander's health and to the mission. But she finally said, "We've already been discussing it. She says the ziggurat walls are less thick on the top half. Much of that is a hollow area, a big internal chamber that houses the dragon."

"*That's* where she wants to break in?"

"If we can climb up there somehow in the next few minutes, she might be able to burn through it quickly, while the guards and the pirates are still busy with each other."

"Uh huh, and who will the *dragon* be busy with?"

That was Cas's question too. Maybe they would be better off trying to shoot the guards and forgetting the idea of sneaking in. She was about to voice the suggestion when Sardelle spoke again.

"Jaxi says he's unconscious."

"The dragon?"

"Yes."

"All right." A soft thump sounded—Zirkander hitting the tree with his palm? "Let's not delay any longer. We'll circle around the back and find a way up."

"Hope you brought a ladder, sir," Duck said. "Those tiers each look to be a good fifteen, twenty feet high."

"We have rope. We'll manage. Ahn, lead the way, will you?"

"Yes, sir."

Cas backed away from the rim, making sure there were a few trees between her and the edge before she started walking. Unfortunately, the trek to the other side took them past the mass grave again. Her gut protested traveling through that odor once more. Especially now that she was worried Zirkander might have been infected. After showing the first symptoms, how long did a person have before his mind changed and he turned into one of those crazy souls? And how long until death followed? The idea of Colonel Zirkander, the hero pilot of Iskandia, falling to some sickness in a remote jungle after he had survived so many aerial battles… It was inconceivable.

She blinked a few times and pushed the thoughts out of her head. She had to concentrate on the mission, that was it. They would finish it and find a way to fix him, to fix everyone. Tolemek could do it.

"No stairs over here, either, eh?" Zirkander said as the group looked down to the back side of the ziggurat. The sound of gunfire echoed from the front, but they could no longer see the pirates or the door. Moss blanketed the tiers of stone walls, and in some spots, vines dangled down, dripping water. Even from the rim, the climb looked like it would be slick and challenging. "Makes you wonder whose job it is to scamper up there and light that fire."

"Yes, sir," Duck said, instead of making one of his usual flippant comments. He must be worried too.

"Well, Raptor-eyes, is it safe to mosey down there?" Zirkander asked. "See anyone skulking in the shadows, waiting to shoot us?"

"Nothing moving down there, sir," Cas said.

She led the way down the steep slope, watching both corners

of the ziggurat as they descended. She didn't expect anyone trying to breach the front entrance to run back here, but one never knew.

The tall, wet grasses batted at her clothing, leaving them damp. She wondered if Tolemek had found some secret entrance or had slipped in the front. And what of her father? Had he found a way in already? She had been watching the crater nearly continuously since his appearance, but she had not seen anyone sneaking in the front.

The slope leveled out, and she pushed her way through the grass to the base of the ziggurat. She grimaced when she stood next to the stone monolith and looked up. From above, she hadn't appreciated its sheer mass and towering size, but even the wall rising to the first tier stretched high over her head, closer to Duck's estimate of twenty feet than fifteen.

"I've got a rope." Zirkander came up behind her with a slender cord and collapsible metal grappling hook extended and ready. "Give me some room."

"I can do that, sir," Duck offered, as the rest of the team joined him.

"I'm not dead yet," Zirkander said, an unaccustomed growl to his voice.

"Yes, sir," Duck said softly.

Zirkander swung the hook on the end of the rope a few times, then released it. It sailed up, landing with a clank that was lost under the gunshots echoing through the crater. They sounded louder down here than they had from the rim above.

Zirkander pulled gently on the rope until the hook found some notch in the old, porous stone, then tugged harder, leaning his body weight against it. Cas almost offered to go up first, since she was the lightest one, but she held her tongue, not wanting to be growled at. He climbed up the rope without bothering to take his pack off. They probably could have left their gear behind and simply taken weapons and some ammunition, but maybe he was trying to prove that he was still capable and that nobody needed to worry about him. He made the climb, slowing only a couple of times, when his boots slipped on the slick moss, but something about the way Sardelle gazed after him made Cas think she was indeed worrying about him, no matter what he wanted.

"Next," Zirkander called down softly.

The gunshots out front had stopped. Cas was tempted to take a quick look to see if the pirates had made it to the entrance or all been mowed down. It was difficult to believe the risks those people were taking for some vague possibility of treasure. Unless… maybe they had been affected by the disease too? Was some derangement guiding them at this point?

"Next," Zirkander called again, and Cas realized she remained alone at the bottom, Duck and Sardelle having shimmied up more quickly than expected.

Having no delusions about her own weight-carrying abilities, she left her pack leaning against the wall—Sardelle's was there, too—and shifted her rifle, so it hung across her back. She grabbed the rope and pulled herself up, knees banging against the stone. The moss wasn't as insulating as one might have thought. Before she had gone more than a few feet, she found herself being tugged up. She soon joined the others on the first tier. Again the breadth of the structure amazed her. They had to walk more than fifteen meters inward before they could throw the rope again and start climbing to the next level.

They continued that way until they were over halfway to the top. The gunshots hadn't resumed, nor did Cas catch any voices, but it could simply be that all of the remaining people had gone inside.

"This far enough?" Zirkander asked, sounding winded.

More winded than usual? No, he and Duck had been pulling up Cas and Sardelle so they could ascend more quickly. That was all. Cas grimaced, wishing she could stop thinking of him as a victim.

"Jaxi would like to go one more level," Sardelle said.

"*Would* she?" Zirkander asked. "Would she be offended if I simply tossed her up there?"

"She would like me to point out that the stasis chamber has a protective charge around it to ward off people, animals, and objects, and that those of us with flesh and bones will likely burst into flames if we touch it. She believes she'll be unaffected. She's only thinking of you. You know, Ridge, despite your threats to toss her places, she's rather fond of you." Sardelle wrapped her arm around him.

"I would hate to see the conversations she has with people she's not fond of."

"Yes, you would."

"Stasis chamber?" Cas asked. "What is that?"

"It's where you go to nap for three hundred years, as I understand it," Zirkander said.

"Or three thousand," Sardelle said.

"What?" he asked sharply.

"Jaxi was looking through Tolemek's eyes earlier and studied a panel on the wall down there. It—"

"Tolemek's inside already?" Cas shouldn't be shocked—where else would he have gone?—but she was surprised he had already reached the dragon's chamber. She touched the stone wall. "Is he in that center area you spoke of now?"

"She's not sure. She doesn't think so." Sardelle stepped away from Zirkander, drew her sword, studied it for a moment, then stepped back from the wall and threw the blade.

Startled, Cas stumbled back. But the sword sailed well over their heads as it arced up to the next tier. She expected a clank of the metal striking the stone, but it never came. Instead, a faint crimson light emanated from above them.

"I see," Zirkander said. "It's not acceptable for me to throw her, but you can fling her around whenever you wish?"

"A perk of being her handler."

"Hm. While she's doing whatever she's going to do up there, can you explain this panel and how this dragon is now three thousand years old, please?" Zirkander twirled the end of the rope again and tossed the grappling hook.

I'll explain it. This relaying of messages through human mouths takes too long.

If Cas had stumbled before, she nearly fell over this time. Duck came even closer to pitching over. He put a hand on her shoulder to steady himself.

"Did you all hear that?" he asked.

"Yes, but I always hear her these days." Zirkander locked in the hook and climbed toward the next level.

"*Her?*" Duck asked.

Cas was only slightly less stunned. Even if she had known the sword could talk to the others, she had assumed that as a normal, non-magical person, she would never hear it.

Think again. It's more difficult for me to speak to those who aren't receptive, but I've been chatting with Sardelle's soul snozzle for almost two weeks now.

"Her what?" Duck rubbed the side of his head.

"Only two weeks?" Zirkander asked as he disappeared over the edge. "It seems like *much* longer."

"Be nice," Sardelle called up softly. "She was just thinking fondly of you since you're going up to get her."

"I just came up here for the view," Zirkander said over the edge. When he looked over his shoulder, the crimson glow coming from in front of him lit up his face. His eyes widened.

Cas headed for the rope. If the sword was burning a way in, she wanted to be there for it, especially if Tolemek was nearby inside.

Here's what I've gathered so far, Jaxi spoke into her mind. *And yes, I'm talking to all of you at once. It's tiring, so listen closely so I won't have to repeat myself.*

"Yes, ma'am," Duck said.

I didn't know much until I saw the panel on the stasis chamber. I didn't even know there was a stasis chamber. I should have guessed. How else would a dragon have survived into this era when all of its brethren have long since died off or otherwise disappeared?

Cas climbed up the rope. Zirkander had moved away from the edge, too distracted to help pull her up this time, so she grunted up the wall, her rifle heavy on her back.

I had been thinking this dragon might be part of some remote, long lost clan that lived in seclusion on these wild islands, but here's what I think actually happened, and this is all a guess, mind you. The dragon appears to be unconscious. He certainly hasn't answered any of my greetings over the last few days.

As soon as Cas poked her nose over the edge of the stone, intense heat beat against her face. The sword hadn't landed on the bottom of the tier up here, as she had assumed, but it had flown all the way to the wall, where it was now wedged between two of the massive blocks that comprised the ziggurat. The blade radiated red light and heat, and the stone was disappearing. No, Cas amended, when she spotted the liquid pooling underneath the sword. The stone wasn't disappearing. It was *melting*. That was a pool of molten rock with steam wafting into the night air above it.

As Sardelle already knows, humans originally received the stasis chamber technology from the dragons over a thousand years ago—it's more an intricate creation of magic rather than technology as you would call it. I'd read stories about how they had used it in the past, but it was generally to keep laboratory specimens alive or, ah, humans that they cared for. I wasn't aware that dragons ever used it.

"Humans that they *cared* for?" Duck asked from below. "Like lovers?"

That was the case in the novel I read. It was a historical text, but a work of fiction, so I can't be certain if that was truly ever done.

"It was a historical romance novel is what Jaxi means," Sardelle said.

Hush. The details aren't important. My point is that dragons had little reason to ever use the technology on themselves, as far as I've read about. They were long-lived and so powerful that it usually took a battle with another dragon to slay one. But for some reason, this dragon chose to entomb himself in a stasis chamber—or someone forced him to be entombed. That's a possibility too. Judging by the model of the chamber, this isn't the most recent example of the technology. It's old. That's why I'm guessing this is a three-thousand-year-old dragon. Well, not technically. Just as Sardelle isn't technically three hundred and thirty years old. But it was born *thousands of years ago. I'm not sure what its real age is. Just from what I've glimpsed of the physical form, I don't think he's actually that old.*

"Sardelle is three-*hundred* and thirty?" Duck asked.

"Surely you didn't think *I* was the mature one in the relationship," Zirkander said.

"Well. Uh, no, but… Never mind."

"I think he just decided it isn't prudent to suggest that one's commanding officer has *never* been the mature one in a relationship with a woman," Sardelle said.

Zirkander nodded. "Likely so."

"So why is the dragon unconscious?" Cas asked, watching the hole in the stone grow larger and larger. Each giant block was over ten feet long and five feet thick, but the sword had already burned through the first one. Somehow it moved inward as it worked, instead of simply falling down when the stone around it melted away.

I could guess, but I can't tell just by looking at him.

"Is it possible the dragon is sick?" Sardelle mused. "We had speculated, Tolemek and I, that its blood was being turned into a biological weapon, but…"

"Sick in a way that's making human beings who come in contact with it sick?" Zirkander asked. "Human beings who then pass the illness on to each other?"

"Not just humans," Cas said, thinking of the winged tiger.

That's a thought. The stasis chamber would have also worked as a form of quarantine. So long as it wasn't opened.

"Which it obviously has been," Zirkander said.

Yes, the protective barrier remains above the dragon, but there's a door and the Cofah have been accessing the chamber. Someone found a way in. As we're about to do. The crimson light wavered and grew less intense. The heat lessened, as well.

Sardelle walked over but stopped a few feet from the tunnel now melted into the wall. "We'll have to wait a moment before we can walk on this." She waved at the molten rock hardening in front of her. The wall had been eaten away, and a faint light shone from inside, but the thickness of the stone made it impossible to see through without getting closer.

"What's our goal when we get in, sir?" Duck asked.

"Stop the Cofah from sending any more blood out of this facility," Zirkander said.

"Does that mean, uhm?" Duck glanced toward the hole. "Do we have to figure out how to kill a dragon?"

Sardelle frowned at him, and Cas winced. She had deliberately avoided asking that question with her around.

"If this is the last dragon in the world, to kill him would be a great crime," Sardelle said. "If anything, we should figure out how to help him. If the Cofah are using him—"

"That's what we need to find out," Zirkander said. "If the Cofah are using him, or if he's a willing accomplice."

"If he's unconscious, I doubt he's willing or unwilling," Sardelle said.

"We should find Tolemek and his sister," Cas said. "She would know more about what's been going on."

"If Tolemek wanted to be found, he shouldn't have run off," Zirkander said, his voice stern. He pulled up his rope, coiled it, and walked to the hole the sword had finished burning, his back to her.

Cas didn't have a response, anyway. Tolemek should have waited for them. It had to be safer to stay in a group, especially if... Damn, she wished she knew who her father's target was.

"Is that the barrier you warned us of, Sardelle?" Zirkander pointed through the hole and downward. "I just saw a drop of molten rock hit something invisible and burst into flame."

Sardelle eyed the still-steaming sides of the tunnel, but squeezed in beside him. Even though the sword had eaten some twenty feet into the wall, the hole itself narrowed at the end, and only one of them would be able to go through at a time. If there was anywhere to go through *to*. Cas was too far back to see much, but she sensed that open space the sword had warned them about.

"Yes," Sardelle said. "Only the top portion is still turned on. The rest seems to have faltered or was deliberately turned off, more likely. Some Cofah archaeologist may have been here a long time, studying the instruments to figure out how to do that. The language on the panel is the dragon tongue, one of their three written languages. They used to use their minds to etch words in stones. That doesn't matter now, but what's interesting is that there are components to the chamber besides the panel, but they're not visible. Jaxi has seen examples in textbooks. I think—*we* think—the ziggurat was built *around* the dragon in his stasis chamber."

"As some kind of temple?" Zirkander asked. "To worship it maybe?"

"That would be my guess. The ancestors of some of these tribes people must have stumbled upon this spot at some point in the past and constructed this. Or maybe it was another race. The architecture and statues we've seen certainly seem more sophisticated than what's common in the villages. It's also possible that some of those ancient people had dragon blood and were capable of doing some of this building with magic. Hollowing out this crater and devising that latticework up there." Sardelle pointed toward the greenery overhead, the greenery that had kept the team from seeing this spot from their fliers. Had those ancient people also intended to camouflage this area from those with the capability of flight? The dragon riders that were mentioned in lore? "It's too bad your father didn't come along," Sardelle said. "He might have found this interesting, as well."

"I tried to tell him that. He has a singular mind. No time for side projects."

"Like children?" Sardelle asked softly.

Zirkander grunted but didn't say anything else.

Cas shifted from foot to foot, wanting a look into the hole, more because she needed to see what security difficulties they might face in sneaking in. Were there any people on guard down there? Admittedly, she wanted to look for Tolemek too.

"So if we climb straight down, we'll hit that shield?" Zirkander asked.

"Yes," Sardelle said. "And be burned. Or incinerated, if Jaxi is right."

"Neither sounds palatable. Those holes in the wall—are those tunnels or just vents?"

Sardelle didn't answer right away. Maybe she was accessing her magic.

"Can I have a look, sir?" Cas asked.

Zirkander stepped back and waved her forward.

Careful not to touch the melted walls, Cas slipped past Sardelle and inched forward until she could crouch and see through the opening. Her heart lurched at the first thing that came into view. The dragon. A massive, silver, vaguely reptilian figure slumbering on its belly with its thick tail wrapped around its side. Even if it was unconscious and maybe sick, it was an impressive creature. She imagined she could feel the power radiating from its form. Maybe it wasn't her imagination.

She tore her gaze from the dragon and studied the walls, looking for the holes Zirkander had mentioned. There. In several spots, about twenty feet below their current level, holes opened up, hinting of inward passages. They weren't wide or tall—no more than three feet by three feet—but if they continued back into the walls, it ought to be possible to crawl through them. She couldn't see any sign of the barrier Zirkander had mentioned.

Pirate boy tossed a pebble and it burst into flame, came Jaxi's thoughts in Cas's mind. *He was in one of those passages. The Cofah spotted him, and he turned around and went back inside. I've lost track of him. If we can get some distance between us and the dragon, my senses may let me pick him up again.*

"He's not our primary concern," Zirkander said. "What's in that room down there? Can you tell?"

Their laboratory. That's probably where you want to go. There are samples of blood, as well as machinery. There were some men in there earlier, but they're gone now.

"Looking for Tolemek?" Cas understood that they had a mission and that he couldn't be their priority, but she worried about him, nonetheless. She had a hard time *not* thinking of going after him. It made her wonder if earlier in the week she had been mistaken when she had said she didn't have the capacity for love. Was this what love was? An obsessive need to know if someone was all right?

"Or maybe checking out that pirate activity," Zirkander said. "I'll assume they aren't aware of your father yet." He sighed and shoved his fingers through his hair. "I do hope that whatever his mission is doesn't interfere with ours. All right, I really hope none of us *are* his mission." He looked squarely at Sardelle.

Cas didn't say anything. She couldn't help but feel guilty that it was *her* father here, possibly about to make their lives difficult. Or worse. Why couldn't it have been some other assassin?

"Unless one of you two sees another option," Zirkander said, "we're going to have to drop down on a rope and try to swing into one of those holes. Without falling on the barrier that apparently incinerates rocks and anything else."

"Sounds fun, sir," Duck said, his voice making it clear that it didn't.

"I'll go first," Sardelle said.

"No," Zirkander said. "This isn't your mission."

Cas didn't point out that nobody had given *him* this mission, either. She supposed a self-assigned task could drive a person just as much as one handed down from the king.

"Besides," Zirkander added. "I'm hoping you can save my butt if I fall off the rope. Shield it or something."

"That will only work if my shield is more powerful than the one projected by the stasis chamber controller. I can't promise that."

"Then I'll try to hang on, eh? Look, I'm just planning to find that lab and destroy everything at this point. If anyone wants to stay out here, that's understandable. I won't order anyone to follow me." He looked at Duck and Cas. Did that mean his offer didn't apply to Sardelle? "In case I fail, in case *we* fail, someone needs to survive, get back to report to the king."

"I'm going in," Cas said. Not only was Tolemek in there, possibly getting himself shot at, but she wouldn't have abandoned Zirkander, either.

"Me too," Duck said.

"I am *not* going to miss seeing a dragon close up," Sardelle said.

"All right, all right, just offering. Ahn, scoot over, will you? I need to find something to fasten this hook to. Jaxi melted this smoother than a sheet of wax."

Flame burst from the stone floor near the lip of the hole. Cas scampered back from the sudden heat warming her face.

"What the—" Duck started, but he was shuffling back, too,

and she didn't hear the rest of the curse.

Under the flames, more molten rock formed, but instead of simply pooling, it slid sideways, defying gravity as it spread across the level stone floor. It wasn't until the heat and fire disappeared that Cas realized what had happened.

"Jaxi made a nub for my hook?" Zirkander asked.

"Jaxi made a nub," Sardelle said.

"She's being quite handy. I may have to forgive her for mocking me and calling me… that thing."

"Soul snozzle?" Duck rubbed his head.

"That's the one." As soon as the rock hardened again, Zirkander fastened his grappling hook. He leaned out, scanning the chamber below, then let his rope dangle through the hole. "Let me get into the tunnel first and see if it's a feasible way into the ziggurat. It would be nice if one of our magically gifted party members could break that panel down there and shut off the barrier, but I assume it's protected." He looked at Sardelle, his eyebrows raised.

"By far more power than I'll ever possess."

A dragon made that, Jaxi added. *I cannot stress enough how much more powerful they were than humans are.*

"Even humans turned into swords?" Zirkander asked.

Alas, yes.

Zirkander took a deep breath, then turned his back to the chamber and slid through the hole, his hands tight around the rope. Before he disappeared below the edge, Cas glimpsed the sheen of sweat on his forehead, illuminated by the light from below. His eyes seemed glassy, too, but he gave them all a familiar quirky smile before descending out of sight.

Sardelle crept out to the edge to watch him. Cas probably should have been keeping an eye on the route behind them, but she eased forward, too, needing to see if Zirkander made it. Besides, she ought to hear anyone climbing up the levels of the ziggurat behind them, a grappling hook clanking on the stone if nothing else.

Zirkander slid down the rope carefully, glancing down often, not at the dragon, but at that laboratory that lay mostly out of sight behind the same glass wall that held the control panel. Had someone come back into the room? Cas dared not ask. She doubted that barrier blocked sound. She wondered if it would block the dragon itself if it woke up and noticed intruders on a rope above it. It might not like having its long nap interrupted.

When Zirkander made it two thirds of the way down, he stopped, glanced at the laboratory one more time, then shifted his body weight back and forth. He swung himself, like a pendulum. Cas poked her head out, trying to spot his target. There was a hole in the wall, perhaps the very hole Tolemek had been kneeling in earlier.

Rock crumbled under Cas, and one hand slipped away. She was lying on her belly, so she wasn't in danger of falling, but a jolt of fear charged through her, anyway, as her arm dropped. A pebble and some dust *did* fall, and she winced as one bounced off Zirkander's shoulder, then hit the barrier ten feet below him. As promised, it lit up with a blaze, incinerated instantly.

Zirkander glanced up. Cas could only mouth, "Sorry."

He didn't stop working his weight on the rope. He had built up some momentum, and was almost reaching the hole with his swings. The hook creaked in the tunnel beside Cas. She hoped Sardelle could make sure it held fast with all of the twisting and swinging going on below. Even with the two of them, it would be difficult, if not impossible to hold up the colonel's weight if the hook gave way.

Zirkander checked the laboratory again, then seemed to find the swing he liked. He let go of the rope, flying toward the wall. Cas held her breath. If his aim was a foot or two off, he would strike rock and bounce off. But he disappeared into the hole. The empty rope bounced and danced in the air. For the first time, Cas noticed the end was charred. It must have struck the barrier too. Zirkander was lucky the fire hadn't burned all the way up the rope.

"One down," Sardelle murmured, then slid out of the hole before Cas could ask who wanted to go next. "There are two men in the lab down there, so be quick and try not to make noise," she advised before sliding down out of sight.

Or drop rocks on the barrier, Cas added to herself. She hadn't heard much when that one struck, but it was quiet in the chamber, and it wouldn't take much for someone to overhear.

Duck came forward to kneel next to Cas. "I took a peek around the corner but didn't see anyone on the road out front," he whispered. "It's quiet out there."

"Because everyone's in here," Cas murmured, watching Sardelle.

She had reached the spot where Zirkander had stopped. Like he had done, she started swinging. Interestingly, she didn't have to throw as much of her body into it to gain momentum. Some magical assistance? Cas worried a little about her own ability to repeat Zirkander's feat. Did she weigh enough to cause the rope to sway back and forth effectively? If not, she hoped Sardelle could help.

Sooner than she would have expected, Sardelle let go of the rope. She flew through the air and disappeared into the hole.

"You want to go next or should I?" Duck asked.

"Go ahead," Cas said. "Catch me if I fall, all right?"

"I'll do my best."

Duck slithered over the edge. As he slid down the rope, some movement below caught Cas's attention. Frowning, she tried to see around him and to the room. Had someone passed near the glass wall? No, it had been closer to the center of the room. When Duck started swinging back and forth, she saw the movement again, movement his body had been blocking. And she gulped. The tip of the dragon's tail was twitching.

"Please let that mean he's having a good dream," Cas breathed. Then she clamped her mouth shut. How good was a dragon's hearing? She didn't even see ears on the creature, but that might not mean anything. Snakes didn't have ears, either, but they could sense things around them through the earth.

Distracted by the tail, Cas almost missed seeing Duck make the leap toward the hole. His aim wasn't quite as precise as Zirkander's and Sardelle's had been, and he smashed into the corner of the opening. Cas bit her tongue to keep from gasping, afraid he wouldn't be able to find purchase, and that he would fall and disappear in flames the same way the pebble had. But Zirkander caught Duck and pulled him in before he could drop. Cas's second fear was that the noise would have been all too audible below—she had distinctly heard the thud of him hitting the rock. The rope bounced around, and if anyone walked out and looked up, it would be clear what was happening.

And if the *dragon* looked up... She could only guess what might be the result of that. Its tail had stopped twitching. Did that mean it had fallen deeper into its stupor? Or did that mean it had woken up and was simply waiting for the appropriate moment to pounce?

For a moment, Cas waited, poised on the edge, debating. She could go back out and try the front entrance, see if she could sneak past—or eliminate—the Cofah guard, but she had no idea what the situation was out there now. Even if she made it in that way, would she know how to find the group? She had no idea as to the layout of this place. Tolemek was already missing. Zirkander wouldn't want to lose anyone else, especially not one of the officers in his command.

Yes, there he was. Leaning out and waving for her. He alternated looking in her direction and glancing at the dragon and that room. He had to be worried about the noise too. Cas doubted waiting would help the situation.

She grabbed the rope and eased off the ledge. As soon as she started descending, she was glad she had left her pack outside. Even the weight of the rifle on her back pulled at her balance. But she skimmed down as quietly as she could, using her feet as brakes. When she drew even with the opening, she nodded at the others, relieved to see Sardelle and Zirkander watching her. She started swinging, but as she had feared, she didn't have as much weight as the men, and she struggled to make the length of rope sway back and forth.

Then she had a strange sensation of being assisted. Sardelle had backed away from the ledge, but she had to be doing something. Air whispered past Cas's cheeks as she sailed through the air, each swing longer than the last. She threw her body into it, eager to escape into that hole. She felt so vulnerable out here, visible to anyone below.

The thought made her glance down to check that tail. But it wasn't the *tail* that was moving.

The dragon's large, silver head was rising from the floor. It tilted, and one of its eyes came into view, one of its *open* eyes. The large yellow orb stared into her heart, filling her body with a fear unlike any she had ever felt, even when her flier had been in the middle of crashing.

"Cas," came a loud whisper from the wall. Zirkander. "Now," he urged. "Jump!"

More because she was trained to follow orders than out of any intelligent thought or reason, Cas let go of the rope as she neared the end of the swing. As she flew toward the hole, a powerful cry sounded in her mind, far louder and more intrusive than anything Jaxi had uttered.

Intruders!

CHAPTER 12

FROM THE SHADOWS OF THE narrow passage, Tolemek rolled his last knock-out grenade around the corner and down the hallway. In the tomb-like silence of the ziggurat, he could hear it bumping along the uneven stone floor, but the murmur of voices didn't stop. He pulled out his dagger and waited. He almost withdrew his pistol, too, since the Cofah should be aware that he was in their base by now, but these guards didn't sound hypervigilant, or even aware that they had intruders. The massive alarm he had expected had never come, at least not that he had heard. He had, however, chanced across more soldiers with slit throats, and suspected he had the other infiltrator to thank for the anemic pursuit from the guards.

"...think it'll quiet down now?"

"I don't know. I didn't mind the excitement. This is the most boring post in the world."

"I'll take being bored over being dead."

"True, but living is no guarantee around here. Every morning I don't wake up sick, I'm thankful. This place *is* creepy. Wonder what those fools thought they were doing coming up here."

"I don't—where's that smoke coming from?"

The sound of footsteps drifted around the corner, one man jogging forward to check on it. Tolemek rolled onto the balls of his feet, ready to charge down the corridor and deal with the men if he had to, but the grenade had another twenty seconds' worth of sedative to spit into the air. If he ran in, he risked receiving a whiff himself. Better to let the men take the full dose first.

"This ball thing." A thump sounded, and Tolemek's smoke grenade flew past his intersection and disappeared down the corridor, ricocheting off the walls.

So much for a full dose.

Holding his breath, Tolemek charged around the corner. The

closest guard, the one who had kicked it, was leaning against the wall, his eyes drooping shut. But they popped open when he spotted Tolemek.

The guard reached for a pistol holstered at his hip. His movements were slow, and Tolemek had time to throw a knife first. It struck the soldier in the wrist, and his pistol fell from his grip. Tolemek grabbed him by the shoulder and punched him in the gut. The man might have fallen, but Tolemek kept him upright, aware of the second soldier racing down the hall at him, a weapon raised. This one's reflexes had not been dulled, but with the other Cofah blocking the way, the guard did not fire.

Tolemek leaned out and flung one of his goo webs at his face. These two were wearing normal uniforms, not the heavy suits and helmets, and it would have worked, but the man ducked. The web flew past, plastering to the wall instead. But the distraction gave Tolemek time to dig out a vial and hurl it at the soldier's feet. Glass shattered, and thin liquid splattered across the floor, lubricating the stones. The guard's boots flew into the air, and he landed hard, his head striking the wall on the way down. Careful not to lose his own footing, Tolemek kicked the soldier's hand, sending his pistol flying down the corridor.

The first man had recovered his wits, and he grabbed Tolemek's arm, trying to twist into him for a shoulder throw. But enough of the sedative had hit the guard's senses that his movements were sluggish. Tolemek read the attack and deflected the groping arm. He ducked and slammed his elbow into the man's sternum, then followed by ramming him against the wall several times. The brutality made him uncomfortable, and he wished his sedative had knocked the guards out instead, but the man's eyes eventually rolled back into his head, and he slumped.

The man who had fallen had not struck his skull hard enough to be knocked out, but he was struggling to get to his feet, the passage all around him more slippery than ice.

Tolemek caught a flailing arm and pulled the man to his feet, then pressed a knife to his throat.

"Where is my sis—the girl?" he asked, making his tone as cold as possible. "I have vials that contain far deadlier substances than lubricants."

Usually that would be a bluff, and Tolemek would shy away from seriously harming his own people, but the fact that the soldiers were forcing his sister to interact with that dragon, to risk catching that disease, while they hid in the laboratory and wore those protective suits… It infuriated him. The rage flowing through his veins made him want to run through the base, shooting everyone in sight.

The guard set his jaw and glared back without saying a word.

"Do you know who I am?" Tolemek whispered.

The man's eyes narrowed, but he kept his jaw clenched.

"The pirates call me Deathmaker." Without moving the knife from the man's throat, Tolemek dug into a pouch on his belt. He withdrew a tiny gray ball less than a centimeter thick. "If I throw this on the ground at your feet, you die. Oh, I could simply cut your throat and save my tools for later use, but I enjoy seeing my gases work, melting the skin off my victims, burning through muscle and then down to organs, eating them—eating *you* from the outside in, while you live to experience every moment, until your heart finally stops. After hours of torment."

Tolemek was preparing an answer to the next obvious argument, that he wouldn't throw such a gas around while he was nearby, but some of the mulishness had faded from the guard when he had shared his infamous nickname. He licked his lips, his gaze darting both ways down the corridor.

"No help is coming," Tolemek whispered, hoping he spoke the truth. "Where's the girl?"

"In the lab."

"Which way?"

Tolemek thought he was going in the right direction, but it wouldn't hurt to ask. Of course, the man might lie to him.

But the fight had gone out of the guard. He tilted his head to the side, toward the direction Tolemek had been heading.

"Good." He wanted to race off, but could not leave guards lying around, especially conscious ones. "Take off your trousers and give me your belt."

It took him a few minutes to tie up the men and find an

alcove to stuff them in, and he lamented the loss of time. When he returned to the hunt, he had the guards' pistols, one in each hand, and he ran in the direction the man had indicated. He was out of vials and knock-out grenades, and contrary to what he had told the guard, he didn't have any smokes capable of eating human flesh. He would have to go forward with more conventional weapons—and hope he didn't run into an army.

Tolemek jogged down the corridor, feeling a sense of urgency, of limited time. He turned a corner, then two more, hoping he was still heading toward the center of the structure. Earlier, he had been sure, but with all the turns, he worried that he had lost his sense of direction.

Finally, voices sounded in the distance, and the light grew brighter ahead. Soft clanks came, like a hammer banging on nails. Odd.

Tolemek increased his pace, came to another intersection, and leaned his head around the corner, checking in all directions. A glint of glass caught his eye. The lab? He couldn't see a door yet, but everything else down here was made from ancient stone. He barely kept himself from breaking into a jog. But as he strode down the hall, the voices and clanks grew louder. He heard at least two people talking, and who knew how many more weren't saying anything? Tolemek wished he had saved the knock-out grenade and not wasted it back on those guards.

When he leaned around the next corner, he spotted two men in those bulky suits standing outside of a glass door. They weren't wearing the helmets, but they did have rifles. The door they guarded was part of a glass wall, and other uniformed men moved about inside, packing things in crates. A couple wore the heavy suits, helmets included, but most looked like soldiers who had been recruited to help. This was indeed the laboratory Tolemek had seen from above. The dragon's bulky form was visible on the far side, beyond another clear wall.

Unfortunately, one of the guards outside of the door spotted Tolemek, and he did not have time to count the exact number of people in that lab—or formulate a plan.

"Harmek," the man barked, jerking his rifle around.

Using the corner for cover, Tolemek raised his pistol, hoping to fire first, then duck back before he was hit.

Before he squeezed the trigger, a loud voice resonated in his mind, a fierce cry of, *Intruders!*

Surprisingly, the guards seemed to hear it too. They both jumped, and the one who had been aiming at Tolemek stumbled back, smacking into the glass wall and nearly dropping his weapon. Tolemek took advantage of his distraction and shot with both pistols. One bullet slammed into one man's chest, the suit doing nothing to deflect the attack. His aim wasn't as good with his left hand, and he only clipped the other guard in the shoulder.

He thought about charging out, anyway, trying to overpower the soldier before he recovered, but the men behind the glass had heard the fighting. Tolemek threw his knife instead, then ducked back behind the corner. The injured man did not react quickly enough to dodge, and the blade clipped his throat. Tolemek did not know if it was a killing blow, but the guard should be out of the fight. Good, because the glass door slammed open.

Expecting the men to race outside after him, firearms leading, Tolemek backed up a few steps and prepared to fire at the first person who rounded the corner. But something clanked instead, and a canister bounced into view. Tear gas. He remembered the brown canisters with their skull and sword symbol well from his army days. It was already spewing yellow smoke. Tolemek held his breath and squinted his eyes to slits, then rushed forward and grabbed it.

The heavy glass door was swinging shut, the men inside waiting for the smoke to incapacitate him before charging out. He snatched up the canister, ignored the way it burned his palm, and flung it at the gap before the door closed. It glanced off the edge, and he thought it would bounce back toward him, but the obstacle only deflected the canister slightly. It still bounced inside.

Someone inside the room fired. Tolemek threw himself back around the corner, afraid the bullet would cut through the glass and slam into him. But the thick wall cracked without breaking, and the men inside were the ones who had to duck. Someone shouted a curse at the unthinking soldier.

Tolemek backed several steps down the corridor, made sure nobody was creeping up behind him, and yanked off his vest and shirt. He rushed to tie the shirt around his nose and mouth. The material would not do much to filter out the airborne gas particles, but it was better than nothing. The smart thing to do would be to run away and hide again—there were at least six men in that laboratory, maybe more, given that the tables, equipment, and crates inside made it hard to count. But he couldn't back down, not when he was this close to reaching Tylie.

Nobody had run out after him yet, so he took the moment to wipe tears from his eyes and to reload the pistols before advancing again. The yellow smoke tainted the air inside the enclosed laboratory. Tolemek was surprised the men hadn't kicked the canister back through the door again, but he glimpsed motion in the distance and understood why they might have been distracted. Even through the smoke, he could see the dragon moving. It had risen to its feet, only part of the massive body visible—the laboratory ceiling was much lower than that of the big open chamber beyond it.

The creature's thick silver tail slammed into the glass wall, and Tolemek jumped back. He did not know if it was trying to attack the people in the laboratory, or if it was simply agitated. Intruders, it had called out, as if the Cofah were permitted here, but Tolemek and the others were not.

Even with his shirt over his nose and mouth, he took a huge breath before advancing to the laboratory. He crouched low, where the smoke hung thickest in the air, and tried to open the door. They had locked it. He pulled out some of the caustic paste he had used to break himself and Cas out of the Cofah prison the night they had first met. He dabbed a line of it across the lower half of the door, even as the smoke attacked his eyes. Tears streamed down his cheeks and into the shirt, which did little to protect his nostrils from the searing gas. Tendrils escaped down his throat, too, irritating it so that he struggled mightily not to cough. He wanted nothing more than to flee from the smoke's influence, but he made himself wait for his goo, as Cas called it, to burn through the glass.

Fortunately, the door wasn't as thick as the wall, and after a moment, he was able to remove the lower panel.

"Got it," someone inside said at the same time as a *ker-thunk* sounded in the ceiling. A vent fan turning on.

Tolemek set aside the panel, hoping the door still appeared closed to those farther back in the lab. Once the smoke cleared, the evidence would be obvious, but he ought to have a few seconds.

He crawled inside and headed for a solid stone wall on one side of the laboratory. He wanted his back to it, but he also wanted to check two curtained doorways he had spotted before the smoke had filled the room. Smoke that was now being sucked upward to a vent in the ceiling. If he wanted to eliminate some of his enemies, he had better do it soon. These people weren't going to let him walk out of here with Tylie.

"He's in here," someone barked.

"Don't—" The second voice broke off in a chain of coughs.

Tolemek spotted the figure hunching over, shot, then quickly moved to the side, anticipating return fire. He wasn't disappointed. Two soldiers shot at him, or at where he had been, the bullets ricocheting off the wall. He could barely see the men, so they had to be having trouble seeing him too. The one he had shot fell to the stone floor. More people coughed in the corner, and Tolemek fired in that direction, using the noise to guide his aim. His own throat and nostrils itched, with mucous streaming from his nose. He would not be able to hold back his own coughs much longer. He fired again, afraid his luck wouldn't hold out, and that they would locate him and shoot him. All he struck was one of the chemistry worktables. Glass shattered, and some green liquid dripped out onto the floor.

Another thump sounded, the tail striking the wall again.

"What is the dragon doing?" someone demanded, the man's voice sounding hollow, like he might be wearing a mask to protect against the smoke.

"It's acting crazy. Get the girl to talk to it."

Tolemek had reached the first curtained doorway, and he thought about ducking into it, but he had to make these people leave—or take care of them in another way. Their mention of Tylie only convinced him further that she was nearby, that he couldn't leave.

"Forget the dragon. Get that damned pirate."

They knew who he was? Or was he simply being lumped in with the pirates that had attacked out front? Maybe they didn't know about the Iskandian group yet.

Tolemek leaned out from behind a cabinet and shot toward the corner the men were crouching in. They had found cover, as well, and his bullets did nothing but hit the worktables and other furnishings. One glanced off a centrifuge, and a nearby rack full of crimson vials rattled. Someone fired back, and he skittered farther along the wall. His elbow bumped a cabinet, and bottles rattled and clanked inside. He wiped at his eyes and looked at the contents. Numerous chemicals and powders. He spotted a bottle of hydrochloric acid and tugged it out. He found a pouch of potassium nitrate on the bottom shelf. If they had tried to drive him to distraction with tear gas, it was only fair that he throw some compound at them. But he needed a burner. And some copper.

He fired twice more to keep them pinned down as he moved along the wall, searching for what he needed. Of course, they fired back, trying to keep *him* pinned down, as well. This was one of those moments when it would have been nice to have allies. Too bad he hadn't waited for them to come along.

Whispers came from the other corner. They had to be plotting something.

As Tolemek spotted a burner, another thump came from the wall, this one the loudest of all. Glass shattered and broke, with shards flying inward. Tolemek ducked, but several sharp pieces struck his hands and bare chest.

Fools! Is no one seeking the vermin that have invaded this place? Free me from this cage, and I will find them. My fate may be inevitable, but I will not die like this, intruders. Do you hear me? The powerful voice resonated in Tolemek's mind, causing an instant headache.

Someone groaned on the other side of the room. Because he had been hit by glass? Or because the dragon's voice affected him even more strongly?

All Tolemek knew was that the men were distracted. He flicked on the burner and found the copper he had been hunting for. He grabbed a jar and searched for a mask, so he would not end up killing *himself* with his concoction. If that other guard—or maybe he was a scientist—had one, there had to be more.

Tolemek? came a soft call in his mind, sweet and gentle after the dragon's roar.

Tylie! Where are you? He kept working as he responded to her, pulling a mask with a filter off a rack, then returning to the burner. The urge to simply leave this mess and run back through one of the two curtained doorways tickled his mind.

Not there. Tylie almost sounded amused. *Down here.*

An image entered his mind, one of the very laboratory he crouched in. But he was looking down at it from above. He couldn't see himself—or the men. It was as if this was some picture that had been drawn earlier. Then it moved, the view shifting, almost making him dizzy as he struggled to focus on it and on what he was mixing on the burner. It took him to the far corner, where those men were waiting, and he spotted a large grate in the floor, such as might be used for draining water into a sewer. Except it was bigger than that.

Not much bigger, Tylie thought dryly.

You're down there? Fresh anger surged through Tolemek's limbs.

Yes.

Right now?

Yes. I can hear you all shooting at each other. And something stinks.

Most of the gas had been cleared by the fan, but the air was far from fresh. Tolemek looked down at his new project, with dread filling him. *Are you right under that grate, or can you move to the side? So something wouldn't drip on you?* Drip, hell, his concoction would eat right through that metal…

I'm to the side. In a little room, with some mummified corpses.

Are you joking? Tolemek thought of the sarcophagi he had

passed on the upper level.

No, they thought the crazy girl would enjoy the company of the dead. Soldiers are strange, Tolemek. This last, she added sternly, a clear dig at his former occupation. She sounded incredibly sane at the moment, more so than she had when they had communicated twenty minutes earlier. What had changed?

He's awake, Tylie thought simply, as if that explained everything.

All right, I'm getting you out of there. Stay back, far *back, from the grate. Do you understand?*

Yes.

A pistol fired, the bullet clanging off the wall two feet above Tolemek's head. He flinched, almost knocking over his fresh brew. He had donned the mask, but it wouldn't protect him from acid burning through his skin.

"...the pirate still over there?" someone whispered.

"The curtains moved. I think he might have gone down the storage hall."

Yeah, keep thinking that. Tolemek found the sturdiest gloves he could, then grabbed the jar he had heated, its contents steaming and sloshing inside. He slid a lid atop it, carried it around a tall bookshelf, then risked standing to his full height. He threw the jar, hoping most of it would spatter on the men instead of flying free before it reached them.

In return, someone fired again. Tolemek dropped to his belly on the floor and crawled back to his corner.

A scream of pain came from the other side of the room. The nitric acid had spattered at least one of them. A second cry of pain joined the first, and he allowed himself a feeling of grim satisfaction. Whatever sympathy he might have had for soldiers stationed out in this backwater, he had none of it for anyone keeping Tylie in a hole in the ground. A hole adorned with sarcophagi. Bastards.

Furniture scraped and fell over. Something clattered to the ground—someone's pistol? The cries of pain continued. "Get it off," a man bellowed.

Others shoved through the lab, knocking over equipment and

cabinets. One charged out the door. From his position, Tolemek could have shot the man in the back, but he decided the soldier had enough trouble. He wasn't the only one. The others sprinted after him, crying for water and ice.

Though Tolemek also wanted to sprint, he forced himself to take it slow, keeping his pistol up and staying behind cover as he approached the corner with the grate. The dragon was still moving on the other side of the shattered glass—the wall continued to stand, but cracks streaked in every direction, and shards littered the floor. As he kept an eye on the giant creature, Tolemek stepped lightly to keep from crunching them under his feet. He couldn't yet be certain all of the guards had fled the lab. At least the dragon had stopped hammering at the wall. Only his head and neck were moving now. It was hard to tell from down here, but he seemed to be lifting it to peer into the holes in the wall up there, perhaps into the very passage Tolemek had been in earlier. Did that mean the dragon could thrust its head through that barrier? Or had he turned it off somehow? Tolemek had assumed he was a prisoner, but if the dragon could access the control panel, what kept him here?

The thousands of pounds of rock that the humans built over his head while he slept, Tylie thought.

Can't he break through it?

He is very weak. This is the first time I've seen him stand since they brought me here.

The corner of the grate came into view. As did holes in the metal and stone where the acid had eaten through it. Tolemek was glad he had kept his gloves. At the moment, they were stuffed in his belt, but he would put them back on before—

A man in a helmet leaped around a cabinet, a pistol in his hand. Tolemek ducked at the same instant as it went off. It was so close that it ripped off some of his hair, but it didn't strike him, and he lunged, barreling into the man. In the fall, he lost his pistol, but he was too busy punching his foe in the gut to care. The grate lay under the man, the grate they had thrust Tylie through and then locked for the gods knew how many weeks. He pounded his rage into his opponent, slamming the man's head against the iron bars. A hand groped for his face, but he squinted his eyes shut and kept hammering his enemy into the floor. Finally, the man stopped moving.

Tolemek rolled him off the grate, found his pistol, and kicked the extra one across the room. It disappeared under a cabinet. As Tolemek shifted to look for the grate opening, he spotted a dark chunk of hair on the floor. He blinked, realizing exactly how close he had come to being shot in the head.

I never cared for that hairstyle, anyway.

Funny, Tylie. Want to explain to me why you're so... cogent when the dragon is awake?

By cogent, you mean not crazy?

Uhm. Tolemek didn't know what to say—or think. Never before had Tylie seemed to think there was anything strange about her speech or mannerisms, not since she had first started acting strangely. In a moment, he would crush her with a hug, but he had to get through the lock on the grate first. The shank had been corroded by acid spattering on it. Tolemek doubted the iron would have dissolved all the way through, but he grabbed it and pulled, nonetheless, hoping it might snap. It didn't.

"Give me a moment," he said and reached for his corrosive goo again. It could burn through metal far more efficiently than simpler acids. While he tugged it out and brushed some on the lock, he kept his pistol close, guessing the soldiers would return, likely with reinforcements.

As for Phelistoth, it's hard to explain, Tylie thought. *I'm not sure I understand it completely. He's been awake so little, and we've had so few actual conversations. But we're connected.*

Tolemek returned his vial to his pocket. While he listened to Tylie and waited for the substance to eat through the metal, he tried not to think about how concerning it was that his little sister might be "connected" to a dragon.

His subconscious mind has been reaching out to me from his living tomb here, seeking help. He knew that even with the stasis chamber, his body could not last much longer. This was not the logical, rational part of his mind, only the part that knew he must survive. It sent telepathic calls out into the world, hoping someone could respond to him, hoping that a cure for his illness might have been discovered in the countless generations that have passed since his kin locked him away in here.

As in quarantined him? Is his illness what's affecting people out here now?

Yes. It's not his fault. He was only trying to survive. I didn't understand any of this then, just that his presence was there in my mind, and it was so strong that I couldn't think straight. All I knew was this overwhelming desire to come to this place, to help him somehow. When the military came for me, I was happy at first, because they asked me all about him and wanted to bring me here, but I was scared too. I saw in their thoughts that they wanted to use him. I knew he was sick, and I was afraid he wouldn't survive. I was... afraid of what they would do to me too.

So if the dragon was affecting your consciousness, your ability to think, he was the reason Father thought you were crazy all those years? The lock fell open. Tolemek shifted his position so he could tug open the grate.

You thought I was crazy, too, I seem to recall, she thought dryly.

I just knew you needed help. And that I didn't know how to give it.

I know.

Tolemek peered into the gloom. Her captors hadn't even thought to provide her with a light? He was about to lower himself down, when a shadow came in from over his shoulder.

He grabbed for the pistol even as he realized it couldn't be a guard, not from that direction. He looked toward the shattered wall, to where a huge silver head faced him through the glass, two large reptilian eyes burning into his soul with such intensity that he almost couldn't breathe.

For a sick-and-dying dragon, he still looks deadly, Tolemek thought. He also looked like he was thinking of breaking through the rest of the glass with his snout.

This is the liveliest I've seen him. He's incensed about the Iskandian intruders. He thinks they're here to kill him, and he doesn't want to die by enemy hands. I would love to see him healthy again. He's too weak to break out of here now. He certainly couldn't fly. Tolemek, dragons are meant to fly.

At the moment, Tolemek was more concerned about whether dragons were meant to eat people.

He's protective of me, but he won't hurt you. I told him you're my brother.

If he's protective, how come he let the soldiers lock you up down there? Tolemek didn't want to say as much, but he wondered if Tylie might be making some of this up, or believing something because she wanted to believe it.

They haven't tried to hurt me, and he's not sure what the ramifications might be to me if he hurts any of the men here. Also, they've told him that they're working on a cure for him. That they've been taking his blood samples and studying them here and also sending them to the best labs back in Cofahre.

Tylie... they're using his blood to fly aircraft and create weapons. I've seen them.

She didn't respond immediately, and he wondered if she was relaying the information to the dragon. He also wondered when she had learned to speak telepathically to people. And how she was able to keep from getting sick if the dragon was contagious.

Not everybody catches the disease. We have strong blood, Tolemek. He said so.

A gunshot fired in the distance, reminding Tolemek that he didn't have unlimited time. Hoping the dragon wasn't going to break through the glass and eat him, he lay on his belly and extended an arm downward.

"Tylie? Can you reach my hand?" He could make out her shape among the shadows, as well as the shapes of two large stone sarcophagi against the walls of her room—her dungeon. He didn't think she was more than eight or ten feet down. If he had to, he would leap in and boost her up, then figure out a way to climb out himself.

Come down here, she urged.

"What? You can't reach?"

Sssh. Someone is coming.

All the more reason to leave.

There isn't time. Tylie walked out of the darkness to look up at him, her brown eyes earnest. And worried. *Come down here, and close the grate behind you. We have to hide.*

Tylie... I can handle a couple more soldiers. He touched the pistol resting on the floor next to him.

Not this one. This isn't a soldier.

How can you—

Now, Tolemek! Before it's too late and he sees you.

Every instinct screamed for him to stay where he was, that he would be trapped and at a huge disadvantage if he dropped into the dark room, but Tylie's words rang in his head with the authority of a general's command. He couldn't disobey.

He grabbed the grate, lowering it most of the way, then slid through, using his head to keep it from slamming down. He didn't let go with his hands until the cold metal rested on his knuckles. There was no way to keep it from making *any* noise, but he tried to ensure the clang would be as soft as possible. Surprisingly, as he let go, he didn't hear the grate bang down.

When he landed on the floor, thick patches of mold squishing beneath his feet, he looked up to make sure it had indeed closed all the way.

Phelistoth softened it, Tylie explained. *He's very weak and can't call upon much magic, but that was a simple matter, even for a sick dragon. Come over here in the darkness, please.*

This was a request, rather than a command, and he didn't feel the urgency—the power—that had compelled him to obey the last one. But now that he was stuck down here, hiding in the shadows and being quiet seemed like a good idea. He reached out a hand, intending to give Tylie a hug, but her warning stopped him before he reached her.

He's entered the lab.

Tolemek hadn't heard anything, not a footstep or the clunk of that door opening and shutting. *Who? And how do you know? Is the dragon telling you, or... something else?*

Even with his new knowledge that he possessed dragon blood, it was disconcerting to think of his sister as having power. Already developed power, not the latent power Sardelle had spoken of.

I can't really do anything except for talk. I'm still... normal. A person, I mean. I suppose I wasn't ever normal. All trace of that commanding tone was gone now, and she sounded like a young girl, one hurt that he had been thinking about the strangeness of her powers rather than thinking about her.

Tolemek reached out again, and this time he found her and pulled her into a hug. She hugged him back and buried her face in his shoulder.

I'm so glad you came. I was afraid I'd never see you again, or Mother, either.

He noted that she didn't mention their father. Not surprising, since he had been the one to send her to the asylum.

And my friends, Yeesha and Tabi. It's been so long. I wonder if they even remember me... She didn't sound certain about that.

Tolemek wished he had been home recently and could promise that the girls from the neighborhood did all remember her, but he didn't want to lie. *I'll find a way to take you back home to see everyone. And I have some new friends now that you might like.* Granted, she might not find a bunch of adults interesting. She might be seventeen now, but did she consider herself a grownup? Her childhood had been so abbreviated. *One of them is... someone who can teach you how to use your powers better.*

Assuming they had made it into the compound. It had been some time since Jaxi had poked her nose into his thoughts. And that gunshot he had heard—who had fired it?

Good. Scoot back now, and be very quiet. He's searching the lab.

Who? Maybe Zirkander was the one sneaking around up there. Or it could even be Cas. If anyone could move silently, it would be she. *Are you sure it's a man?*

Yes. He has a lot of weapons. He's looking for something. Or someone. He's a hunter. I can tell.

That didn't sound a lot like Zirkander, not unless he had his flier with him. This had to be someone else.

As soon as he accepted that realization, the image of the murdered guards jumped into his mind.

Don't breathe. He's almost right over us.

Tolemek stayed utterly still and listened as hard as he could. He had yet to hear so much as a footstep, and yet, he didn't doubt Tylie. Maybe it was some magical sixth sense of his own, but he also believed someone was up there. And then he heard something, the faint rustle of pages being flipped.

Is the dragon still up there? Tolemek couldn't imagine where else he would have gone, but wondered what he thought about the intruder. He didn't hear the tail thumping against the glass.

Yes, but all he can do is watch. He's overexerted himself. He's struggling to remain conscious. After an uncertain pause, Tylie added, *If that happens, it may affect me. His subconscious is... it's hard to explain, but we're linked.*

Why you?

I was the only one who could hear his calls and who responded. Maybe I was the only one to hear them at all. I don't know.

Tolemek wanted to ask how the Cofah had found the dragon and picked her out of the asylum as someone who could communicate with it, but the rustling up above had stopped. He pointed his pistol at the grate.

He's not moving. Tylie leaned against Tolemek's side. *He may know we're here.*

The shadows shifted up above. Tolemek had the sense of someone walking around the grate, being careful not to step on it, to show himself. Maybe it was nothing; maybe he was examining the divots left by the spattered acid. Or maybe he was waiting with his garrote for Tolemek and Tylie to show themselves.

CHAPTER 13

C AS CRAWLED THROUGH THE DIM passage after Sardelle, Duck, and Zirkander, trying not to let her rifle scrape on the stone walls, but the thought that a dragon might be about to hurl gouts of fire down the shaft after her didn't lend itself to moving slowly and with care.

Only the gold dragons can breathe fire, the soulblade spoke into her thoughts.

"Comforting," Cas muttered, certain the dragon could find some other way to slay her if necessary.

"We have to cross a vertical shaft or go down it," came Zirkander's voice from up ahead. He was leading the crawl through the three-foot-wide passage.

"The lab is down," Sardelle said.

"Can you find it?"

"I think so. If not me, Jaxi says she can."

"Can Jaxi tell how many soldiers might be between us and that lab?"

Keep your firearms handy, the sword spoke into everyone's thoughts.

"Wonderful. Down we go." A faint rasp of clothing on stone followed this statement, and Zirkander disappeared from view.

Cas followed Sardelle and Duck down the shaft, her back to the rock, and her legs stuck out to brace herself. She had to hold her rifle in front of her. The descent reminded her of the night she had met Tolemek, when they had descended a millennia-old latrine shaft to escape that Cofah prison.

Gunshots fired in the distance, and her heart lurched. Was that him now? Shooting at the soldiers? Or being shot at by them?

She couldn't descend any more quickly, not without cracking someone in the head, but when she landed next to Sardelle, she already had her rifle raised and ready. She didn't truly expect trouble right away—the gunshots were muffled and distant—but two men in Cofah uniforms jogged around a corner in front of her. Their eyes bulged with surprise. Cas fired. She caught the first one in the chest, even as he loosed a round. His flew wide, banging off the stone wall behind her, but the second had time to aim a pistol at her. She snapped the rifle lever, chambering a second round, but knew she would be too late.

An instant before the soldier fired, a pistol boomed behind her ear. The man flew backward, slamming into the corner wall with far more force than should have happened as a result of being shot.

"Thank you, Sardelle," Cas said.

"You're *welcome*," Zirkander said, waving at the bloody hole in the man's forehead. It looked like they had struck at the same time. Cas didn't care, so long as she hadn't been shot.

"I guess that means we're not sneaking anymore." Duck was facing the other way, watching for trouble.

"We haven't been sneaking since the dragon shouted into everyone's head." Sardelle sighed and pointed in the direction Duck was facing. "The lab should be that way."

Zirkander stepped aside, gesturing for her to lead, his expression wry. Or maybe pained. After the crawl through the tunnels, he was sweating even more than before. His eyes were bloodshot, and his face flushed with fever. Duck's face had a flushed hue to it, as well. Would she be the next to develop symptoms? She implored the gods to at least let her finish the mission, to help her comrades and to find Tolemek.

More gunshots fired. They sounded closer this time.

"Are those coming from the lab?" Cas thought of her father. He was the epitome of stealth, so it was hard to imagine him getting caught in a firefight. But what about Tolemek? Would he start shooting at his own people? Or was it more that his own people were shooting at him?

She quickened her step, soon passing the others to stride along at Sardelle's side. The gunfire stopped. She wanted to break into a run, but Zirkander was lagging behind, despite a determined set to his jaw.

They turned a corner at an intersection and almost stepped on a body. The dead man had been flipped over and slouched against the wall, his neck sliced open.

"That's my father's work," Cas said quietly. Maybe he was the one shooting people in the lab after all.

"Handy," Zirkander muttered.

Sardelle pointed down the new passage. "We're almost there."

"Anyone else disturbed by the people eating brains?" Zirkander asked, stepping past the body and waving a hand toward the carvings on the walls.

"I was hoping that was merely cereal in a skull-shaped ceramic bowl," Duck said.

"I'm trying not to look," Sardelle said.

Ignoring the decorations, Cas reached the next corner first. A hint of an odor lingered in the air, something that made her nostrils sting. They had reached the lab, but it was a mess. One of the big glass walls was shattered, and furniture had been shot up and toppled. Fancy chemistry apparatuses were smashed all over the tables and floor.

A twinge of disappointment ran through her. Tolemek wasn't there. Even though she knew he was hunting for his sister, and she had no idea where the girl was, Cas associated Tolemek with labs. It would have felt right for him to be here.

"Look," Sardelle breathed beside her, then pointed at the lab, or rather *through* the lab, to the huge figure on the other side of it. The dragon might have looked up at her earlier, but it wasn't moving now. Its head lay between its arms, almost like a snoozing dog.

"A very *big* dog." Cas didn't see anyone in the lab, but she approached the door with her rifle at the ready. Those furnishings could hide an army, and there were curtained doorways on one wall too. "What's the plan, sir? Smash everything that isn't smashed? Find any vials of blood and take them for Iskandia?"

"Find the vials," Zirkander said. "And then... Sardelle, how would you like to chat with a dragon? Convince it to leave the Cofah and join us? Or at least fly off to some remote island that isn't affiliated with either government."

"I don't think it's going to be able to fly anywhere. It—*he*—is dying."

Cas was listening to them as she opened the door to the lab, the top half of it, anyway. The bottom had been sawn away. Or maybe burned away? She touched the edge, thinking of Tolemek's corrosive goo. Had he been here already? Maybe he had caused all the damage. But then where had he gone?

She stepped inside. The odor was stronger, despite a fan sucking air through the ceiling. She paused inside the doorway, her shoulder blades itching. They weren't alone. She was sure of it.

"Any ideas on how to keep the Cofah from continuing to use him?" Zirkander asked. "As a military man, I have to admit my first thought is to blow up this installation, the same as we did with the volcano, but my father would kill me if I destroyed ancient ruins. I'm also skeptical as to whether I brought along enough explosives to handle it."

"I would say set him free, but I'm worried he's willingly working with them," Sardelle said.

Duck followed Cas into the lab. "Someone made a mess in here."

"Someone who may still be here," Cas murmured.

"Ah?" Duck glanced at her face, then raised his rifle too.

They went in opposite directions, Cas along the stone wall with the doorways in it and Duck along the glass. She stopped when she reached the first curtain. It was swaying slightly on the wire it hung from. Because of the ventilation fan? Or because someone had just brushed past it?

Cas looked back at Sardelle, wondering if she could sense anyone else nearby. But she was drifting across the center of the lab, her gaze locked on the dragon's form, a pained crease to her brow. Maybe his presence was overwhelming her senses, or even hurting her. Either way, Cas would have to search the old-fashioned way.

She nudged the curtain open with the muzzle of her rifle. A dark, unlit hallway stretched ahead of her, the sides lined with crates and stacks of books. The Cofah had humped a lot of gear up here along those narrow jungle trails. They must have cleared a real road somewhere that led all the way down to the water.

Not seeing any movement down the hallway, Cas let the curtain fall shut again. Doorways opened up in that direction, but she might get herself lost in a maze if she started checking each of them. Besides, the lab was what they needed to secure.

A soft clank came from one corner of the room. Zirkander lifted an apologetic hand. "Just me. Looking for their stash of dragon blood. I'm assuming they have some here, and I intend to liberate it from them. Or at least make sure they can't send it off to power any more unmanned fliers."

"You would think the dragon would be mad about them taking its blood," Duck said.

"*His* blood," Sardelle murmured. She had crossed the lab and stood with her hand pressed against the shattered glass wall that separated her from the dragon.

Cas hoped she wasn't planning to go out for a visit. It—he— might appear unconscious now, but that could be a ruse. Maybe he was trying to lure them in, so he could more easily attack them. He might be the very reason that wall was shattered. Had he seen Tolemek and tried to get to him?

"It—he should want to work with us instead of them," Duck grumbled. "But the way he called out 'intruders' when he spotted Cas sounded about as promising as a fox with its snout down the vole's den. Promising to the vole, anyway."

Cas checked behind the second curtain. The hallway and its contents were almost identical to the first.

"Something happened over here," Duck said.

"Something happened *everywhere*," Zirkander said.

"Yeah, but the ground is all chewed up over here. It's strange. Like acid burned it."

Acid? Or some goo that Tolemek had concocted? Cas turned the corner and headed toward Duck. She passed Sardelle, who still had her hand pressed to the glass. Cas thought about suggesting that someone should be standing guard back in the tunnel they had entered through, but she didn't know if Sardelle might be communicating with the dragon or trying to learn something important. Besides, Zirkander was facing the door as he poked around, and he still held his pistol.

"There's a big grate in the ground too," Duck said.

"Perhaps," a familiar voice said as Cas walked up, "you could open it and help us out?"

She rushed to the grate, barely noticing when she clanked the end of her rifle on a table and knocked over an empty beaker. "Tolemek? Are you all right?"

"So long as you're not some assassin who seeks to shoot one of us, we're fine."

"Us?" Duck asked. "Did you find your sister?"

"Yes."

Cas pulled open the grate, worried anew by his mention of an assassin. Had her father attacked Tolemek? Driven him down there? If so, why would he have left them there instead of finishing his grim task? "Did my father... did you see him?"

A long pause came from below, and a woman whispered something Cas couldn't make out.

"Your father?" Tolemek asked.

"He's here. I would have told you, if you hadn't run off."

"I didn't run off. I strode boldly away. Duck, I'm going to boost Tylie up to you. Will you help her out?"

"Of course." Duck stepped past Cas and crouched beside the hole.

"I hear some voices in the distance." Zirkander had moved to the door and stood with it open, his ear cocked. "Might want to move things along. We may have visitors soon."

Cas hesitated, knowing she should go over and stand by the door with him to prepare for an assault, but also longing to see Tolemek, not to mention the sister that had been a part of his quest for years.

She came into view first, a brown-haired, brown-eyed girl of sixteen or seventeen—the layers of dirt smearing her face made it hard to guess more than that. The Cofah obviously didn't think their prisoners deserved bathing rights. Her gaze slid past Cas, barely registering her, and focused on the dragon. Her eyes were glassy, vacant.

Duck caught her beneath the armpits and lifted her to the floor. Tolemek jumped, his fingers wrapping around the edge of the pit. He pulled himself up and hugged Cas. He was grimy, too, and smelled strongly of that unpleasant smoke, but she hugged him back, relieved he hadn't gotten himself killed when he had been running—striding boldly—off on his own.

"I'm sorry," Cas said. "Is my father the one who forced you down there?"

"No, at my sister's suggestion—" a strange, almost bewildered expression flashed across his face, "—we hid down there. I didn't know who was coming or what he wanted, but she thought he was extremely dangerous. He certainly was quiet. I wasn't sure he was gone until I heard you talking up here."

"Ah, I was going to be alarmed if he was making a new hobby of stealing men's shirts and stuffing people into holes." She patted his bare chest, wondering how he had lost it. He still had his vest—its various vials and tools prodded her through the leather.

"No, but Cas..." Tolemek stepped back to look her in the eyes. "What's he doing here? Did you know he was out here?"

"I knew someone was out here, at least I suspected it, but no, I didn't know he was the one following us until an hour ago. He warned me not to come in here." As if she would have abandoned her team, her friends. "He wouldn't say who sent him or what—or who—he's after."

"He came in here, but I don't know if he found what he sought. I think he heard you coming and left." Tolemek turned toward his sister—she was staring at the dragon, much as Sardelle was, as if some enthralling theater troupe were performing on the creature's back. Cas could only assume that those with sensitivity to magic felt something she didn't. Oh, she sensed the power emanating from the being—it hung in the air, as tangible as if it curled around them like a thick mist. But she had no trouble looking away and focusing on other matters.

"Tylie?" Tolemek touched her elbow. "This is Cas, that's Duck, and that's Sardelle over there. She's the one who might be able to help you."

Tylie glanced at Sardelle, shook her head, and pointed at the dragon. "He's the one we have to help. You have to find a cure for him. He can't last much longer. If he dies…" She swallowed, her voice thick with emotion. "We can't let him die."

Tolemek spread his hands, giving Cas a quick what-do-I-do look. She had no idea how to help him. Tylie was more cogent than Cas had expected, but she sounded younger than she should have for her age, like a child with a simplistic view of the world.

"I doubt that's within our power to stop, Tylie," he said gently.

"Duck?" Zirkander called softly. "Want to help me over here? We're going to have a fight on our hands soon. It sounds like they're gathering all of their forces."

"Maybe we could find a back door out of here." Duck waved toward the dragon's chamber. "Or if you still have the rope, maybe we could climb back the way we came. Assuming the dragon won't eat us if we go out there."

"We're not done here yet," Zirkander said. "We should probably destroy the lab—the rest of the way—and then we have to make sure the Cofah can't get any more blood." He frowned thoughtfully at the dragon. "Though I suppose if he's dying anyway, that solves that problem for us."

Tylie hadn't been paying much attention to the conversation, but these words made her whip around and stare at him. "We're *not* going to let him die. Tolemek won't. He's a great scientist. He can find a cure." She looked around her, eyes growing wide as she seemed to see Cas, Duck, and Sardelle for the first time. She shrank back toward Tolemek. "You're Iskandians. Tolemek, they're…"

"Friends," he said firmly. "I'll explain it all later, but I've found sanctuary in Iskandia. I'm working there. They gave me a lab of my own. And I have…" He stretched a hand toward Cas, but didn't finish the sentence.

She wished she had given him a less nebulous answer back in the pirate town, let him know that he *did* have her. He hadn't lowered his hand, so she clasped it and nodded.

Tylie frowned doubtfully at that handclasp, but she didn't comment again on the company. She gripped Tolemek's arm.

"You can save him. I know you can. You're so much smarter than any of the scientists here that were studying the disease."

Tolemek had been shaking his head, but he paused at her last words. "They were studying it? You didn't say—earlier you didn't seem sure they were actually doing that."

"They said they were," Tylie said, but her words didn't sound confident.

"Actually, it makes sense that they would have been," Sardelle said. "Some of them were dying from it, too, after all. And Tolemek..." She glanced toward Zirkander and lowered her voice. "If the dragon isn't a compelling enough reason for you to see if you can find a cure, Ridge has started showing symptoms of the disease."

"That's supposed to make me want to help?"

Cas frowned at him, and so did Sardelle. Tolemek sighed and lifted an apologetic hand. "Sorry. No, you're right. We've all been exposed at this point, so it *would* be useful to find a cure. Maybe if they've already made some progress..." His face grew bleak as he looked around the lab, taking in the broken equipment strewn all over the floor, as well as the bullet holes lacing the cabinets. "I'm now wishing I hadn't so wantonly shot up the place."

The crack of a pistol made Cas jump. "Sir?" she asked—it had come from the doorway.

"I think that was a scout." Zirkander waved toward the corner of the corridor that led to the lab. "I scared him off, but I'm sure he'll be back."

More rifles fired, and bullets blasted against the glass wall a few feet away from the door where the colonel stood. Tolemek grabbed Tylie and pulled her down behind a desk. Cas ducked, too, but she planned to head for the door to help Zirkander as soon as she was certain a bullet wouldn't fly through the wall and take her in the face along the way. The spray had damaged the glass, sending spider webs of cracks out in all directions.

"Guess I didn't scare him off, after all," Zirkander said. "The glass is thick, but it's not going to hold forever. We better take this into the tunnels, try to back them off so Tee doesn't have to worry about a bullet in the head. Because he's going to find a cure for us, right?"

Cas glanced back in time to see Tolemek's scowl.

"Yes, because curing diseases is so often the work of a half hour."

All Cas could do was wave and hope he could do it, hope that whatever the Cofah had been researching would help him along.

"Wait," he called as Duck and Sardelle headed after her. "I don't mean to sound needy, but if there truly is an assassin skulking about, it would be nice if someone watched my back while I worked. It's hard to concentrate when you're expecting a bullet between your shoulder blades at any moment."

Cas paused. He was right. For all she knew, *he* was her father's target. Zirkander and the others might need her marksmanship on the front line, but... She looked back at Tolemek. He needed her. Sardelle had the power to keep the Cofah at bay. She could—

"I'll watch him," Zirkander said, surprising her by coming up beside her. "You're more fit than I am right now. I can manage to sit on a desk and point my pistol at any shadows that move, but you'll be more capable of keeping them from advancing. Duck will help you, and Sardelle will be there too." He nodded at Tolemek. "Jaxi said she would help you, Tee."

"Did she? Joy."

Cas shook her head. "Sir, I should stay. It's my fault that my father's here, and I should be the one to protect Tolemek."

"I don't see how it could possibly be your fault that you're related to him and he's here. But I wasn't opening this up for debate." Zirkander jerked a thumb over his shoulder. Another spray of bullets fired, but this time, they bounced away before striking the glass. Sardelle must have raised one of her shields. Did she truly need the help of a couple of riflemen? Maybe she could hold off the Cofah on her own.

"She's not as effective with the dragon's presence muting her awareness," Zirkander said, as if he had guessed her thoughts. "And she said she would be busy watching over Tolemek's shoulder." He touched his temple. "She's the only other person here likely to know how to help with this cure. I need you to protect her. You and Duck."

Cas knew she shouldn't hesitate, but she couldn't help but

feel she was the best person to protect Tolemek and Tylie if her father showed up. She knew him; she'd been *trained* by him. She met Tolemek's eyes, silently asking what *he* wanted. But he was no help. He gazed back at her for a moment, then walked over to a desk full of books and handwritten journals. He put his back to her and dug into the notes.

"Lieutenant," Zirkander said. "I'm not making a request."

"Yes, sir." Cas glanced once more at Tolemek's turned back, then headed for the door.

* * *

While Tylie watched from the corner, Tolemek flipped through the logs, scanning the entries as quickly as he could, hoping he would find what he needed in the mess. And hoping that what he needed was actually there. The Cofah might not have spent any time looking for a cure, instead accepting the losses of their troops as a necessity in order to obtain the blood.

That observation made him pause and look up, his thoughts focused inward. The blood. If the dragon was contagious with this virus, didn't that imply that handling his blood wouldn't be safe, either? The Cofah scientists wouldn't have dared ship it out to different parts of the empire if it was possible they would start an epidemic. Even if they hadn't been working on a cure, they would have had to find some way to filter the blood, extricate the virus from amid the cells. That alone should give him a starting place. *If* he could find the information.

"That where you're going to work?" Zirkander pointed to the desk, then climbed onto a table between two cabinets, putting his back to the wall. It was a spot where he could see over the furnishings in the lab, but where he was protected from most sides.

"Yeah. You actually going to watch my back?" Tolemek would rather have had Cas, but he hadn't wanted to put her in the position of having to choose between him and her commander. Mostly because he was afraid the equation wouldn't come out in his favor. Zirkander should want to make sure Tolemek survived, so that he could find a cure, but the way he had ordered Cas away had struck him as odd. "I wasn't sure I believed your reasoning with Cas."

Zirkander frowned down at him. "I didn't want her to be in a situation where she would have to shoot her own *father*. That was my reasoning."

"Oh." Tolemek's cheeks heated. Chagrined that he hadn't thought of that himself, he struggled to focus on the words in the logbooks. He kept wanting to think of Zirkander as a villain, because he had always been one of the Cofah military's arch enemies when Tolemek had been a soldier. It was disappointing that the man refused to live up to expectations of nefariousness.

Zirkander sat now, his pistol resting in his lap, watching all of the doors to the lab. Sweat beaded on his forehead, and dark semicircles had formed under his eyes, but he didn't look like he would let the virus keep him from his duty. "I, on the other hand," he said, "wouldn't be all that upset over shooting the man."

"Cas hasn't talked much about him with me." Tolemek couldn't quite bring himself to ask if she had revealed more family details to Zirkander.

He wasn't finding much in the logs, which seemed more dedicated to reporting the check-ins of people on duty than scientific findings. He drummed his fingers on the desk and looked around the lab.

"I assume he cares about her, but it's not all that apparent. He doesn't talk to her. I don't know why parents are mystified when they raise a kid to be competent and independent, and then the kid ends up choosing her own career." He was speaking loudly, perhaps to be heard over the gunshots down the corridor, or perhaps because he hoped Cas's father would hear him.

"If he hears you, he might shoot you instead of me."

"That would be better than turning into a crazy man who attacks his friends before dying," Zirkander muttered so softly Tolemek almost didn't hear it. "I haven't had the opportunity to try parenting yet. I suppose it's easier to judge from the outside. Those competent, independent women aren't all that easy to handle." He smiled faintly.

"You seem to be doing all right." Tolemek tried not to sound bitter. He loved Cas and appreciated all of their similarities, right down to the distant father figure who couldn't quite understand his children. But he kept struggling to accept that Cas didn't seem to feel as strongly about their relationship, or at least wasn't ready to admit to as strong of an emotion as love. And then there was Zirkander and Sardelle, always sharing smiles and leaning against each other, flirting with each other. They hadn't known each other much longer than Tolemek had known Cas, but they seemed much more comfortable with each other. Much more... in love.

"Oh?" Zirkander used his sleeve to wipe sweat from his brow, then took a deep swig from his canteen. "Glad to know it comes across that way."

"You don't think it's going well?" Tolemek poked into the drawers of other desks and picked up notes left on tables, searching for something more useful than the logbooks.

"It's going well." Zirkander put his canteen away, gave Tolemek a thoughtful look, then added, "But it's a little hard to be with a woman who doesn't need protecting, and is in fact far better at protecting people than you are. Far better at everything, really. I'm not complaining, mind you, and I wouldn't change anything about her. I'm just admitting that my ego has been a little battered of late, and that I'm struggling to feel needed around her."

"She is the one with the bigger sword."

Zirkander snorted. "Yes. And that's a good thing, that she's here to protect us, and that, for some reason, she's fond of me. The fact that sword size enters my mind and matters to me at all, it's a failing, I suppose."

"I like hearing about your failings."

The faint smile returned. "I thought you might."

Tolemek didn't look back at Zirkander, but he wondered if the man knew of the argument he and Cas had engaged in. Or maybe he could simply tell that Tolemek had a problem with her divided loyalties, something he had already acknowledged as a failing in himself. Still, it did make him feel better to know that Zirkander and Sardelle might not have quite the perfect relationship that he had witnessed from the outside.

"He's falling deeper into unconsciousness," Tylie said softly from her corner, a mournful note in her voice. "I think when he roused himself earlier, it stole the last of his reserves."

"Understood." Tolemek forced himself back to the task. He could ponder his love life later. If he could only find something useful in this mess.

Remembering the vials of blood he had seen by the centrifuge earlier, Tolemek jogged to that corner, checking on Tylie on his way past. She was watching him, her eyes large and hopeful, and he tried not to feel her expectations weighing on him like the yoke of a cart too heavy to pull. Since the dragon had fallen unconscious again, she had been less coherent, less able to grasp the situation around her. What would happen to her if that dragon died?

Tolemek stopped in front of the centrifuge. There had been a binder over here, hadn't there? Yes, there it was. He grabbed it and a vial, but paused, his hand hanging over the rack. There had been six or eight vials there before. There were only two now.

"I think I know part of our sniper's mission." Tolemek waved at the rack.

"He took some?"

"Yes, but not all of them. Four or six vials maybe. I only saw this rack from the other side of the room before."

"Hm. We already sent back samples for the king," Zirkander said. "But it's possible—no, probable—that he was sent out before Kaika and Apex returned. So he could conceivably be working for the crown. But he could be working for someone else, too, some high bidder who heard about the dragon blood somehow. It was top secret, but that doesn't mean information doesn't slip out."

The binder absorbed Tolemek's attention, and he forgot to respond. It held the information he had been hoping to find, a long list of tests, along with notes about filtering the blood. And how they had failed to filter the blood. He snorted. He could have guessed that. If the virus was too small to see under a microscope, it was much smaller than a cell. Unless something larger could attract and bind the smaller proteins somehow.

He rubbed his face. As much as he appreciated his sister's faith in him, this wasn't his specialty. It sounded like the scientists had already tried means of filtering and had abandoned the strategy. Tolemek flipped the pages, hoping to get past the failed tests and to a spot where the researchers had found success.

Halfway in, the tactics switched to attempts to kill the virus without killing the blood cells. "Ah, now we've got something," he muttered, pacing back toward the desk.

"A cure that doesn't involve cutting into people's skulls?" Zirkander asked.

"Uh, a cure that's not going to help you at all."

"That's not heartening."

"Can it help the dragon?" Tylie asked, leaving her corner to stand beside Tolemek.

"Maybe. If I can find a way to deliver a sun's worth of radiation to the dragon without frying everyone else in the ziggurat." Tolemek peered around the laboratory, searching for inspiration. What had worked in vitro wouldn't necessarily work in a dragon.

"Care to explain?" Zirkander asked.

"It's fairly simple. After trying countless ways to filter the blood or kill the virus without killing the cells, someone sterilized a vial on a whim. Maybe the scientist had noted the resilience, or pure magical power, you might call it, of the dragon's blood. Sterilization would kill human blood cells, the same as it killed the virus, but the dragon cells survived. All they've been doing is irradiating the blood, then crating it up and shipping it out."

"So you can help the dragon, but you can't help any of the people that have been afflicted with this already?" Zirkander didn't tear up and mention the state this left him in, but it had to be on his mind.

"You can help the dragon?" Tylie repeated, clasping her hands in front of her. She either did not realize that Zirkander was sick or could not grasp the ramifications of it in her current state.

Tolemek wanted to heal the dragon if only so he could release

Tylie from whatever bond he had formed with her, and so those glimpses of sanity he had received down in that tomb would return permanently.

"I have to figure out—" he scratched his stubbled jaw and stared through the cracked glass at the dragon, "—how in all the cursed realms am I going to irradiate an entire dragon?"

"How does one irradiate something small?" Zirkander asked. "As you'll recall, I was folding paper fliers in my science classes, so you'll have to explain it in little words."

Tolemek snorted. "Exposing something to energy that's capable of stripping electrons from atoms. This destroys or slows down bacteria, microorganisms, and viruses, or at least renders them incapable of reproduction. You can deliver the radiation with a radioactive substance or generate it electrically."

"I'm not sure those words were little enough." Zirkander raised his eyebrows at Tylie, as if to ask if she understood.

She leaned against Tolemek's arm. "My brother is smart."

"No, I just read books." He hugged Tylie, but then returned to his walk around the lab, hunting for whatever equipment they had used. "They may have just done it with heat, honestly. Thermal radiation."

"Heat?" Zirkander asked. "You know Jaxi melted a hole in that twenty-foot wall up there earlier, right?"

Tolemek paused. Was it possible the sword could emit enough heat to kill the virus in the blood? Or maybe all they would need was ultraviolet light? He thought he remembered reading about short wavelength light being used in Iskandia to sterilize drinking water down in some mines. He didn't think it would be enough to simply strike the exterior of the dragon with intense ultraviolet though. They would have to find a way to remove the blood, irradiate it, and return it to the dragon. Probably. Maybe. He wished he knew more, that more science of this nature had successfully been done in the world. As resilient as a dragon might be, this one was nearly dead. He might kill it if he experimented. And where would that leave them then?

Tylie was watching him pace, her eyes full of faith.

He swallowed. Even if he could cure the dragon, where would

that leave Zirkander and anyone else infected?

Healing the dragon might make him feel favorably toward you, came Jaxi's thoughts in his head. *He might be able to then help with healing the humans.*

Tolemek would never admit it later, but hearing Jaxi's voice in his head reassured him, reminding him that he didn't necessarily have to do this with pure science and technology. Sardelle and the soulblade could bring other powers to bear. Still...

If he had the power to kill the virus infesting its body, wouldn't he have done that three thousand years ago? Tolemek asked.

Not if he didn't know how. I've been listening to you babble on about atoms and radiation and whatever else, so I could relay the information to Sardelle, and I haven't the slightest idea what you're talking about. She seems to get it, even if she doesn't know the terms you're using, but I doubt a healer three thousand years ago would have had even the faintest grasp.

Would you be able to create ultraviolet light?

Of course. What is it?

Tolemek snorted, then tried to form an image in his mind, a table of the light spectrum produced by the sun. Maybe using a picture would be more helpful than a bunch of words that hadn't existed when Jaxi had walked the world.

Yes, thoughtful. Thank you. Let me think about it for a moment. We've got more trouble out here.

Gunshots fired in the distance, followed by a far greater rumble, then a crash. Tolemek stared toward the corridor, afraid that had been a rockfall or some other devastating explosion. Cas, Duck, and Sardelle had gone that direction to keep the Cofah from returning to the lab. He wished he could see what was happening. He would have to trust that Jaxi would have warned him if anyone had been hurt.

Zirkander stood up, his head nearly brushing the ceiling. He squinted toward the dragon, then climbed off the table and walked toward the shattered wall.

"See something?" Tolemek asked.

"The light level in there seemed to change. Maybe it was my imagination."

Tolemek had been looking in the other direction and hadn't noticed a change, but he walked over with Zirkander. He didn't know if there was much more that he could do without Jaxi's help.

The dragon hadn't moved. The floor and walls hadn't changed, and the panel was emitting the same steady glow it always had, its light responsible for much of the lab's illumination, as well as the chamber's. Zirkander leaned close to the glass, almost pressing his chin against it as he looked up.

"Hm."

"Hm?" Tolemek leaned close, too, though he didn't know what they were looking at. He didn't see anyone crouching in the passage he had used earlier or in the big one that Jaxi had burned in the wall.

"I think the barrier's gone," Zirkander said.

Tolemek stared upward, trying to tell. "It might just look different from below. Did you look before?"

Zirkander picked up a shard of glass from the floor and walked toward the door.

"Are you sure you want to go out there?" Tolemek glanced at the dragon, thinking of the way its cold, reptilian stare had been leveled at him.

Zirkander didn't answer. He pushed open the door, walked out a couple of feet, and tossed the piece of glass upward. Instead of being incinerated, the shard simply fell back to the stone floor with a soft tink a couple of meters from the dragon. His eye flicked beneath the lid, but he didn't otherwise move. His breathing seemed labored, and Tolemek didn't know how much longer he had to come up with something. He could feel his sister watching him.

On his way back inside, Zirkander jerked to a halt so quickly that Tolemek reached for his pistol. He glanced around the lab and readied for an attack. But Zirkander wasn't looking through the glass—he was staring at the panel next to the door, the one that presumably controlled the stasis chamber and the protective barrier. He pulled something out of the side, something that hadn't been visible from Tolemek's position in the lab. A dagger.

Zirkander stuck it through his belt, held up a finger, then walked along the outside of the chamber. Following the wall, he turned a corner and disappeared behind the dragon.

"What happened?" Tylie whispered, her eyes toward the open air where the barrier had been.

"I don't know," Tolemek said. It was the truth, but he had a guess. He had been worried that he—or maybe Tylie—would be the assassin's target. But maybe it was the dragon.

Zirkander came into view again, shaking his head as he returned to the door. He paused to look up for a long moment before entering.

"No sign of him?" Tolemek guessed.

"No." Zirkander leaned against the wall, closing his eyes. "I was watching the lab, but he must have come through without me noticing. Either that, or he came down from above and went back that same way. There aren't any other ways out of this chamber." He sighed, his shoulders sagging. He looked like a man who hadn't slept in days. "It didn't occur to me... I don't know why it didn't occur to me, that he might have been sent to deal with the dragon."

"What?" Tylie spun toward him, her long hair whipping about her face.

Zirkander opened his eyes and spread his hand. "I'll watch from here." He pushed the door open so he could stand in the middle. He gave Tolemek a tired, wry smile. "Maybe I should have had Ahn stay in here, after all."

A boom sounded from somewhere down the corridor that held the others.

"No," Tolemek said. "You made the right decision. I need you to call Sardelle back, if you can." He eyed the dragon again. "We're going to need Jaxi."

CHAPTER 14

CAS CROUCHED, USING THE CORNER for cover. An invisible magical barrier stretched across the corridor, shimmering yellow every time a bullet was deflected, so she probably wouldn't have needed to bother, but standing out in the open went against her instincts. Duck knelt behind her, looking over a crude map he had found in one of the dead soldier's pockets.

"I wish they would leave," Sardelle said from the center of the corridor. Apparently, her instincts trusted her magic, because she didn't feel the need to hide behind the wall.

Sweat gleamed on her forehead. Cas didn't know if it was an early symptom of the illness or a sign that the work taxed her. She hadn't yet drawn her sword.

"I don't wish to kill them for doing their duty," Sardelle added softly.

Cas had fewer qualms about that and almost said so, but she doubted that was something she should be proud of. At times, it bothered her how much of her father there was in her. "The colonel just said to keep them out of the lab, right?"

"Yes, but there would be more time for research and for attempting to communicate with the dragon if the Cofah were not here." Sardelle sighed. "I can't stand here, doing this indefinitely."

"We'll take shifts if it comes to that. My bullets aren't as flashy, but they're good at convincing people to leave me alone." Cas shifted her weight. Her thighs were starting to burn. "Duck, anything enlightening in that map? There's no way they can get around us, is there?" Earlier, the soldiers had tried to attack en masse, sending a barrage of rifle fire at Sardelle's barrier. There was even a cannon squatting in the corridor up there. But the firing had been less frequent during the last fifteen minutes, and

Cas had glimpsed the same two men leaning out from behind cover and taking shots.

"Looks like we're guarding the only route to the lab," Duck said. "Those storage tunnels dead end."

"Nothing above us or below us?" Cas thought of the volcano lab, where defenders had attempted to crawl through ducts above the ceilings to attack them.

"Unfortunately, this map is only of the ground floor here. Guess there aren't any crow-like cartographers in this crew that could figure out how to display different levels."

Cas raised her brows. "Crow-like?"

"Sure, crows are smart."

"Smart enough to make maps?"

"Nah, they don't need maps. Got it all in their heads."

"There aren't ducts," Sardelle said, nodding toward Cas. She must be remembering the other lab too. "But I do sense that there are other tunnels around here, above and below us. Most dead end and are filled with sarcophagi, but it's possible they could get fairly close to us. Still, these blocks are all ridiculously large. And dense. Without Jaxi to burn holes, it's hard to imagine how they could reach us or slip behind us to reach the lab."

"But they're up to something, aren't they?" Cas asked. "There are only a couple down there, where there were several before. Maybe we should push through to deal with them. Before they have time to use their crow wiles."

Duck snorted. "I told you, they're not as smart as crows. Maybe robins."

"I'm reluctant to go far from the lab," Sardelle said. "In case there *is* another way around. I—"

One of the Cofah fired at the barrier again, and Cas thought that might be why Sardelle had paused, but after a moment she said, "Tolemek needs Jaxi. He has an idea."

"About curing people?" Duck asked.

"About curing the dragon." Her lips thinned. "We're hoping one will lead to the other. Somehow."

"Sardelle," Duck said, "you *have* to help him come up with a fix for the colonel. He can't die out here. Not like this."

The haunted expression in Sardelle's eyes said that such thoughts hadn't been far from her mind. "I will."

"Wait," Cas said. Given the somber topic, she felt awkward speaking up, but they had to think of survival and of dealing with the enemy. "Can you do something to those men before you go?" Cas waved to the intersection past the barrier, where the two soldiers were keeping themselves out of sight except when they leaned out to fire. "Knock them out, maybe?"

"It's difficult to force people to fall asleep when they're in a highly alert state," Sardelle said.

"Can you try? Now that there are only a couple left, maybe it will be easier? I want to go find out where the rest of them went, and it will be easier if I can get past those two."

"Go find out?" Duck frowned at her. "By yourself?"

"I'm sneakier alone." She might not have her father's gift of stealth, but she had more skill at it than the average pilot. "Besides, someone needs to stay and guard the lab entrance."

"That's *both* of our jobs."

"It's our job to keep the Cofah off Tolemek's back while he works on a cure. That's what I plan to do."

"But—"

"What if some squad blows the walls open in the lab and charges in, shooting at everyone? Give me your map, please."

He scowled at her. Cas expected an argument from Sardelle, as well, but she had her eyes closed. When she opened them, she said, "They're unconscious, for the moment. I trust they won't be killed while they're sleeping."

"I can find some rope to tie them," Cas said.

Sardelle inclined her head, then walked toward the lab.

"Stay here, Duck." Cas plucked the map from his fingers—he didn't try to keep her from taking it, but he didn't relinquish it easily, either. "Don't let anyone in. I won't be gone long."

He scowled at her but didn't object.

Cas trotted to the intersection. It was empty except for the two soldiers slumped on either side of the corridor. Since she had left her pack outside, she didn't have any rope with her, but she carved up their clothing and used the fabric for the task. She would have preferred to lock them away somewhere, but aside from the two lab entrances, the ziggurat was short on doors and locks. She studied the map briefly and decided an opening to her right was most likely to parallel the corridor Duck was guarding.

Soft footsteps sounded in the corridor behind her. Assuming it was Duck again, she turned, intending to remind him that she outranked him, if only by a month.

"Going exploring?" Zirkander asked. Duck was peeking around the corner behind him.

Cas grimaced. She shouldn't have mentioned her plan to Sardelle. She must have told Zirkander right away.

"There were eight or ten men here a few minutes ago," Cas said. "If they're gone, I'm assuming they left to plot something. I'd like to look for them." She watched the side passages as she spoke, aware that they were in the open, vulnerable to anyone who walked out of a doorway.

Zirkander must have been thinking the same thing, because he stepped back and waved for her to do the same. Cas slumped. He wasn't going to let her go. Didn't he see the folly in sitting there, waiting and reacting instead of going on the offensive? If they were in the air, he would never succumb to such a strategy.

"You're not going hunting for your father, are you?" he asked.

"What? No. I mean, if I see him, I can try to stop him, but…" She hated to admit it, but she finished with, "I'm not sure that's within my power." She searched his face, trying to guess what had prompted the question. His eyes were bloodshot and glassy, and she couldn't read anything beyond that he was tired. And sick. "Did you see him, sir?"

"He was in the lab. He destroyed the device keeping the barrier over the dragon, but he was gone before I spotted him."

"That's how his interactions with people usually go." The dragon. Was that what her father was here for? It made sense, now that she thought about it. If Tolemek or even Sardelle had been his target, he could have waited until they returned to the city to strike. That didn't necessarily mean they were safe, but she would be less distressed if he killed the dragon than one of her friends.

"Go," Zirkander said. "If you find them and need help, come back and get us. I'll be with Duck. Jaxi is about to possibly blind everyone in the lab, so it seemed a good time to leave." He smiled weakly.

Cas didn't understand the joke, but she nodded, glad he trusted in her abilities enough to let her go. She hoped to live up to that trust. She also hoped Zirkander would still be alive when she got back. He looked like a half-drowned rat with his damp hair clinging limply to his head.

"Thank you, sir." She thought about giving him a hug, but lieutenants didn't hug colonels, even dying ones. She nodded again, then jogged down her chosen route.

Before turning the corner, she glanced back. Zirkander was dragging one of the unconscious men back up the corridor. Yes, good idea to lock them up in the lab instead of leaving them out to be found or wake up and free themselves.

The passage Cas entered wasn't lit. She didn't know if that made it more likely or less that the men had gone in this direction. Her father could have navigated it without light, but she removed a lamp from one of the sconces and lit it before starting down the passage. She left the glass open, so she could blow it out quickly if needed.

Cas passed several alcoves holding sarcophagi, but she only glanced inside them long enough to ensure nobody was crouching behind them. During one of these checks, she spotted a dark smudge on the floor. She touched her finger to it and held it up to the lamp. It wasn't a smudge; it was gunpowder. Had the soldiers come this way carrying explosives?

She told herself not to assume anything, that it might have been dropped during any of the months that the Cofah had occupied the ziggurat, but it was dry when she rubbed it between her fingers. In this humid climate, that wouldn't have been the case if it had been lying there for long.

She crept forward, searching for more signs that men had come this way recently. Cobwebs stretched across the upper corners of the tunnel, but those that might have dangled lower had broken off. She quickened her step, hoping she had time. If men had come this way with explosives, they could have only one thing in mind. If they blew their way into the lab, who knew what damage it might do? Hurl heavy furniture onto people? Cause volatile chemicals to explode? Either way, Tolemek and Sardelle would be in trouble, especially if they were preoccupied with the dragon.

The light bounced off a wall ahead of Cas. A dead end. She stared at it, disappointment filling her. Maybe the gunpowder hadn't meant anything, after all. Maybe they had been storing kegs down here and had simply knocked some of the powder out when they had moved them. Except she didn't see any sign that this corridor had been used for storage. She patted the stone wall. Maybe those ancient architects had built in trapdoors. But after a minute of groping around and finding nothing, she sighed, defeated. She would have to go back and check other nearby tunnels.

"You sure this is the spot?" a distant voice asked.

Cas froze. It hadn't come from her tunnel. It sounded like it had come straight out of one of the walls.

"I'm sure. Now climb."

Cas touched the wall, resisting the urge to knock on it to see if it was hollow. If she could hear those speakers, they would also hear any noise she made. Instead, she slid her fingers along the wall, again searching for hidden doors. She reached the first alcove without finding anything. A single sarcophagus rested in the center of it, positioned parallel to the tunnel. The carved stone box rose higher than her waist, with less than a foot of air between it and the low ceiling. There wasn't much room on either side, but she squeezed around one end to look behind it. She almost snorted. A dark, square opening awaited her, with more spilled gunpowder dusting the floor in front of it.

She poked her lamp into the opening, identified another tunnel, albeit a much lower one, and crept into it. She listened intently, wondering if she should cut off the lamp. The last thing she wanted to do was alert the soldiers to her presence. On the other hand, the idea of crawling through the tight passage in pitch blackness made her uneasy too. It shouldn't, but who knew what ancient booby traps might be waiting for her? Or what spiders and scorpions.

Cas grunted silently at herself. Some brave sniper she was.

"Where should I set the charge?"

Though it was soft, she clearly heard the voice. It couldn't be far away, but sounded like it came from a higher elevation. Rustling noises drifted to her, too, along with the grinding of boots on sand. How many men were up there? Two to set the explosives, but then more to rush through after the bomb went off?

Her light glinted off something metal up ahead. A ladder.

They weren't going to blow their way into the side of the lab. They were going to bring down the ceiling. Her stomach tightened with anxiety. She had to hurry. But she had to be careful. She *had* to have the advantage of surprise. Even then, in these close quarters, she wouldn't be able to get many shots off before they saw her and fired back.

Cas blew out the lamp and set it by the base of the ladder. Blackness swallowed her. She couldn't see any light coming down from above, so she hoped she was as close to the men as she thought. What if passages wound around back here, and it took a long time to reach them?

"Here? All right, that should do it."

"Ssh. They're right below, boar licker. Let's not alert them, eh?"

Cas slung her rifle across her back and climbed up the rungs. In the dark, she had to feel her way up, and she kept patting above her, expecting the ladder to end. She rose higher than she expected and would have kept climbing, except the voices sounded again.

"Back everyone up. We want to go through *after* we blow a hole, not *as* we blow it."

She gaped. The voice had come from below. She must have missed a passage leading away from the ladder shaft. Hoping she wasn't making a mistake, that she had to go up and over something and then down, she retraced her steps. A hint of light came from somewhere, lessening the depths of the darkness around her. There. She *had* missed a hole in the wall. She felt around the edge with her hand. It was ragged, with the stone cut away recently. She could climb through it, but the soldiers must have struggled.

The silhouettes of men came into view as soon as she poked her head through. They weren't straight in front of her, but hunkered off to the side. Here and there, pipes and ducts rose up from the floor, and a soft hum reverberated through her boots. It took her a moment to realize they were on top of the lab. This space must have been made so people could install and maintain those fans and deliver a water supply to the scientists.

Cas crept forward and hid behind a vertical duct pipe. She counted eight men up ahead, two off to the side and six others waiting and watching them. Some of their backs were to her, but some would see her out of the corners of their eyes if she moved much. The darkness should hide her now, especially since they were all looking at the flame of a lamp—a lamp about to light a fuse to a pile of explosives. She gulped as one of the men shifted, and the kegs came into view. If those were full of gunpowder, they would not only blow a hole, but they might cause the entire ceiling to collapse. And the stone above, as well. Even though this structure must have been built sturdily to last for centuries out in this jungle, Cas couldn't imagine the original architects had been thinking it would have to withstand explosives.

As the enormity of the situation came to her, the unlikeliness that she would survive eight-to-one odds, Tolemek's face appeared in her thoughts, his dark eyes full of concern as he gazed down at her. She wished she had given him a kiss before walking out of the lab. More than that, she wished she had told him good-bye, just in case something happened. Or maybe she should have told him… that she loved him. If she didn't, would she worry so much every time he was out of her sight? Would she wonder what he would think before she did something reckless? Would thinking of never seeing him again—and of him never knowing what had happened to her—bring tears to her eyes?

Cas blinked those tears away before they could fully form. There was no time for regrets now. She had to stop these men.

She slid her rifle off her back, preferring its accuracy to that of her pistol. The problem was taking care of all of those men before they returned fire. Even in the dark, she could tell they were well armed. Rifles and pistols protruded from their silhouettes.

If she were in her flier, she would have a machine gun with incendiary bullets. She might blow up the kegs before they were ready and take a number of them out in the blast. Except that would still bring down the ceiling, most likely. Cas slid her hand along her duct, wondering if it was thick enough to protect her if they shot at her. No, the metal felt thin. A bullet would rip right through it.

"Ready."

"Light it."

Cas cursed to herself. She wasn't ready, damn it. A plan, she wanted time to come up with a smart plan. But all she could do was rely on instincts—and hope they were good enough.

Her last thought, as she squeezed the trigger, was that the others should at least hear the gunfire and have time to get out of the way down there.

She shot the man lowering the match to the fuse and was firing at the second before anyone reacted. But once they understood what was happening, they spun toward her as one. Cas rolled away from the duct, stopped on her stomach, and shot twice more. Bullets were already flying in her direction, slamming into stone and tearing through that flimsy ductwork. She rolled again, hoping they couldn't see her in the shadows, not the way she could see them. Not that it mattered. A wild shot blasted into the darkness could kill her as easily as a well-aimed one fired at her heart.

Something slammed into the back of her head. A piece of stone? She wasn't sure. She scrambled to a stop behind a pipe, doing her best to stay silent, so they wouldn't get a bead on her, and took a second this time to make sure of her aim. Three forms were either unmoving or rolling and gasping on the ground. That meant she had missed once. She couldn't afford to miss. The Cofah were on the move now, the same as she was, and they had rolled out of the light's influence. Even as she was taking aim at a flash of orange from someone's firearm, one of the other men shot out the lamp. Cas fired, then rolled away again.

A bullet slammed into the pipe she had left. Water sprayed everywhere, spattering her cheek and back. She hoped the sound would dull any noise she might make. With the light out, utter darkness had descended. Smoke clogged the air and tickled her nostrils. She would *not* sneeze.

More rounds pounded the wall behind her and skipped off the stone all around her. They knew she was on the ground, and they were aiming low. The next pipe she bumped into, she climbed. It wobbled precariously, but supported her weight. They were still firing, four men, she guessed. She found her way to the ceiling and groped about, hoping for a support beam. There wasn't one. She would have to fire from the top of the pipe. It wouldn't be the first time she had shot one-handed. But she needed a target. Unlike the Cofah, she didn't have ammo to waste. She had two more shots before she had to reload.

She listened, trying to pick out heavy breathing or whispered words. The soldiers had stopped shooting. She hadn't fired for a moment. Maybe they thought they had hit her.

The soft clanks of someone loading rounds drifted across the room. She leaned away from the pipe, listening and aiming. Right about… there. She shot, and a cry of pain erupted.

"Shit, how many of them are there?" someone demanded, breaking the silence. "I thought I got one."

"Get out of here. Too many."

More rounds fired, but she could hear the thuds of the men running for the exit. They hadn't figured out she had climbed up yet, and their shots hit the ground beneath her. So much smoke filled the air that she wouldn't have been able to see even if there had been light. She could only use her ears to aim, this time shooting toward the footfalls—the men seemed to be running together as they shot. Her rifle was out of ammo, so she gripped the strap in her teeth and pulled out her pistol.

She thought about letting them go—she had stopped their plan, so did she need to cut them all down? But Duck and

Zirkander were below. As capable as they were, Zirkander wasn't at his best, and she would hate herself for the rest of her life if an enemy soldier she let go ended up killing one of her comrades.

If the men hadn't blown out their lamp, they might have made it out, but in the dark, they couldn't see the exit any more clearly than she. Someone ran into that duct and grunted. Cas took advantage and fired, having a sense of exactly where that was, despite her numerous rolls and dodges since then. The man shouted in pain and rage.

"He's up high!" the wounded soldier roared.

Cas promptly dropped to a crouch, catching her rifle as she fell so it wouldn't clang against anything. She fired three more times with the pistol, aiming at the sounds of people groping around, trying to find the exit. The bullets thudded into flesh instead of clanging off stone. Doubting they had all been mortal wounds, she followed the wall toward the kegs, or where she thought they were. She stretched her hand out in front of her, wanting to use them to duck behind so she could reload. But nobody else was firing. She crouched behind the kegs and listened, trying to still her own breathing to ensure she wasn't making noise. The sound of someone escaping down the ladder reached her, but from the labored and uneven way he thumped down the rungs, he must be injured. He shouldn't be in the mood to go after her team. But the others? In the dark, she couldn't tell if someone might be feigning death, waiting for her to reveal her position so he could shoot.

A soft clunk came from the opposite corner, and a startlingly bright beam of light streamed up from below. Cas squinted, raising a hand.

Sardelle's head poked up. She wobbled, as if she was standing on something shaky—or someone's shoulders more likely. The ceilings down there weren't low.

"Cas?" she asked.

Cas hesitated to respond, still not certain there weren't soldiers capable of firing back. But she didn't want Sardelle to be a target, either, and with the light streaming up around her, she was easier to see than a sun. Cas stepped out from behind the kegs.

At the same second, someone fired from the ground near the ladder. Cas shot, even though she knew it was too late. With the light seeping up from below, she easily hit the soldier, but that wouldn't matter if—

She looked back and found Sardelle gazing blandly in her direction.

"Oh. I forgot. Your magical shields." Cas slumped against the kegs.

"Yes," Sardelle said. "That's why they volunteered me to come up first."

"And because you didn't want me standing on your shoulders," came Tolemek's voice from below.

Cas mopped sweat from her face, relieved to hear him. From Sardelle's calm tone, Cas assumed nobody else had been injured while she had been gone.

"I would have come up earlier, except nobody knew there was a panel here. We were debating on how to saw our way through the ceiling to come help, but, ah..." Sardelle's head turned slowly as she took in the entire area—or maybe all the bodies slumped in the entire area. "It seems you didn't need help."

Cas didn't say anything. Sometimes, she was proud of her skills, but it never seemed like she should be when death was the result. Weary and battered, she shambled toward Sardelle. She paused at the opening. "Maybe we shouldn't leave the gunpowder here."

"I can render it ineffective," Sardelle said.

"What's going on down there?" Cas wondered about the intensity of the light. Candles and lamps couldn't account for that kind of brightness. "We might need it for something."

"Roll it over," Tolemek called up from below. "Zirkander would be upset if he didn't get a chance to blow something up before leaving."

Cas snorted. "You're thinking of Captain Kaika."

"They have similar mentalities. Now, get yourself down here so we can make sure you're not injured, please."

Cas pushed the kegs over to Sardelle, who floated them down to a floor that was awash in light. Cas squirmed through the hole and dropped down, her legs trembling as the enormity of that battle and how close she had come to being shot washed over her. Before she could decide if she wanted to collapse somewhere or try and maintain her stoic soldier's facade for the rest of the night, Tolemek engulfed her in a hug.

"If Zirkander sent you up there alone to deal with those men, I'm going to kill him," he growled into her ear. "Seven gods, are you all right?"

"Fine," she murmured.

He brushed his fingers through her hair, and shrapnel fell out. "Fine?"

"Mostly. Anyway, it was my idea, not the colonel's. I thought you might not like having your ceiling blown in."

He gripped her shoulders, naked concern in his eyes as he looked her up and down, searching for injuries. Seeing that concern brought her thoughts from before the battle rushing into her mind, the words that she had lamented leaving unspoken. She opened her mouth, thinking to share them now, but he spoke again first.

"Does he *know* you went?" Tolemek demanded.

Maybe this wasn't the right time for proclamations of love. Not when he was busy being irritated by someone else. She wanted to quell his irritation—and to bring his focus to her. She stood on her tiptoes, placed her hands on either side of his cheeks, and kissed him.

He blinked, and some of the ferocity bled out of him. He returned the kiss, his grip on her shoulders shifting and growing more gentle as he wrapped his arms around her. One hand came up to stroke the back of her head, and she smiled, her lips against his, when more shrapnel tinkled to the floor. She thought about kneading the tense muscles in his neck and back, but she was still on duty, and they were still in the middle of enemy territory. Reluctantly, she broke the kiss.

"That's nice, thank you," Tolemek rumbled, his voice softer now, "but this doesn't mean I'm not going to punch Zirkander in the face as soon as he's well enough to take it."

"He would have stopped me, but he was too sickly and weak," Cas said.

"Really," came a dry voice from the doorway. Zirkander shambled in, his shoulders back, looking like he was trying his best *not* to look sickly or weak. "The things you people say about me when I'm not around." He shook his head but met Tolemek's eyes as he passed by and said, "I told you. My ego. It's getting squished down so far, nobody will be able to find it soon."

"Good," Tolemek grunted.

"Hope yours doesn't have that problem. How many soldiers did you single-handedly take down, Cas?"

"Enough that my father would probably be proud." Her lips twisted. She had no wish to make the man proud, not at this point in her life, and not for this.

Zirkander seemed to read between the lines. He gave her a friendly thump on the shoulder as he passed, then walked over to one of the kegs. "No reason why we can't go back out the way we came in, right?" He nodded toward the dragon's chamber.

Cas finally had a chance to stand on a stool to see over the cabinets and cluttered tables and investigate the source of the light. But someone had leaned boards and crates all along the glass wall overlooking the chamber. Powerful beams of light seeped through the cracks, making the lab daylight bright.

"Ridge, are you planning to blow something up?" Sardelle asked with faint disapproval.

"I was thinking of making that corridor disappear so Duck and I can do something more interesting than watching it. Like lying in the corner under that desk over there and taking a nap."

Sardelle strode to him, bumping her hip on a table but scarcely noticing. She blinked away moisture in her eyes as she took his hands. "Ridge, nobody's going to be upset if you sit down and rest."

"*Lie* down and rest," he said, squeezing her hands. "Don't misquote me now."

She leaned against his chest, and he wrapped his arms around her, resting his chin on her head. Cas looked away, giving them their privacy.

Tolemek was gazing down at her, and she clasped his hand. "What's going on in there?"

"Jaxi is attempting to irradiate the dragon."

"Uh. What?"

"The scientists have been removing the virus from the blood samples through radiation. From the logbook I found, it seems dragon cells are hearty enough to withstand everything from chemicals to deadly herbs to heat that would destroy the cells of any other animal, reptile, or bird."

Cas didn't have much knowledge when it came to science and medicine, but what she got out of his words was… "Are you saying you might be able to cure the dragon, but you're not going to be able to cure us?"

"Sardelle believes that if we're able to restore the dragon to health, he might have the power to help us, perhaps direct his energy more precisely than Jaxi can and target just the virus within us."

Cas eyed the light blasting in through the cracks between the boards. "If that could be done, why couldn't other dragons heal this one three thousand years ago?"

"Nobody knew what a virus *was* three thousand years ago," Sardelle said. "Even in my time, we were only just beginning to understand the concept of things that were too small to see being able to affect us. And by *we*, I mean healers. The general population didn't even know that cleanliness helped stop the spread of disease. And for all their power and magical ability, dragons were never known for being great scientists or intellectuals, so it's very likely that they didn't understand how to attack something too small to see. But perhaps with some instruction…" She spread her hand, palm up.

"Let's see if Jaxi is able to help him first," Tolemek said. "Right now, she may be doing nothing more than giving him a sunburn."

He made a face, then rolled his eyes.

"I'm betting Jaxi had a comment for him," Zirkander muttered.

"Something about talking about her behind her back," Tolemek confirmed. "I didn't realize swords had backs."

Cas stuck her hands in her pockets, feeling superfluous in the conversation. "Anything I can do, sir?" she asked. "Help you with that powder?"

Zirkander started to nod, but Sardelle frowned at him. "Are you sure you want to risk structural damage simply to block off that tunnel?" she asked.

"Depends. By structural damage, do you mean blowing those disturbing cannibalistic carvings off the wall, or do you think a small, controlled blast could bring down the ziggurat?"

"I've seen you fly, Ridge. I don't think you know the meaning of the words small or controlled, especially when it comes to explosions. Why don't you come over here and rest?"

"I—"

A massive boom blasted through the lab, and Cas found herself hurled into the air. Someone crashed into her, and all of the light disappeared. Her back slammed into something, and she crumpled to the ground, but it wasn't stable at all. It quaked and bucked underneath her. A cacophony of noise buried her, hammering her ear drums so hard, she wanted to wrap her arms around her head, anything to drive out the sound. But things were falling all around her—she couldn't tell what in the dark. Furniture? People? The ceiling? The roar sounded like a rockfall, and she groped around for something to hide under, even as she doubted it would do any good, not if the entire ziggurat was collapsing.

She'd no more than had that thought when something struck her head. The world was already black, but her mind followed, unconsciousness stealing awareness.

CHAPTER 15

PANIC WELLED IN TOLEMEK'S THROAT as he groped about in the darkness, trying to find Cas, and where was Tylie? She had been in the corner near the dragon's chamber. Had she managed to hide under something? The ground was still shivering, the aftershocks of the earthquake—or whatever that had been—that had been set off by the explosion. Everything in that lab that could have fallen probably already had, but rocks continued to thud and clatter to the ground all around him.

Tylie? he asked with his mind, thinking she might try to reach him that way if she was buried under debris and couldn't call out. *Are you all right?*

Tolemek was about to repeat the question out loud and ask for Cas, too, but a white light came on, distracting him. Faint at first, it grew in intensity. That had to be Sardelle. At least *some*body else had survived.

The light revealed much. Utter carnage had befallen the lab. Not a single piece of furniture remained standing, most of the ceiling panels had fallen, and shards of glass littered everything. He couldn't see anyone amidst the mountains of wreckage.

"Ridge?" Sardelle called plaintively. "Are you… is anyone…?"

"Here," Tolemek croaked, even though he knew he wasn't the one she wanted to hear from. He pushed a ceiling panel off his side and crawled out from a pile of rubble that had nearly buried him. Sweat streamed into his eye, and he wiped it away. Not sweat, blood. It didn't matter though. He wasn't hurt that badly. But he needed to find Cas.

"Blessed gods," Sardelle whispered.

He glanced at her, expecting that she had found Zirkander dead under the rubble, but she was staring across the lab, toward the dragon's chamber. Tolemek almost didn't look—the dragon was the last of his concerns at the moment—but Tylie had been over in that direction. He pushed himself to his feet to see over the piles of debris and gaped at the wreckage.

If he had thought the lab utterly destroyed, the dragon's chamber was another matter altogether. The glass wall had been blown out, and nothing except rock was visible beyond it. A huge pile of rock that rose higher than the ceiling of the lab.

"The whole ziggurat fell," he breathed. The part of the structure over the chamber anyway, the entire top half of the pyramid. There wasn't a sign of the dragon. Or Jaxi. If the soulblade was still emitting light, it wasn't visible through the tons and tons of rock.

"Tylie?" Tolemek called. "Cas?"

"They're under the rubble," Sardelle said. "Give me a minute, and I can be more precise. I—" She winced and touched a hand to the back of her head. Blood streaked one side of her face, too, and dripped from her fingers.

Tolemek had been closer to Cas, so he crawled in that direction first, but he kept trying to call out with his mind to Tylie at the same time. He wished he had asked Sardelle to teach him to speak into people's heads. Or the way she could sense where people were. Why had he shied away from accepting his skills instead of embracing them?

Rubble stirred near the side of the lab where the front wall had once been. This one, too, had shattered, completely collapsing, only piles of glass shards remaining. It bit into Tolemek's hands and knees as he crawled over it, but he didn't care. If that was Cas, she might not be able to breathe. She might be bleeding to death under the debris.

He clawed at the rubble, cursing when glass dug into his palm. Where were those gloves he had used earlier? They had fallen out of his belt. He tore his vest off, wrapped the leather around his hand, and dug through the chunks of wood and glass. He heaved aside a broken tabletop, and a hint of skin came into view.

"Cas! Is that you?"

"What in all the levels of hell happened?" came a squeaky male voice from the corridor beyond the lab. Duck. He stared inside with eyes rounder than gold coins. "Sir? Colonel?"

"Get in here and help move this junk," Tolemek snapped.

Duck glanced at Sardelle, who was also digging into a rubble pile, then scrambled over the mounds of broken glass to join Tolemek. He almost sent him to search for his sister—nobody was looking for her, damn it—but he had uncovered an arm. Cas's arm. This wouldn't take much longer. He would have her out and then... He gulped. She wasn't moving.

"Cas?"

"Is the colonel under here too?" Duck asked as he pulled a beam off her legs.

"I don't know where he is." Tolemek flung a hand toward Sardelle. "She knows."

"I've got him," Sardelle said, flinging heavy objects aside without touching them. Her eyes burned, her plaintive tone from before gone and replaced with one of grim determination. And rage. Whoever had done this was going to be in trouble. "Duck, when you're done there, Tolemek's sister is in that corner. I can guide you to her."

"Is she all right?" Tolemek asked, shoving aside a broken ceiling panel, revealing Cas's face. Her eyes were closed, her short hair matted with blood.

"Better than Ridge," Sardelle said.

Duck touched his fingers to Cas's throat, something Tolemek had not dared do. She was alive. There was no way she couldn't be alive, not somebody who could survive a gunfight with a squad of Cofah soldiers. She couldn't die from this. She couldn't.

His vision blurred, and he had to wipe his eyes before he could see Duck, trying to read the expression on his face as he withdrew his fingers.

"She's alive," he said.

Tolemek nodded, relief stealing the strength from his limbs. If he had been standing, he would have crumpled to the ground. He didn't think he could talk, so he didn't try. After pushing away the rest of the debris burying her, he slid his arms under Cas's shoulders and hips. He found the energy to stand up, lifting her with the intent of putting her somewhere safe—less covered with glass—but he didn't know where. The corridor Duck had been guarding had broken glass scattered on the stone floor, but that was it. He almost headed in that direction, but what of the soldiers? If they had caused that rockfall, they would send someone to check on the results of it soon. He headed for the flat stone top of a workstation instead. He had to set Cas down somewhere safe, then find Tylie. Fortunately, Duck was already heading in her direction, though he paused to stare at Sardelle, who was kneeling beside Zirkander. His eyes were also closed, his face cut, the front of his uniform dark and damp with blood. Sardelle had a hand on his chest, her chin drooped and her eyes closed.

Tolemek navigated past them, the footing more awkward than walking on logs floating in a river. He tripped, nearly losing Cas, and her eyes fluttered open.

"Cas," he said by way of greeting. His throat was so thick with emotion that he couldn't manage more. Not knowing what internal injuries she had suffered, he resisted the urge to squeeze her.

"I hurt," she whispered.

"I know. I'm sorry." He continued to the workstation. "I need to find Tylie, but you'll be all right. Sardelle will finish with Zirkander, and she'll help you." Looking down at her wan face, he felt guilty about leaving her, even if it was only to go to the other side of the room.

"Tolemek?" she murmured, lifting a hand slightly.

"Yes?"

Her hand rested on his shoulder, and she opened her mouth, but hesitated. Then she said, "Every time I see you today, you're wearing fewer clothes."

He snorted softly. "It's a tropical climate."

He sat her on the table, pushed glass off it, and started to lay her down.

"Wait." Cas's hand tightened on his shoulder. "Tolemek?" she asked again.

"Yes?"

She swallowed and met his eyes. "I love you."

"I…" He had hoped for those words from her, but he had not expected them. Almost overcome with emotion, he had to close his eyes for a moment before he could find his voice and respond. "I love you too."

"Good."

He smiled. "Good."

This time, she let him lay her down. Her rifle was still strapped to her back. She frowned when he tried to remove it, so he left it. If she wanted it poking her in the shoulder blades, so be it. What did it matter? She loved him. Something he would savor more later. Right now, Tylie needed him.

"Wait here for Sardelle," he said.

Cas's eyebrows twitched, but she didn't defy him.

As soon as his hands were free, Tolemek ran across the hills of debris, heading for the corner where Duck was already digging. "Have you found her?" he asked. *Tylie?* he tried again with his mind.

"Not yet, but Sardelle said she's here." Duck shoved aside a filing cabinet with a grunt, the drawers falling open and papers flying everywhere. He hadn't been bloodied when he had come out of the corridor, but his hands were cut up now.

Still using his vest for protection, Tolemek dug in. He was vaguely aware of glass crunching behind him, of someone moving past them, climbing over the mounds of debris that had once been the glass wall. Sardelle? No, that was Cas. He frowned. Why hadn't she stayed put? Nothing except a dark mountain of rock waited out there.

"Cas, what are you doing?" Tolemek demanded, torn between needing to keep digging for his sister and wanting to grab her and pull her back inside, make her lie down and rest. "You were unconscious two minutes ago, damn it."

She waved back at him, but that was all the acknowledgment she offered. With her gaze darting around the dark chamber—what remained of it—and her rifle in her hands, she looked like a panther on the prowl.

"I see a hand," Duck blurted.

Tolemek looked down and redoubled his digging efforts. He

doubted there was anything out there alive, not after that huge rockfall, but he would have to trust Cas to take care of herself if there was.

* * *

Cas was aware of the tinkle of glass and thumps of debris being pushed aside behind her, but she tried to focus her awareness on the chamber—what remained of it. The night sky opened above her now, the entire top third of the ziggurat having fallen into this chamber. The dragon head statue from the pinnacle had survived the plummet and had rolled into one corner, the brazier tilted on its side and the fire out.

She stepped as quietly as she could atop the shifting rocks. Every time she bent slightly or inhaled deeply, a stab of pain came from her ribs. Her head ached like someone was hammering a spike into her skull, the feeling intensifying every time she turned it. Tolemek's suggestion of lying down wasn't a bad one, but she couldn't rest while the team was in danger, and she had no doubt that danger remained here. She had no idea if the dragon had survived—it seemed unlikely that any living creature, powerful and magical or not, could have—but *someone* had set the explosives that had taken out the roof. And she had an idea as to who that someone was. Who else here wanted the dragon dead? No one.

He might have already left, assuming his task complete, but her father was a thorough man. She wagered that he wouldn't leave until he knew for certain that he had succeeded. Whoever had hired him might even require some proof that the deed had been accomplished.

As she followed the base of the rubble mountain, she moved away from the lab until the others disappeared from view, hidden by the rock. Most of the light disappeared, too, leaving deep shadows on this side. The latticework of vines that spread across the crater high above kept out most of the starlight. She had to rely on her senses, on her ears and—

She crinkled her nose as the faintest hint of gunpowder drifted to her on a draft. Had the explosion been set off somewhere nearby? No, she was walking where the dragon had been resting. To take down the roof, the explosives must have been placed up in one of those tunnels, or perhaps even on the wall up higher. She shouldn't be smelling it down here, unless the person who had been handling the gunpowder was close by.

Cas halted, rotating slowing, trying to pierce the gloom with her eyes. Her own senses itched, and she had a feeling someone was trying to see her, as well. She had stayed close to the wall, both so it would be at her back and so its shadows would camouflage her. But against her father, she doubted any camouflage would be enough. Was that some movement halfway up the rock mound? She pointed her rifle in that direction.

"I was wrong to suggest you remain outside," came a soft, familiar voice from the shadows.

Cas swallowed. Even though she had come out here, knowing she was most likely hunting her father, she didn't know what she should do now. Shoot? Over a dragon that had been hours from death anyway? Over her own injuries, injuries she had received as a result of the explosive he had set? She wasn't sure she could manage indignation over that, but what of Zirkander? She had glimpsed Sardelle kneeling over him and didn't know if he was alive and she was working some magic or if he was dead and she was mourning him. It was that sight that had driven Cas out here. She might forgive her father for a lot of things, but if his actions took Zirkander's life...

Had he even considered that fellow Iskandians were in here? Had he thought about aborting or changing his mission when he had learned Cas was in here? Or had he decided that he had done his duty to her by giving her that warning?

"You are competent enough to survive much," he said, his voice still soft, too soft for anyone in the lab to hear.

She thought he sounded proud of her, but at the same time, she would be shocked if he weren't pointing a firearm in her direction, the same as she was pointing one at him.

"Your mission was to kill the dragon?" Cas asked, talking to buy time, to figure out what she meant to do, but also because she needed to know if anyone else in her party was a target. Just because he had *started* with the dragon didn't mean he didn't have orders to kill someone else.

"Kill the dragon, collect blood samples, yes."

"How did you know he was here? That he existed? Those were top secret orders."

"The king is not the only one with spies," he said.

Cas still couldn't pick him out among the shadows, even though she must be looking right at him. Still, if she shot, she was fairly certain she would hit him. With his instincts, he might anticipate her intent and shoot first. He had been doing this all of his life, after all.

A whisper of sound came from his direction, not a voice but something else. A knife being pulled from a sheath? Maybe he didn't have a pistol aimed at her, after all.

A hint of light came from the shadows, a pale green glow like that of some of the goos in Tolemek's collection back home. But this was no goo, nor was it like the globes of illumination that Sardelle waved into existence. This was a sword, a long, heavy-looking blade that reminded Cas as much of a meat cleaver as a war tool. The glow came from the weapon.

"You have a soulblade?" Cas asked. Her father was the last person she would have expected to show up with a magical sword. And the fact that it glowed, did that mean it was attuned to him? That he had some of that dragon blood Sardelle spoke of? Wouldn't Sardelle or Jaxi have sensed it in her if it ran in the family?

Her father gazed down at the sword, turning it over with his hand. "I was told it's some kind of dragon sticker and has the power to cut through almost anything, including dragon hides. Admittedly I wouldn't know the difference."

"Who gave it to you?"

"My employer." A slight smile ghosted across his face, his features illuminated by the soft glow. "It's on loan."

He pressed the tip against the rocks at his feet and leaned into it.

After seeing Jaxi drill through the wall up above, Cas wasn't shocked when the rubble melted away from the blade. Smoke rose, and the air smelled of burning rock.

"You don't think the dragon is dead already?" Cas hadn't felt any movement under foot, no shifting from the rocks.

"It likely is. In its state, it wasn't a particularly worthy opponent. But I must return with evidence to prove that the mission was completed if I wish to be paid."

"Why does that even matter? You have enough money to last you the rest of your lifetime. Why come all the way out here for that?"

"The challenge, of course. To be the best. To leave a legacy and a reputation for the business… if my daughter will come be a part of it."

Cas hadn't lowered her rifle, and she didn't now. The rocks melted away, and he sank lower, unfazed by the smoke rising around him. Heat wafted from the new hole, enough that Cas could feel it. Oddly, it didn't seem to affect him, even though he stood in the middle of it. Some benefit of the sword? She wondered how far he would have to dig to reach the dragon. And if she should do something to stop him. Wouldn't she have already attacked if he weren't her kin? Her shared blood? She hadn't hesitated to stop the Cofah soldiers from harming her teammates. But the dragon was probably already dead and wasn't on the team, regardless.

That dragon is the only one who can heal your commander, genius. Better keep him alive.

Cas flinched at the sudden intrusion in her head. She immediately smoothed her face, not wanting her father to see her surprise. Even if the shadows still cloaked her, they couldn't be as deep, not with that sword glowing over there.

Is he still alive?

Yes, we were making great progress before this ugly stoat blew up the pyramid. But obviously, we're both at somewhat of a disadvantage here. I'm going to melt my way out, but I don't know if I'll be able to beat Kasandral.

Who?

Not who. What. *That's the sword he's holding. Dragon sticker—the irreverence slays me. An Iskandian king wielded that fifteen hundred years ago. Stop him, or I will.*

Cas didn't know if the soulblade *could* stop her father from under tons of rock, but she didn't know that Jaxi *couldn't*, either. It didn't matter. If the dragon was the only one who could heal Zirkander, then Cas had to keep him alive.

"Stop, Father." She had never shifted her aim away from him—even though he had lowered nearly to his chest as the ground melted away around him—and she tightened her finger on the trigger. "I can't let you kill the dragon."

"You won't shoot me, Caslin."

"No, but I will," someone said from the side at the same time as a pistol went off.

Utter shock flashed across her father's face as a bullet slammed into the side of his shoulder. He dropped the sword and leaped from the hole. A second shot fired, but he was sprinting across the rock, disappearing into the shadows now that he wasn't holding the glowing blade.

Cas should have fired, too, but was secretly glad that someone else had taken over, at least for this task. She stared at Zirkander, shocked that he was up and even more shocked that he had succeeded in sneaking up on her father. He heard *everything*. She usually did too.

Did you not hear him coming? Such a shame.

From the sarcasm that accompanied Jaxi's words, Cas assumed she had done something to mute Zirkander's approach.

Good guess. Now could you all get off of us, so we can try to bust out of this prison?

Zirkander gave Cas a salute and a wry smile that suggested he had heard the command request, as well, and shambled back toward the lab. Sardelle might have helped with his wounds, but he still looked like a man half in the grave.

Cas gazed in the direction her father had gone. He had been struck, but that hadn't been a fatal blow. He could yet be trouble. She would watch Zirkander's back the rest of the time they were out here, but first she climbed up to the fresh hole the sword had melted. Heat still radiated off it, but it wasn't so warm that she couldn't stand on it. The sword had stopped glowing, and it lay where her father had dropped it. She hopped in, grabbed it, and the blade started glowing again. Apparently, it didn't care who wielded it.

It's not that bright. Not like me. Just a tool made for poking holes through dragon scales, back when battles were frequent and dragons carried people into flight.

I'll stick to my flier. Cas climbed out and scrambled after Zirkander.

So long as you're not leaving it here. That's a famous relic, and it would be a crime to abandon it in this dismal jungle.

Cas didn't mention that her only thought in collecting it was to make sure her father couldn't come back and grab it, not easily, anyway. Also, when they returned home, maybe they could find a record of who owned the artifact and thus figure out who had hired her father.

Before she reached the lab, Cas came across Sardelle, kneeling in the rocks at the edge of the pile, one of her hands splayed on what had once been a piece of the wall.

Zirkander had stopped next to her. "Do you need help with anything?"

Sardelle shook her head. "Go inside, please. It's going to be dangerous out here again."

"Retrieving Jaxi?"

"Among other things."

Cas passed them, barely noticing the conversation. She had her eyes on Tolemek. He knelt beside his sister, his hand on her forehead, a deep frown on his face. Duck stood behind them, his hands in his pockets, his eyes lowered. She hadn't died, had she?

Cas blinked back tears as she picked her way toward Tolemek. She had barely met the girl, but she knew how much Tylie meant to him, how long he had been trying to find a way to help her. She wasn't bleeding, the way everyone else who had been buried in the rubble had been, but her eyes were closed, her skin pale.

Duck looked up first at her approach.

"Is she alive?" Cas mouthed, not wanting to interrupt

Tolemek's moment. His head hung, his ropes of hair dangling about his face, and she couldn't see his eyes.

Duck shrugged. "Breathing. But he can't wake her up. She doesn't have any big bumps on the head, so we're not sure how or where she was injured. Dug her out from under a desk that was still standing, so it didn't seem like she should be that hurt."

Tolemek lifted his gaze, and Cas's heart ached at the distress in his eyes.

She leaned the sword against a pile of broken furniture, walked around to his side, then knelt and put an arm around his shoulders. He slumped against her.

"She said she's linked to the dragon somehow," Tolemek said. "I'm afraid... I don't understand it, but I'm afraid if the dragon dies, she might..."

"Didn't you hear Jaxi?" Cas searched his face. She had assumed that communication had been to all of them. "It sounds like the dragon's still alive."

His brows rose, and he looked toward the mound of rocks. The very large mountain-sized mound of rocks.

"You said they're tough," Cas said.

"I said they have tough blood. He was already almost dead. Did he—"

Out on the pile, rocks shivered, shifting and falling. Cas couldn't tell if Sardelle was responsible—she was still kneeling out there—or if the dragon stirred, trying to unbury himself. Or maybe Jaxi could move the boulders to free herself.

Zirkander shuffled into the lab. He was still holding his pistol, and the way he glanced over his shoulder made Cas wonder if he was expecting her father to return to shoot him at any moment. He could barely walk. He sat in the hollow between two rubble piles, and leaned his head back and closed his eyes, as if he didn't have the strength to keep them open any longer.

Cas bit her lip and stared at the rock mountain, hoping the dragon lived, that Jaxi had helped it enough that it might now have the strength to help others. She wished she understood more of the disease and what exactly the soulblade had been doing out there.

The rocks went from trembling to rolling down the mound in droves. Sardelle lurched to her feet and skittered backward. Cas would have kept staring at it, but she still had her arm around Tolemek, and he shifted.

"Tylie?" he asked.

The girl's eyes fluttered open. "Phelistoth," she blurted. She rolled away from them and scrambled to her feet.

"Tylie," Tolemek said again, stretching out a hand toward her.

But she was already running and stumbling across the mounds of debris.

* * *

"Phelistoth?" Duck asked. "Is that a curse or a name?"

"The dragon's name." Tolemek pushed himself to his feet and jogged after Tylie.

For a moment, his sister looked like she would charge up the mound of rocks—a dangerous risk the way they were tumbling away from the pile, some larger than a human being. But she stopped next to Sardelle.

"Phelistoth?" she called.

Several boulders flew into the air, and the dragon's head—now more dust-colored than silver—emerged from the pile. He tilted his fang-filled maw toward the sky and roared, a great reverberating roar that would have made a lion turn meek.

Tolemek's reaction was to step back—far back—but Tylie ran closer, as if she meant to climb up the rock pile to the dragon's head. Even if they had some connection, all those sharp teeth worried him, along with the fact that she could be pummeled by one of those boulders. He scrambled after her, but Sardelle surprised him by stretching out an arm to stop him.

He could have charged through her, but the dragon had stopped moving and was staring down at them with baleful eyes. Somehow Tylie didn't find this alarming. She had reached the top of the rocks—the dragon was still mostly encased, aside from his head and long sinewy neck—and balanced on a boulder to reach out and touch those dusty scales.

Sardelle is explaining the situation, Jaxi announced. *Apparently, she believes she's more tactful than I.*

Tolemek watched Tylie, ready to catch her if she tumbled—or if the dragon's humorless yellow eyes turned toward her. *She's explaining the part of the situation where the dragon should make sure not to crush my sister?*

Actually, the part where I need his help healing all of you.

Remembering Zirkander's situation, Tolemek felt selfish. It surprised him to realize that he didn't want to see Zirkander die, not anymore. Seeing him humiliated or his ego battered, that would likely remain a pleasurable experience, but he agreed with the others that it wouldn't be fitting for him to meet his end out here.

Charitable of you, Jaxi thought dryly, *but there's still a chance you'll become infected. From what the dragon has observed, one in two people who come within five miles of him become infected. The suits those geniuses are wearing don't matter one way or another. Also, if you eat something that was infected, you could also be hanging from your toenails over a lake of lava. Most of the villagers with symptoms probably hunted animals that came down off the mountain.*

"Oh." Tolemek should have guessed that when they started seeing the carcasses. "Any way we'll be able to heal the rest of the people on the island?" He probably should have asked the question in his head, since nobody else knew he had been chatting with Jaxi, but Sardelle nodded, as if she had already been thinking about that.

"I'm asking, letting him know it's a problem for miles in all directions and seeing if there's anything he can do. It's actually because he's a dragon that he's so virulent. The same power that lets him telepathically communicate with a girl on the other side of the world gives anything infesting him a boost. Humans probably need to be in very close contact with each other to transmit the disease, so I'm hoping it will die out eventually with him no longer infectious."

"And us," Zirkander said.

"And us."

"Colonel Zirkander?" Tylie called from her spot beside the dragon.

Tolemek blinked. He hadn't told her Zirkander's name, had he? Certainly not his Iskandian rank.

A dragon's telepathy skills make mine look small and quaint, Jaxi thought. *They don't speak or hear, not like humans, but they know what everyone around them is thinking, person, animal, or soulblade.*

Zirkander pushed himself to his feet. "Is it time to sacrifice me to the dragon?"

"He's going to attempt to destroy the virus in your brain," Sardelle said. "He says he can see it now that he knows what he's looking for, and that he can target only the virus, not the rest of your body."

"He can *see* it?" Tolemek hadn't even seen it with his microscope.

Jealous? Jaxi sounded amused.

Maybe.

Me too. He's kind of smug about it, really. And arrogant. He's talking about how he could have cured all of the dragons who had been afflicted with this virus if he'd simply known about this. As if he's even done anything yet. I'm the one who healed him, and what does he say? He offered advice on improving my technique.

Does this virus have anything to do with why there aren't any dragons left around today? Tolemek asked, trying to ignore Jaxi's little tirade. *Did others die before being put in a stasis chamber?*

I don't know. You'll have to ask Ridge's history-loving lieutenant, but I don't think there's anything in the books about a great disease or plague that humans suffered at the same time. They should have been affected too if it was the same disease. Also, if the dragons saw their ends coming, they could have used more stasis chambers. I don't think there have been fossils found that implied a massive dragon die-off. I was always told that they simply left this world.

"How close do I have to get?" Zirkander had walked to the edge of the rubble heap. He seemed to find those big yellow eyes baleful, as well, because he wasn't hurrying to get closer.

Tylie patted the dragon on the neck, then scrambled back down the rocks. She joined Tolemek, clasping his hand and smiling up at him. "He can help us. All of us."

"Good." Tolemek didn't see the confusion in her eyes that

had been there when the dragon had been unconscious.

Step back, a voice much deeper and stronger than Jaxi's announced in his head. In everybody's head, judging by the way the entire group hustled backward.

The dragon pushed himself to his feet, sloughing more rocks away. His head and upper body disappeared from Tolemek's view, above the lab's ceiling. He stretched like a cat waking from a nap. Boulders rolled away from him, as if they weighed less than drops of water. Since he had been barely conscious before, this seemed a vast improvement, but Tolemek didn't know if he was fully healed or not.

Of course he is. Jaxi sniffed—an impressive sound for a sword. *I do excellent work.*

Jaxi was visible now, too, the hilt of the blade poking out from under a rock. Sardelle retrieved her, wiped her off, and sheathed her. Tolemek knew from experience that this wouldn't silence Jaxi.

Of course not. It would be tragic if it did.

The dragon's head lowered into view and turned toward Zirkander. *You.*

Chatty, isn't he? Tolemek thought.

A single dragon eye flickered toward him, and he decided to keep his thoughts silent, insofar as he could.

Zirkander took a few uncertain steps forward and placed his foot on a boulder. "Do I—"

Something invisible smashed into him. His arms flew out, his head fell back, and his entire body stiffened, as if he had been struck by lightning. He toppled backward, landing hard on the stone floor.

"Ridge!" Sardelle blurted.

Tolemek's first thought was that Cas's father had shown up again with some new attack. Indeed, Cas had taken a step forward, her rifle raised. Zirkander's eyes were open, but they didn't move. *He* didn't move. Sardelle raced to his side. Tolemek stared at the dragon. Had he done this? Instead of curing Zirkander, had the dragon killed him? Why? Because he was Iskandian? Hadn't anyone explained that the Cofah had been the ones keeping him subdued? Using him?

"Tylie," Tolemek whispered, squeezing her hand. "What just happened? Does the dragon know we're on his side?"

Tylie only smiled.

Zirkander gasped and blinked.

"Ridge?" Sardelle whispered, laying her hand on his shoulder.

He blinked a few more times and focused on her. "I... what happened?"

"You were dead," she said, "for a moment. Your heart wasn't beating."

He suspended the animation of the entire body so he could more easily target the offending invaders. Jaxi sounded smug, as if this had been her idea.

"That's alarming." Zirkander smiled and lifted a hand to her face. "I'm glad you were here to hold my hand. Big sword and all."

She leaned down and kissed him.

"That's even better," he murmured.

"Do we all have to do that?" Cas asked, lowering her rifle.

"Kiss each other?" Tolemek wrapped an arm around her. "I recommend it."

"I meant get hurled to our asses."

"Ah. I don't—"

A wave of power slammed into Tolemek and his heart stopped. Terror clutched his mind, all rational thought gone, and then he lost consciousness.

He didn't dream or remember anything else until he woke up, lying flat on his back, staring at the broken remains of the ceiling panels above him. He gulped in air, having the sense that he hadn't been breathing before then. Confusion encased him, and for a moment, he didn't know who he was or where he was. It was those dangling ceiling panels that brought him back to the world, back to the ziggurat.

"Cas?" he croaked, rolling onto his side. He almost rolled into her knee.

"Right here," Cas said, dropping her hand to his chest. Her short hair stuck out in a hundred directions and the way she slumped to one side suggested her ribs hurt. "We were all knocked out, except for the colonel. He got to stand guard—sit guard."

"Sit guard," Zirkander grumped from a few meters away. "Let's not tell the general about that one, all right?"

Duck and Sardelle still lay on their backs, their eyes open but blinking with confusion. Zirkander sat next to Sardelle, cradling her head in his lap.

"Duck," he said, "you all right?"

"I'd be better," Duck said weakly, "if someone was holding my head and fondling my hair."

"Uh," Zirkander said. "I guess I could if you want to crawl over here."

"I meant a woman, sir."

"Well, if you're going to be picky, I can't help you."

Tolemek hunted around for Tylie and found her climbing to her feet already. She looked like she had been knocked out, too, but she walked toward the dragon on unsteady legs. He had settled on his stomach, his tail stretched out behind him, and he watched her approach, his eyes not so chilly as they had been when regarding Tolemek and the others. Tolemek still wouldn't call the expression inviting. There was a distinctly reptilian alienness to Phelistoth's face, reminding him that this was not a human being and couldn't be counted on to act or feel the way one did.

Tylie walked up to the dragon's side and leaned against him, her face to his scales.

"Is that, uh, safe?" Zirkander asked quietly, glancing back at Tolemek. As if he knew.

"He did save your life," Sardelle murmured, gazing up at Zirkander, not shifting her head out of his lap yet.

"He did. But I can't say I got the impression he was incredibly pleased to be doing it." Zirkander touched his palm to his chest and shuddered slightly. "He doesn't have a gentle touch."

The dragon's tail had been lying straight out behind him, but it swished a couple of times, then curved around his body. Tolemek had a vision of Tylie being squished by it—even flat on the ground, it came up to her waist—but it curled around her, almost gently. Protectively.

Thank you, came a whisper into Tolemek's mind. Tylie. She smiled at him, a gleam of excitement in her eyes that he hadn't seen since she had been a little girl, plotting some adventure in the woods behind their house. *Be safe.*

Are you going somewhere? Tolemek asked, a hint of panic welling in his chest. This sounded like a farewell. *Sardelle came to teach you.*

Later.

The tail tightened around Tylie and lifted her into the air.

Zirkander's mouth dropped open, and he patted at his side, groping for his rifle.

But Phelistoth merely deposited Tylie on his back, then released her. She sat astride him, as if he were some giant horse, then dropped to her belly, an arm stretched out on either side of his spine. Tolemek reached out, wanting to object. That didn't look safe at all. Didn't the dragon riders of old have some kind of saddle? A way to strap in?

Duck pointed at her. "Is she going to—"

The dragon's legs bunched, muscles rippling beneath the sleek scales, then it leaped straight up into the air, disappearing from view. Tolemek's heart lodged in his throat. He raced forward, certain Tylie would fall off and be crushed when she tumbled to the ground. But somehow, she hung on as the dragon cleared the ziggurat, spread his wings, then shot even farther upward. He broke through the latticework over the crater and sailed toward the stars. Tolemek's last glimpse showed him soaring away with Tylie still on his back.

"Uh," Duck said. "Did the dragon just kidnap Tolemek's sister?"

"She wanted to go." Tolemek sighed, feeling bleak—and small. What could he offer Tylie compared to that?

Cas walked over and took his hand in both of hers. She looked up at him, her eyes full of sympathy. They also seemed to say that she was still there for him. "Ready to go home?" she asked.

"I better be. I'm completely out of grenades, potions, and

other compounds." Tolemek slipped his arms around her, closed his eyes, and dropped his face to her hair.

"*Completely?*"

"Completely."

"I'm almost out of ammo," she said. "I guess we better hope we don't have any trouble reclaiming our fliers."

EPILOGUE

BY THE TIME THE WEARY group limped into town, the noon sun beating down on their shoulders, Tolemek wanted nothing more than to sleep for a week. Perhaps a month.

Little had changed in the pirate haven. New ships were docked in the harbor and new people wandered in and out of the taverns. He didn't see any sign that the virus had reached the area yet. Maybe it never would. Tolemek would hope for that because without the dragon, he wouldn't know how to heal those afflicted.

He looked skyward, hoping he might spot Phelistoth and his sister soaring among the clouds. In the jungle, the canopy had been too dense overhead for him to glimpse much of the sky. Alas, he didn't see anything other than seagulls. They had probably left the island, the dragon wanting to stretch its wings after three thousand years. Tolemek worried for Tylie. She had never been on her own. How would she get by?

"She'll be able to find you when she comes down, I'm sure," Cas said from his side, catching him looking up. She carried her weapons as vigilantly as she had when they had first embarked on the mission, including the dragon-slaying sword that she had wrapped in a cloth and strapped to her pack. The thing looked like it weighed at least ten pounds. If she felt tired after the week's events, she didn't show it. Of course, knowing her father was out there, probably wanting to put a bullet between Zirkander's shoulder blades, might keep her alert.

"I told her I lived in Iskandia now," Tolemek said. "I wish I'd been more specific."

"Do you really want a dragon knowing where you live?" Duck asked.

"So long as he shows up with my sister."

"The king might be upset if he heard about a dragon perching on the roof of your lab building."

"Can't be any worse than the hideous one Zirkander has dangling in his flier," Tolemek said.

Zirkander had been in the lead, setting a determined pace along the outer streets of town, wanting to check on his fliers before anything else, but he frowned back at them at this. "My luck dragon is *not* hideous."

"And it's not in his flier," Cas said. "It's in his pocket."

Zirkander's fingers twitched toward his pocket, but he stopped himself. "It kept me alive, didn't it?"

"Barely, sir," Duck said. "Maybe you should get a bigger one. Maybe Phelistoth will come perch on *your* house."

"I don't know if base security would allow that." The field where the fliers had been parked came into view, and Zirkander's attention shifted forward again. He stared, nearly tripped, then broke into a run.

The fliers were still there, but strings of bones were draped all over them—human bones. In addition, the craft were surrounded by pointy poles thrust into the ground with skulls stuck on the top of them. Entire skeletons dangled from the tops of some, and as the breeze blew in from the ocean, the bones rattled and clanked. More than a few of the skulls had rusty knife hilts sticking out of them.

"Uh?" Cas asked. "I better go see what that's about." She jogged ahead, not running quite as quickly as Zirkander. But then, she wasn't as in love with her craft as her commander was. Her rifle, now, that was another matter.

"There's Moe," Sardelle said, waving toward the wiry man walking toward the field from another street, a book open in his hands. He had not noticed the return of his son yet.

"Dad!" Zirkander called from the cockpit of his flier. "Care to explain this?" He tossed a femur to the ground, then hefted a skull over his head.

Moe lifted his head and closed his book. "Oh, good afternoon, Ridgewalker. I was coming to check on your devilish contraptions. You wouldn't believe how much trouble it's been watching over them."

Zirkander lowered the skull and looked into its empty eye sockets. "Oh, I might."

By this time, Cas had climbed into her own flier, and grumpy curses wafted out of her cockpit, along with bones being flung left and right.

"Those are fallen souls who died horribly on account of the curse," Moe said.

Tolemek, Duck, and Sardelle reached the fliers, and Duck also diverted to check on his craft. Tolemek waited, curious to hear the story.

"That's the story you spread?" Zirkander asked.

"I didn't even need to spread it. Fallen souls and curses are part of the local legend, thanks to the indigenous people. And pirates, being a superstitious lot, are quite willing to believe such tales. All I had to do was supply the fallen souls." Moe waved toward the poles and their skull decorations.

"And you did this for a reason, I presume."

"Oh, yes. Pirates kept trying to steal your fliers, and the natives were flinging mud at them and other less than savory items."

Cas tossed a soggy bag out of her cockpit and made a face. "Yes, found one. This hot humid climate turns things aromatic quickly, doesn't it?"

"I volunteer to ride with someone besides Cas on the way home," Tolemek announced.

She glowered at him almost as balefully as the dragon had.

"Nobody else wants your hairy pirate butt on their seats," Zirkander said as he hefted more bones and garbage over the side.

"Sir," Sardelle said, catching Moe's eye, "where did you get the bones for your ruse?"

Moe closed his book. "From the catacombs beneath the library, of course. This town has a far more fascinating history than I suspected. I'd only intended to do some research of this archipelago in general, but I may need to stay here for a while."

"You would like the pyramid, Dad," Zirkander said, his voice muffled since his head was below the seat, his butt sticking in the air.

Tolemek thought about commenting on the position, but decided he had better help Cas instead. He wanted to go home. And strangely, the image that formed in his mind at the thought was that of Iskandia and his lab in the capital, something to do with Cas's whispered, "I love you," perhaps. The memory of that moment made him smile.

"Ziggurat?" Moe flipped open his book again. "I read about that in here, and the dragon-worshipping culture that built it, but it's believed that the jungle took it back centuries ago."

"It didn't, but it's not in the best shape anymore. There were some explosions... and a dragon flew through the roof."

"Explosions?" Moe's eyebrows flew up. "Ridgewalker Meadowlark Zirkander, did you blow up priceless ancient ruins?"

"Meadowlark?" Tolemek mouthed.

I understand that was his mother's contribution, Jaxi shared.

"It wasn't me," Zirkander said. "Why assume it was me? I was busy trying not to die from some horrible disease. Sardelle, tell him."

"You *were* thinking of toting those kegs down the corridor to bring down the roof on the Cofah," she pointed out.

"But I didn't actually do anything." Zirkander flattened a hand to his chest. "I'm innocent."

"Ridgewalker," Moe said sternly. "I don't think you understand how important history is and how irreplaceable relics from the past are."

"How am I getting a lecture when I'm the one who came back to a flier full of bones and... seven gods, is that goat poop?" Zirkander's lip curled. "Sardelle? I need you to wave your hand like you did before, that move where you clean the seats of disgusting organic matter." He cast a plaintive look in her direction.

"Need any help?" Tolemek asked Cas from the ground next to her cockpit.

She shook her head, but she wasn't looking at him. She had stopped cleaning and was frowning up at the sky, a hand shadowing her eyes.

At first, Tolemek thought she had spotted the dragon, but

the creature flying through the sky was mechanical rather than living. A bronze Iskandian flier buzzed out of the clouds over the ocean. Now that Tolemek had seen a true dragon, the craft was truly laughable—what would Phelistoth think when he encountered his first one? Or a Cofah airship?

"That's Wolf Squadron," Cas said.

Zirkander, who had been arguing back and forth with his father about the sanctity of ancient ruins and how they shouldn't be damaged, even if they had been taken over by enemy troops, looked up. The flier descended toward the harbor, and a few shouts went up from ships docked out there, pirates who must have thought this heralded a raid. But the lone craft veered away from the town.

Zirkander lifted a hand—fortunately, he wasn't holding any skulls this time—and waved. "That's Apex."

The flier circled and came in over the trees to land in the field, bumping along the uneven ground and flattening two of the poles before coming to a stop nearby.

"That's definitely Apex," Zirkander added dryly.

"Captain Kaika is with him," Cas said.

"I see that." Zirkander hopped down from his flier.

Tolemek hung back, doubting this had anything to do with him.

Cas dropped down beside him. "That's odd. I could see why Apex might be sent to check on us—though I'm not quite sure how he found us, since we've been island hopping—but why would the general send Captain Kaika back?"

"Perhaps he found out the ziggurat had only been partially blown up," Tolemek said.

Moe frowned at him.

"Sir," Apex blurted, practically flinging himself out of his cockpit. He landed on a couple of bones, but kicked them aside, barely noticing them. Usually, Duck was the young careless one; Apex was Tolemek's age and not nearly so brash. "I'm so relieved we found you."

"How *did* you find us?" Cas asked.

"The dragon and this island are in the news back home. We're not sure who the source was. It's chaos in the city right now. And we weren't sure you would still be here, either."

"Let's have the report, Lieutenant," Zirkander said.

"The king is missing, sir. The queen is in charge, supposedly, but she hasn't addressed the people, and nobody's seen her outside of the castle."

Zirkander accepted the news with a worried frown but nothing more explosive. Until Apex spoke again.

"Sardelle's face is on wanted posters all over the streets of the capital. As a witch."

Zirkander thumped his fist against his thigh. "Damn, what's been going on while we've been gone?"

"Nothing good, sir. We had to sneak away to warn you. Colonel Therrik has been put in charge of the flier battalion, and you've been declared AWOL."

"*What?*" This time Zirkander cursed so vehemently that Apex backed away, sending a worried look up to Kaika. Tolemek wondered if Sardelle would be offended that this information drew more of a distressed reaction from Zirkander than the news about her bounty. "*Therrik?*" Zirkander went on. "That buffoon doesn't know anything about flying except how to puke in the back of my craft. He's in a different brigade altogether. He *was*. Where's General Ort?"

"He made a fuss, and he's been relieved of duty."

Zirkander pushed his hand through his hair several times, as if he might find some answers in there.

"We've probably been declared AWOL, too, sir," Apex went on. "But we had to let you know."

"Thank you." Zirkander faced Tolemek. "I don't suppose there's any chance your sister would like to bring that dragon back, to fly menacingly into the harbor and show the capital that we've been up to important things these last couple of weeks?"

Tolemek spread his hands. "Sorry, Zirkander. I don't think my sister is aware of or cares about Iskandian politics. Also, I don't know how to reach her. If I did, I'd tell her she's not old enough to stay out past midnight, much less fly around the world on a dragon's back."

Apex's mouth descended to his chest at this talk of dragons, but Kaika was the one to ask, "You got a plan, Colonel? Because I didn't go AWOL because of Apex's companionship. Nobody in my company was doing enough about finding the king, and I was definitely getting the feeling some conspiracy was afoot."

"A plan," Zirkander said. "We'll work on one. On the way back home." He waved at the fliers. "Everyone in. Dad, are you coming?"

"In one of those cursed contraptions? No chance." Moe glowered over at Sardelle, who lifted her hands in innocence. "I'll catch the next boat. Have some more research to finish up first, but... check in on your mother for me, will you? If there's any trouble in the city, make sure she's safe."

"I will, Dad."

"Guess this means I'm not getting that nice bath I've been dreaming about," Cas said with a sigh as the others climbed into their fliers.

"I didn't know you dreamed of such sybaritic luxuries," Tolemek said.

"I do. And I dream of people hopping in with me and rubbing my shoulders."

"Random people or specific ones?"

"Scruffy-haired pirates." Cas hopped up, caught the lip of the cockpit, and pulled herself aboard.

"*Scruffy?*" Tolemek asked. "I thought you found me handsome and alluring."

She winked at him. "I'll find you more alluring if you climb in back there and clean those goat droppings off the seat."

Tolemek looked to the sky again, feeling a little envious of his sister.

THE END

PATTERNS IN THE DARK

Printed in Great Britain
by Amazon